Praise for the *Explorers' Clubs* series:

'A magical adventure.'
The Bookseller

'The most huggable book of the year.
An (iced) gem.'
SFX

'Wintry, atmospheric, highly imaginative fantasy.'
Metro

'A fantastic frosty adventure.'
Sunday Express

'A hugely enjoyable, fast-paced magical adventure.'
WRD

'Full of unique takes on classic tropes with some
unexpected twists and turns along the way.'
Times Educational Supplement

'A delightful read.'
The Week Junior

'I can't wait for the next one!'
Havana Brown, aged 12

ot.'

FABER has published children's books since 1929. T. S. Eliot's *Old Possum's Book of Practical Cats* and Ted Hughes' *The Iron Man* were amongst the first. Our catalogue at the time said that 'it is by reading such books that children learn the difference between the shoddy and the genuine'. We still believe in the power of reading to transform children's lives. All our books are chosen with the express intention of growing a love of reading, a thirst for knowledge and to cultivate empathy. We pride ourselves on responsible editing. Last but not least, we believe in kind and inclusive books in which all children feel represented and important.

ABOUT THE AUTHOR

Alex Bell has published novels and short stories for both adults and young adults, including *Frozen Charlotte*. *The Polar Bear Explorers' Club* was her first foray into middle grade. She always wanted to be a writer but had several different back-up plans to ensure she didn't end up in the poor house first. After completing a law degree, she now works at the Citizens Advice Bureau. Most of her spare time consists of catering to the whims of her Siamese cats.

ABOUT THE ILLUSTRATOR

Tomislav Tomić was born in 1977. He graduated from the Academy of Fine Arts in Zagreb. He started to publish his illustrations during his college days. He has illustrated a great number of books, picture books, schoolbooks and lots of covers for children's books. He lives and works in the town of Zaprešić, Croatia.

EXPL★RERS AT PIRATE ISLAND

Illustrated by
Tomislav Tomić

ALEX BELL

faber

First published in 2021
by Faber & Faber Limited
Bloomsbury House,
74–77 Great Russell Street,
London WC1B 3DA
faberchildrens.co.uk

Typeset by MRules
Printed by CPI Group (UK) Ltd, Croydon CR0 4YY

A CIP record for this book
is available from the British Library

ISBN 978-0-571-35973-8

FSC
www.fsc.org
MIX
Paper from
responsible sources
FSC® C020471

2 4 6 8 10 9 7 5 3 1

For my cousin, Tim Willrich.

CONTENTS

Chapter One

Foaming seawater rushed up through the floor of the swim-out hatch and lapped against Ursula Jellyfin's legs. She immediately transformed into a mermaid and swam out of the submarine. It felt wonderful to be in the ocean once again, with the salty water cool against her skin and scales, and the sad, beautiful sound of whale song echoing somewhere in the distance. She dived to the sea floor, admiring the pink shells and pale pearls scattered there, and dipped her tail fin in the soft golden sand. Then she spotted the treasure chest.

It was almost hidden in a big patch of seaweed and was all rusted and covered in barnacles, but the glint of medallions winked at her like giant eyes. When Ursula swam closer she saw that the chest had burst open and was full of precious jewels as well as big, shiny coins. There was a pair of cutlasses and an eye patch there too. Surely it must be a pirate's treasure chest, which meant they were getting close to Pirate Island!

For the last two weeks, Ursula and her friends from the Ocean Squid Explorers' Club had travelled non-stop across the Bubble Ocean, on board the submarine *Blowfish*. Their mission was to reach Pirate Island where the villainous Collector Scarlett Sauvage had set up her new headquarters, and they had no time to lose – there was a lot at stake once they got there.

Scarlett Sauvage was head of the Phantom Atlas Society, an organisation that had been stealing away people and places for years, and locking them up in magical snow globes. Her most recent victim had been the Ocean Squid Explorers' Club itself, and the young explorers were determined to rescue it. Scarlett had also kidnapped a small group of children. She was keeping them hostage to try to persuade inventors to create a weapon for her: something she could use to win over the ice princess, Stella Starflake Pearl.

Stella and her friends from the Polar Bear Explorers' Club had been the ones to discover what the Collector was up to, making them her mortal enemies, but now Scarlett had run out of snow globes and she needed Stella's ice magic to help her create new ones to carry on stealing things away. The Ocean Squid explorers were not going to let this to happen – the world didn't belong to Scarlett, it belonged to everyone. And they wanted to rescue the kidnapped children too. This was especially important to them because Ursula's teammate Max had a sister – Jada – who was one of them.

Ursula scooped up a handful of medallions and then beat her tail hard to return to the surface, leaving a stream of bubbles in her wake. Her head came out of the water and she squinted against the dazzling sparkle of the sun dancing across the waves as she looked for her friends. Sure enough, Ursula spotted their rowing boat coming over the sea towards her, and she swam to meet it.

Their crew of four had docked the *Blowfish* at Starfish Island in order to collect water. Max and Genie had taken the boat, while Jai remained behind on the submarine. He was the sub's captain and his sister Genie was a kraken whisperer. Her shadow animal, Bess, was a gigantic kraken and quite terrifying to look at when you first saw her, but Ursula had got used to her now and didn't bat an eyelid at the sight of the great sea monster swimming along beside the rowing boat, her massive tentacles trailing lazily behind her in the water.

'Ahoy there!' Max said, paddling backwards to slow the boat to a stop.

Max was a robot inventor. He had been expelled

from the Ocean Squid Explorers' Club for conspiring with pirates, but the teammates now knew he had only done this to try to rescue his sister, so Jai had reinstated him and he once again wore the black Ocean Squid explorer's cloak like the rest of them. Max had even made a barber robot so he could replace the shark in his high shave fade haircut with the Ocean Squid crest in honour of the occasion.

Ursula grabbed hold of the edge of the boat with one hand. 'Look!' She held up the medallions. 'I found a pirate treasure chest down there. We must be getting close.'

Genie cheered. 'Our trip was a success too,' she said, adjusting her hat. Genie was really good at making hats, the crazier the better. This one was bright orange and fashioned in the shape of a starfish. And instead of regulation black boots, she wore a pair of bright pink cowgirl boots that sparkled in the sun.

'Did you find water?' Ursula asked.

'Yes, but that's not all. We found this too.' She held out her fist and uncurled her fingers. Sitting in the middle of her palm was a miniature pirate hat, only a few inches long. The tiny feather sticking out from the hatband was bright yellow and made Ursula think of canaries.

'But it's so small!' she exclaimed. 'What kind of pirate would wear that?'

'Pirate fairies,' Max said. 'We found a mini fort on the beach, manned by tiny cannons.'

'Pirate fairies?' Ursula frowned. She knew there were jungle fairies and garden fairies and sea fairies, but she'd never heard of pirate fairies before. 'Are you sure? I haven't read about them in *Captain Filibuster's Guide to Sea Monsters*. Or any of the Flag Reports.'

When explorers went on an expedition they had to fly their club's flag at every opportunity, and when they returned home they had to formally return the flag, along with a written report about everything they had discovered on their journey.

Max shrugged. 'Well, it's either that or pirate gnomes and I don't think a gnome would ever dare go near water. They can't swim – they just sink like stones. I wouldn't be too worried, Jellyfin. Pirates or not, they're only a few inches tall, so I don't think they'd pose much of a threat to us.'

Ursula shook her head. 'You're probably right, but won't they mind that you've taken one of their hats?'

'I don't think so,' Genie replied. 'The fort was abandoned. It looks like everyone left in a great hurry. Their possessions were still there, but there was no sign

5

of the fairies themselves. We saw one of their galleons moored in a nearby cove and that was deserted too. The decks were bare and when we peered in through the portholes, their cabins were empty.' She frowned. 'It was weird because it looked like they'd left right in the middle of what they were doing. I saw a tiny chessboard set up part way through a game and a long table in the galley with a half-eaten meal and all the rum kegs standing open.'

'How peculiar,' Ursula said. 'It sounds like the *Mary Janette*.'

The *Mary Janette* was a famous ship that had been discovered drifting alone at sea. There was no trace of the crew and no one ever found out what had happened to them. There were many theories though, ranging from mutiny, to sea-monster attack, to cursed mummies.

'Perhaps the pirate fairies have gone to join Scarlett Sauvage?' Genie suggested.

She sounded worried. They knew that many pirates were working for the Collector and when the merfolk refused to help her, she had sent some of the pirates to attack mermaid towns. Perhaps the pirate fairies were on her side too?

'Well, either way,' Max said, 'we'd best get back to the submarine before Jai starts getting uppity about the—'

He broke off as a loud, deep *BOOM* filled the air, and they all jumped. Jai had fired the sea cannon from the submarine and they could see ripples spreading out where the ball had landed.

Genie looked at Ursula and said, 'Quick, get into the boat! There must be something dangerous in the water.'

'What could possibly be dangerous around here?' Max asked. 'Jai probably just sat on the cannon button and set it off by mistake.'

But he reached over the side of the boat and helped pull Ursula in anyway. It rocked beneath her weight and her wet tail fin sparkled in the sun.

Genie shook her head. 'Jai never does anything by mistake on a submarine.' She looked worried. 'We should get back at once.' She glanced at her shadow kraken and said, 'You too, Bess! You'll get there faster than us, and Jai might need back-up.'

Although the shadow kraken had no substance and couldn't physically hurt anything, she *looked* real enough, and they had found in the past that a great sea monster lurching up out of the water and waving her tentacles about was usually enough to put off most potential attackers.

Bess obligingly swam off and the explorers took hold

of the oars and rowed as fast as they could. Within five minutes they were back at the *Blowfish* and attaching the ropes to haul the boat on board. Ursula was only half mermaid so she became human again once she'd dried off on land. Max fetched her a robe and she was just slipping it on when they heard the roaring *BOOM* of another cannon firing.

'I guess it wasn't a mistake after all,' Max admitted. 'No one's fool enough to sit on the sea cannon button twice.'

Ursula quickly dried her tail and once she'd got her legs back the three of them ran down one of the gleaming wooden corridors to the bridge. They were expecting trouble when they reached Pirate Island, but no one had thought they were in any danger yet. The sudden sense of urgency took them all by surprise in a most unpleasant way. Ursula could feel prickles of dread creeping over her skin as they threw open the door of the bridge and tumbled over one another to get in first.

'What's happening?' Max gasped as they all wheezed for breath.

'Are you all right?' Genie added.

Ursula was relieved to see Jai standing alone by the portholes, looking quite unharmed. Like Genie, he had brown skin and black hair, and he was wearing an Ocean Squid explorer's cloak, but his had been adapted because he only had one arm, although he sometimes wore a prosthetic.

'Of course I am.' Jai sounded irritated. 'And do you have to barge in all chaotically like that? Can't you see we've got company?'

'Company?'

For the first time, the others looked out the portholes and saw what the submarine had hidden from their view. Spread out on the waves below, there was a fleet of fairy galleons, all flying the pirates' Jolly Roger flag. Bess flailed her tentacles at them threateningly, but the little ships didn't back away. The explorers' path to the open sea was completely cut off, but no one felt particularly alarmed about it. The submarine was gigantic and could easily pass straight through the tiny ships. They could see the pirate fairies had cannons on board, but they were no bigger than a human hand and the little balls inside weren't likely to make so much as a dent against the *Blowfish*'s metal plates.

'Oh dear, this isn't about the hat, is it?' Max asked. 'We honestly thought the fort had been abandoned. Shall I toss it overboard?'

'Hat? What are you talking about?' Jai shook

his head. 'Look, will you all straighten up and stop gasping and spluttering? Come over here so I can introduce you.'

For the first time, the explorers realised that Jai wasn't alone on the bridge after all – there was a fairy perched on the control panel beside him, and she was grinning at them. They would have known, just from looking at her, that she was a pirate. She wore a ruffled white shirt tucked into belted black trousers, with shiny, polished boots. Her wings were sea green, a cutlass hung from her hip and she had masses of curly brown hair, on top of which sat a glorious hat, just like the one Max had found, complete with a ruby feather. But the most telling sign of all was the bright green fairy parrot perched on her shoulder.

'This is Captain Zara Silver,' Jai said. 'She's offered to help us find the Collector.'

The fairy promptly leaped to her feet, swept her hat from her head and gave them a low bow. 'At your service,' she said, before straightening up and replacing the hat with a flourish. She gestured with her thumb at the parrot on her shoulder. 'And this is Ollie.'

'It's good to meet you, Captain,' Ursula said. 'And Ollie.' She looked back at Jai. 'So … we're not under attack?'

'Under attack?' Jai looked alarmed. 'What gave you that idea?'

'You fired the sea cannon,' Genie pointed out. 'Twice.'

Ursula looked out the porthole again and saw that Bess wasn't facing off against the pirate fairies, as she'd first thought. Instead she was waving her tentacles quite happily as several fairies and their brightly coloured parrots flew around her.

'I told you he probably just sat on the button by mistake,' Max said.

'I most certainly did not.' Jai looked aghast. 'I've passed all my submarine health and safety courses with flying colours. I even got one hundred per cent in one of my papers, which the examiner said had never happened before and—'

Max groaned and cut him off. 'All right, all right,' he said. 'If it wasn't a mistake, why *did* you fire the cannon, then?'

'I was simply demonstrating our defensive capabilities to Captain Zara,' Jai said. 'She expressed doubt that we could take care of ourselves trying to get on to Pirate Island.'

'Oh, of course.' Max rolled his eyes. 'How silly of me. And it didn't occur to you that the three of us might be a bit alarmed to hear unexpected and unscheduled cannon fire?'

Jai made an impatient gesture. 'It's your own fault for dithering around. I was timing you. You ought to have been back twenty minutes ago.'

Jai was training to be a captain, and not only did he own all of Captain Filibuster's volumes on sea exploration, he also knew all the Ocean Squid Club and submarine-operating rules off by heart. He could also, unfortunately, be a little inflexible when it came to things like rules, and regulations, and duties, and getting up very early in the morning to scrub the deck. He said that scrubbing the deck helped build a sense of camaraderie and respect for the submarine, whereas Max suggested it only helped build up a ravenous appetite for a very large breakfast.

'We weren't dithering,' Genie protested. 'We stopped to look at an abandoned fairy fort.' She turned her gaze on Zara and said, 'We've never seen a pirate fairy before.'

'There aren't many of us,' Zara replied. 'In fact, we're the only fleet in the world, as far as I know, but half of us are being held prisoner by Scarlett. She grew angry when we refused to join forces with her against you explorers, you see, and she managed to capture half our fleet using her wretched snow globes, including my own crew. When we saw your submarine, we thought she'd returned for the rest of us, so we hid our ships in the cove on the other side of the island. But then we saw your Ocean Squid Explorers' Club flag.'

'Yo ho!' The little parrot said enthusiastically. 'Yo ho!'

'Oh, he can talk!' Genie exclaimed.

'A little,' Zara replied. 'Mostly he just shouts out pirate curses.'

'Why did you refuse to join forces with Scarlett?' Max asked. 'The human pirates seem keen enough to work with her.'

'Fairies have more sense,' Zara replied. 'Besides, the Collector has no respect for fairies. We saw the list of stolen places that Stella Starflake Pearl shared in the newspaper. There were several fairy colonies on there, including the galaxy fairies of Stardust City who everyone thought were lost, and the glimmer-glow fairies from the Emerald Mines.'

'Shiver me timbers,' Ollie said, ruffling his green feathers.

'My crew were supposed to be enjoying some rest and relaxation at a fairy beach party when Scarlett captured them. I was the only one back at the ship, so I managed to escape. Now I'm on a rescue mission, same as you. And if you lot are going to Pirate Island, you'll need someone to help guide the way,' Zara went on. 'You won't last five seconds if you go blundering in alone.'

'How do you know we're going to Pirate Island?' Ursula asked. Their mission was meant to be a secret.

'The papers said you had gone rogue and were going after the Collector on your own,' Zara replied. 'Against the wishes of your club.'

'*Our* club hasn't been able to express any wishes on the matter either way,' Max said. 'It got sucked up into one of the Collector's snow globes too.'

Zara waved a hand. 'The remaining clubs, then. They don't want you to go by yourselves, do they?'

'They think it's too dangerous,' Jai replied.

'And that we're not capable,' Genie said quietly.

The explorers suddenly all felt glum. Their last mission hadn't turned out very well. They had returned the Sunken City of Pacifica back to its original place in the ocean and released it from the snow globe in the belief that they were setting it free. Only it turned out that an underwater volcano was rumbling away in the middle of the city and it had erupted shortly afterwards, destroying everything in sight. The city hadn't been a stolen place after all – its inhabitants had asked the Phantom Atlas Society to take it away until a means to stop the volcano could be found.

No one was hurt because all the inhabitants fled before the eruption, but a great many priceless books and artefacts had been lost, and Ursula and her friends knew that the people of Pacifica would never forgive them, even if they had only been trying to help. They were now in trouble with the other clubs too, even though it had been the clubs' idea to return Pacifica in the first place.

'The newspaper reports didn't specifically mention Pirate Island, did they?' Max asked.

The young explorers had shared Scarlett's location with the other clubs, but it would be a disaster if the newspapers had somehow found out and printed it. It was only through Jada's ingenuity in getting a message to them that they knew where the Collector was, but if Scarlett realised the whereabouts of her headquarters had been discovered, then surely she'd move somewhere else and they'd be back to the drawing board.

So they were relieved when Zara said, 'No, the papers have no idea where Scarlett is hiding, but I know the place well. Pirate Island used to be open to all passing pirates, but ever since we refused to work with her, us fairy pirates are no longer welcome. I visited just two weeks ago to try to see my captured crew, but was refused access and only narrowly missed being thrown in the cells myself. I would like to stop the Collector once and for all, so will gladly help you in any way we can.'

'It's a very kind and gracious offer,' Jai said. 'But I was just explaining that we can take care of ourselves.'

Zara shook her head. 'That's what you think,' she said. 'But no one is allowed on Pirate Island unless they're a pirate, and it's obvious from a mile off that you lot are explorers. Besides, I know some secret routes on to the island that I can show you.'

'That does sound useful,' Genie said eagerly.

'Not so fast.' Jai held up his hand and looked at Zara. 'You're still a pirate and explorers don't work with criminals. No offence.'

'There's more than one type of pirate, you know,' Zara said.

'So you're not thieves?'

'Oh, we are,' Zara replied. 'But we only steal from human pirates. We take back the stuff they stole and return it to its rightful owners.'

'On miniature ships?' Max asked doubtfully. 'Pirate treasure is usually pretty big and heavy.'

'That's where our magic charm bottles come in,'

Zara replied. 'We shrink the loot to fit inside them. Why, we can even shrink an entire kraken and put it in a bottle if we want to.'

'Why would anyone want a kraken in a bottle?' Max wondered, wrinkling his brow.

'Sea-monster aquariums are quite popular in certain towns,' Zara said. 'I saw one in a fancy restaurant once – it had two miniature kraken which used to fight battles during the dessert course.'

'But that's barbaric!' Genie cried. Her hand went to her pendant and she looked suddenly furious. 'Kraken belong in the ocean! Where is this place? I'm going to set those kraken free.'

'It's on Smugglers' Isle, in Barnacle City. You'll never persuade them to part with the kraken, though. They won't sell them for anything.'

'Well, I don't intend to buy them – I'm going to rescue them,' Genie said.

Zara grinned. 'Steal them, you mean. You see, everyone becomes a thief if the circumstances are right.'

Jai shook his head. 'Look, the point is that we only have your word that you're not working with Scarlett. You could be leading us straight into a trap for all we know.'

'That's an excellent point,' Max said. 'No pirate gives

something for nothing. What do you want from us in return?'

'Just what I've already said,' Zara replied. 'I want to rescue the missing part of my fleet, including my crew.'

Jai shook his head. 'It's strictly against the rules to work with pirates. Even fairy ones.'

'It wouldn't be the first rule we've broken,' Ursula pointed out. 'You've said it before yourself – these aren't normal times, so the rules have to be bent a little.'

Jai paused for a moment, then shook his head again. 'We just can't know for sure we can trust her.'

'That's too bad,' Zara said with a shrug. 'I could have been really useful to you. Oh well, I guess we'll just have to hope—'

But that was as far as she got before the roar of cannon fire filled the air, and this time it wasn't coming from the *Blowfish*.

CHAPTER TWO

The submarine rocked in the water, sending everyone flying to the floor in a heap.

'Walk the plank!' Ollie squawked indignantly. 'Walk the plank!'

In the first moments of confusion, Ursula thought the pirate fleet must have turned on them, but then she heard Zara exclaim, 'Impossible! We had lookouts stationed all round the island!'

She flew up to one of the portholes and let loose a stream of pirate curses. The children quickly scrambled to their feet and joined her, staring in astonishment at the huge pirate galleon that had appeared on the other side of the fairy fleet, trapping them in the island's cove.

'But . . . but how?' Jai exclaimed. 'There was nothing there a few minutes ago! We should have seen that ship coming for miles!'

'I think they used a magic disguise painting,' Ursula said. 'Do you remember Stella said in her report that the Collector used one to hide her headquarters at the Black Ice Bridge?'

'That's it!' Max said. 'I can still see a bit of it hanging from the bottom sail. It makes it look like there's only sea and sky there.'

They all saw that he was right. With the magic disguise painting hiding the ship, they'd had no advance warning of its approach and now it was too late.

'Scarlett sent it!' Zara said furiously. 'There's a Phantom Atlas flag flying alongside the Jolly Roger. She's come to get the rest of my fleet.' She flicked a glance at Jai. '*Now* do you believe we're not working together?'

As she spoke, she pointed at the patch of sea where the pirate's cannonball had landed. They could still see ripples floating out from the spot and bits of sail and timber floated where the fairy galleon had been. Ursula gasped as she realised in dismay that the cannon had blown the whole ship to bits. They could see the other fairy galleons hurrying to man their cannons and turn to face their attacker. Zara lost no time and flew towards the door, Ollie whizzing in a green blur behind her.

'I'm sorry,' Jai called. 'We'll help protect you.'

He was already heading for one of the sea cannons, but Zara gave a short laugh and said over her shoulder, 'Thanks, but I think you'll find *we* will protect *you*.'

'I don't think your ships' cannons are big enough to do much damage,' Max said, taking up position by the second sea cannon.

Zara paused in the doorway mid-flight and said, 'Oh, our ships don't fire cannonballs.'

Genie frowned. 'What do they fire then?'

The fairy gave a grim smile. 'Magic.'

And then she vanished through the doorway, hurrying to join the rest of her fleet. Max and Jai turned their attention to the sea cannons but then Genie exclaimed from the porthole. 'She's right, look! Look at the fairy galleons!'

The tiny cannons were firing in quick succession, but the puffs of smoke they emitted were golden rather than grey. The objects they fired were small and round, sparkling and golden. Ursula would have guessed they were miniature gold cannonballs, about the size of marbles – but when the missiles came into contact with the pirate galleon they did not punch holes through its sides. Instead they affected the ship and its crew in startling and unexpected ways.

The explorers watched as one of the fairies aimed

their cannon right at the twin flags flying from the pole. When the golden ball of magic hit them, the flags turned into great, flapping birds that let out terrifying squawks and swooped down at the pirates on deck. Another magic ball hit one of the pirates' cannons and when they tried to fire it, only bubbles came out. A third gold ball hit a member of the crew and they thought the man had disappeared at first, but then Max snatched up a nearby telescope and, peering into it, exclaimed, 'Great Scott! They've turned that pirate into a hamster!'

The others clamoured to have a look, and when it was Ursula's turn she couldn't help giggling aloud at the sight. Several more members of the crew had been hit by the magic balls and they too had been turned into hamsters. Their clothes had shrunk with them, so it looked as if dozens of pirate hamsters were scampering about, swords and duelling pistols tied around their fluffy waists, with little pirate hats balanced upon their heads. The ship's cat was having a field day chasing them around the deck.

'Zara was right,' Ursula said, lowering the telescope. 'They don't need our help at all.'

She recalled what Max had said earlier about how pirate fairies couldn't be particularly dangerous if they were only a few inches tall and thought how wrong he had been. It seemed as if pirate fairies were actually far more formidable foes than their human counterparts. A human pirate might look terrifying and, granted, could make you walk the plank and suchlike, but at least they couldn't turn you into a fluffed-up little hamster forced to scurry around in a frantic fashion to avoid being stepped on or gobbled up by a cat.

Within twenty minutes the battle was over. The fairy fleet had sustained no losses other than that first ship and the humans' galleon was drifting out to sea with its sails transformed into mushrooms, its anchor turned into candyfloss and a whole lot of hamsters instead of a crew.

The explorers went up to the deck of the submarine where they could hear cheers and whistles from the pirate galleons scattered below. When Zara joined them a few minutes later they were relieved to hear that the destroyed fairy ship had been empty at the time because its crew had been serving as lookouts on the island, and no fairies had been hurt after all.

Now that the explorers had seen for themselves that the pirate fairies weren't in league with Scarlett, Jai accepted Zara's offer of help and her ship was brought on board and placed in the submarine's saltwater swimming pool. There wasn't room for the other galleons, so the rest of the fairy fleet were going to stay at Starfish Island and await Zara's return. Ursula was fascinated by the pirate ship and loved seeing it up close. Although nowhere near as big as a human galleon, it was still large enough to take up most of the pool. She saw that it had five individual decks, three lots of sails and a miniature mermaid figurehead. Its name was painted on the sides in sparkling golden letters: *Poisoned Pufferfish.*

'First things first,' Zara told them. 'You'll all need parrots. There's no pirate alive who'll believe you're one of them if you don't have a talking parrot on your shoulder.'

'Shiver me timbers,' Ollie agreed, ruffling his emerald feathers.

'Where are we supposed to get four talking parrots?' Jai asked.

'Parrot Island, of course,' Zara replied.

Jai frowned. 'I've never heard of such a place.'

None of the others had either.

'It's a secret pirate island,' Zara said. 'They've got all kinds of parrots there. Fairy parrots, dancing parrots, yodelling parrots, duelling parrots, et cetera. I can show you exactly where it is on the map.'

Genie dug out the map of the Bubble Ocean that Ursula's mother had given her on one of her visits and spread it on the table. They all gathered round and Zara walked right to the edge of the paper, took a pencil from behind her ear and marked an X on it near Pirate Island.

'There,' she said. 'That's where it is.'

The others peered at the spot she'd marked. 'But that's right in the middle of the Fire-Breathing Octopus Current!' Max exclaimed. 'And perilously close to the Poison Tentacle Sea. No explorer goes anywhere near there these days.'

Ursula shuddered at the mention of the Poison Tentacle Sea. She knew it was one of the most dangerous seas in the world and that the fearsome screeching red devil squid lived there. She thought of the tentacle hanging in the entrance hall of the Ocean Squid Explorers' Club. It was the president's pride and joy, but Ursula disliked it almost as much as she disliked the dreadful mermaid's tail pinned in the trophy room. She'd read the Flag Report that accompanied the squid tentacle and knew that an explorer had died getting it.

The report detailed how Ethan Edward Rook had fallen overboard when the squid attacked the ship and that his brother Julian had leaped into the ocean to save him. In an extraordinary feat of strength and courage, he had managed to cut off the squid's tentacle, thereby saving his brother. But Julian himself had been dragged to the bottom of the ocean by the enraged monster. The last time Ursula had seen Ethan at the club, he'd been standing in the entrance hall, glaring at the tentacle with an expression of utter loathing on his pale face. Ursula felt an almost superstitious dread of the Poison Tentacle Sea and was reluctant to go anywhere near it.

'There's no such thing as a fire-breathing octopus,' Zara said scornfully. 'Whoever heard of such a ridiculous creature? Pirates have made up that story to keep people away.'

'It's been sighted by lots of different sailors and explorers over the years,' Genie said. She loved sea monsters and was an expert on their various forms and habitats.

'It doesn't exist, just the same,' Zara insisted. 'The only octopus that lives around there is the sunset octopus. It's very shy and retiring but it glows bright orange and red at sunset. That's probably what led to rumours that there was a fire-breathing creature in that part of the sea. But sunset octopuses are entirely harmless.'

'I suppose next you'll be saying that reports of the Poison Tentacle Sea are all exaggerated and that it's nothing but sea butterflies and coral gardens?' Max asked.

Zara shook her head. 'Oh no, the Poison Tentacle Sea is extremely dangerous,' she said. 'Absolutely chock full of monsters. Dreadful place. I wouldn't go near it. Parrot Island is close by, but it's still classed as being in the Bubble Ocean, and there's nothing more dangerous there than the Amazonian fire-breathing parrot. You just have to avoid getting sucked into the Bone Current, which sometimes spills into it.'

'If you say so,' said Max, not sounding entirely convinced. 'And what do we do once we have these parrots?'

'Well, then we'll need to create pirate disguises for you too,' Zara replied. 'You don't have any pirate hats lying around, by any chance?'

'No, but I'm good at making hats,' Genie said. 'I can put something together for us all.'

'And how will we be able to rescue the prisoners?' Max asked. 'Scarlett's taken my sister, along with some other children.'

'They'll be in the fort, same as my fleet,' Zara said. 'There's a whole host of cells in the tunnels there.

You'll have a tough time getting inside, though. Pirate disguises will help get you on to the island, but not into the fort itself. Scarlett's really hot on security right now.'

Max frowned. 'Well, do you know a secret way inside?'

Zara looked at him like he was a simpleton. 'It's a fort,' she said. 'It's absolutely impenetrable. Which means it's impossible to get inside, unless you have a key.'

'I know what impenetrable means,' Max said irritably.

'There are pirate guards stationed at the entrance day and night,' Zara said. 'It's got stone walls five foot thick and it's on top of the island's tallest hill, so there's no way of sneaking up on it. You'll have to create a really fantastic diversion. And even then, getting yourselves in and the prisoners *out* is another matter altogether. That's why I haven't been able to rescue my crew.'

'I'm good at lock picking,' Max said. 'And I've been practising on a—'

Zara shook her head. 'The locks can't be picked,' she said. 'I thought you knew what impenetrable means?'

'I'm sure between us we can work out some way to trick the pirates and create a diversion,' Jai said. 'And perhaps the mermaids will have some ideas?'

Before they reached Pirate Island, the submarine was going to make a stop at Mercadia, the mermaid city where Ursula's mother lived. Ursula's father had been an explorer who'd lived at the Ocean Squid Explorers' Club when he was alive, but her mother was a mermaid. After falling in love with Ursula's father, she'd used a sea witch's enchantment to turn into a human. The spell had lasted for five years before she had to return to her original form and the ocean she had come from. Living on land made her ill and she needed the deep coolness of the sea to survive.

Ursula, meanwhile, found herself permanently stuck between two different worlds; she needed sunlight and air sometimes, but she also needed sea and surf too. The Ocean Squid Explorers' Club had always considered mermaids to be their sworn enemies and so Ursula had kept her heritage a secret, until the day Scarlett Sauvage attacked the club and stole it away. When that happened, Ursula had transformed into a mermaid in full daylight in order to rescue the *Blowfish*.

Before leaving on the submarine she had sent her mother a message to explain what had happened and where she was going. But Ursula knew that her mother wouldn't approve of the way she'd gone flying off with a bunch of junior explorers. And certainly their last mission had been perilous enough – they'd had encounters with a colossal sneezing jellyfish and a storm maiden, been attacked by pirates and had to flee an erupting underwater volcano.

As they had never been in one place long enough for a message to reach them, Ursula didn't have any contact with her mother again until they were able to use the firebird. This was a magical creature Scarlett had given to Max so that he could communicate with her when he was supposed to be trying to invent a magical weapon for her.

The explorers thought that using the bird rather than the radio would mean they could avoid having an argument about whether or not they should launch another expedition, but in fact the clubs had used the bird to send responses, and so had Ursula's mother. She had said she was, of course, relieved to hear Ursula was safe, but on no account was she to even think about continuing her mission. She'd said it was far too dangerous, and best left to adult explorers, and so on and so on.

Adults could be so exasperating about things like that. They always thought *they* were the ones who ought to be doing the exploring, and rescuing, and adventuring, even after Stella Starflake Pearl and her friends had shown the world that junior explorers could explore, and rescue, and adventure just as well as any adult. And Ursula had no intention of abandoning her friends, no matter what her mother might say.

However, some of the mermaids had pledged to help them. After Ursula and her friends had helped to save a mermaid ice-cream parlour that was being attacked by the Collector's pirate recruits, Selina, the mermaid who owned it, had been so grateful that she and her friends had sworn to help the explorers stop Scarlett Sauvage in any way they could. And the mermaids they'd met when they visited the luxurious Jaffles Hotel had agreed to join forces with them too.

Ursula was both pleased and dismayed that they were going to the city where her mother lived. She desperately longed to see her, but she also feared she would try to prevent her from leaving with her friends. Still, there was nothing for it. They needed the mermaids' help in their mission to stop the Collector.

When the explorers gathered on the bridge to set a course for the mermaid city, Max cleared his throat and said, 'I just wanted to say thanks. To all of you.' For once, there was no laughter in his voice. 'Jada means the world to me – even if she is really annoying at times. I'm grateful that you're helping me to get her back, especially as it involves going on a forbidden expedition and conspiring with pirate fairies.'

'We're not *conspiring* with pirate fairies,' Jai protested, shuddering at the idea. 'We're working with one. *Temporarily*. Which, yes, is still technically against the rules, but ...' he patted Max's shoulder, 'this is important. Some things are worth breaking the rules for.'

'Your eye twitched when you said that.' Max grinned. 'Say it again! I like that you've come over to the dark side.'

'I *haven't* come over to the dark side.' Jai rolled his eyes. 'I still think rules are important, especially on a submarine, where the safety of the entire crew depends on them.' His eyes flicked towards Genie. 'I just think sisters matter more, that's all.'

And so, with a brand-new member of crew on board, the submarine set off towards the Sunken City of Mercadia.

CHAPTER THREE

Of all the clubs, the Ocean Squid Explorers' one was known for being the most technologically advanced. While the others messed about with sleighs and tents and hot-air balloons that crashed as often as they flew, the Ocean Squid Club owned an entire fleet of superb and spectacular submarines. As a young engineer, Ursula adored the gleaming fleet and had spent many happy hours with her mentor Joe, tinkering with their engines, learning about how they worked, and crawling around in their inner pipes and tunnels.

But they were incredible things to travel in too, even better than floating hotels. They had entire libraries, cinemas, swimming pools, dining rooms and skittle alleys, to say nothing of the bathrooms. Let other explorers get dirty and grubby during their expeditions – Ocean Squid explorers were used to luxuriating in beautiful tubs with sea-flower-scented bubbles and silver plates of candy starfish. And of course the submarines were fast – the fastest mode of transport in existence, with the possible exception of Scarlett Sauvage's flying machine. Everyone knew that nothing could stop a submarine when it was flying through the ocean at full speed. It therefore took the explorers by surprise when something did exactly that.

It was two days after they had left Starfish Island and the explorers had had dinner together as always before splitting up to their various pursuits, leaving the submarine to the automatic navigation system. Max went to the robotics lab to tinker with his robot shark, Jai went to the library to continue work on his book – he was writing a memoir about the exploits of his beloved seafaring cat, Biscuit – and the girls went to the cinema with Bess and Zara. They were about halfway into their sea-monster film, and Genie had just got up to get another bucket of blue-dolphin popcorn when it happened.

The submarine came to a stop so quickly that they all went flying from their various chairs, and any furniture that wasn't nailed down went tumbling around them too. Ursula, Genie, Zara and Ollie ended up covered in sticky blue popcorn and the film reel got stuck in a loop so that it kept playing the same scene over and over again.

'What's going on?' Genie gasped. 'Did we hit something?'

'I didn't feel a collision,' Ursula said, propping herself up.

She was right. Although the sudden change of speed had sent them all flying, there had been no crunch of impact. Besides which, the automatic navigation system would have alerted them if there had been anything in their path up ahead.

'Well, *something* made the submarine stop,' Zara said.

'Dead men's tales!' Ollie squawked from beneath a huge pile of popcorn, flapping his sticky wings indignantly.

Ursula dug the little parrot out and they all scrambled to their feet and hurried over to the portholes, peering out at the dark sea. Unless there was glowing coral, or phosphorescent plankton, or something like that around, it was very difficult to see much outside. There were times when the submarine may as well have been drifting through outer space and this was always guaranteed to give even the bravest and most experienced explorer a bit of a shivery thrill. After all, only a very tiny part of the world's oceans had been explored – some thought as little as ten per cent. The rest of it was a great, mysterious unknown and there could be absolutely anything lurking out there in the water – beautiful, deadly, strange, magnificent things.

The water around the *Blowfish* now was pitch-black and so the explorers had no idea what had caused them to stop. Seconds later, an alarm sounded, summoning them all to action stations on the bridge. Ursula and Genie raced straight for the door, with Zara and Ollie close behind them. The cinema was further away than either the library or the robotics lab, so the boys were already there when Ursula and Genie arrived.

'What's happened?' Ursula gasped.

'We don't know.' Jai glanced around from where he and Max were peering out the portholes. 'We've checked the instruments and it doesn't make sense. There's nothing out there and no strong currents or anything like that. The engines are set to full power, but we've come to a dead stop.'

'It must be some sort of powerful magic,' Zara said with a frown. 'Perhaps a curse from a sea witch or wizard?'

'Why would a sea witch or wizard want to curse us?' Max asked, looking baffled. 'We haven't done anything to them. You don't think they could be in league with the Collector too, do you?'

'Sea witches and wizards don't need an excuse to go around cursing people!' Zara scoffed.

'X marks the spot!' Ollie shrieked from her shoulder.

'They're always at it,' Zara went on. 'I think they just like to show off to each other.'

'There's something out there!' Jai cried, pointing. 'It looks a bit like a mermaid's tail.'

They all turned to Ursula.

'There's no way a mermaid could stop this submarine,' she said. 'The *Blowfish* is far too big and powerful.'

'What if they had water horses to help them?' Genie asked.

Ursula frowned. The magical white horses were formed from the ocean itself and were immensely strong, but the truth was, she couldn't exactly be sure what mermaids could or couldn't do, especially when it came to using the magic of their voices. Growing up in an explorers' club, she'd soaked up some of the humans' fear about mermaids and had always thought of their magic as a dark, dangerous thing that could drown people. So she'd never wanted to listen when her mother had tried to tell her about the wonderful, extraordinary things it could do.

'I don't know,' Ursula said, uncertainly. 'But it doesn't seem very likely.'

'They could be ninja mermaids,' Max suggested. 'I read about them in one of the explorer journals before I got expelled from the club. They're super strong, and very acrobatic, and they're able to do this really cool thing where they—'

'It's not a mermaid,' Ursula exclaimed. 'It's a dolphin.'

The dolphin had swum into view directly in front of the porthole and they could now see it clearly in the dark water because there was a bright purple light surrounding it.

'What's creating that light?' Genie wondered as she peered out.

'It's wearing a glowing sea-flower necklace,' Ursula said.

'And a medallion,' Max said. 'What's that written on it?'

As if he'd heard the question, the dolphin swam right up to the porthole, close enough for them to see the words on the golden disc: 'Bubble Tide Messenger'.

Ursula frowned. 'The bubble tide is how mermaids send messages,' she said. 'Mum and I used it to stay in touch while I was at the club. Normally you speak your message into a shell and then it finds its way to the recipient on the bubble tide. The larger the shell, the bigger the message, but the longer it will take to arrive. Mum works for the bubble tide postal service in Mercadia. I've never heard of dolphins being used before, though.'

Jai shook his head. 'Well, all I'm interested in is how the heck has it managed to stop our submarine?'

As he spoke, the water beyond the dolphin lit up and they saw that the *Blowfish* was surrounded by a gigantic bubble made from dozens of the same purple flowers glowing around the dolphin's neck. He swam back a little bit and continued to gaze through the glass at them with friendly, intelligent eyes. For the first time, Ursula saw that the dolphin had a little bag tied to its sleek body and that this also had the words 'Bubble Tide Messenger' written across it.

'Well, we're not under attack, at least,' Max said. 'I mean, I never heard of ninja mermaids using glowing purple flowers as a weapon before.'

They watched as the dolphin twisted towards its bag, nosed inside for a bit and then turned back to face them with a large shell in its mouth.

'It must be a message,' Ursula said. 'For one of us. I guess I'd better swim out there to fetch it.'

'One of my midget subs will be faster,' Max said. He pressed a button on the nearby control panel, and a moment later one of his robot submarines shot out into the water. It was very small – no bigger than a person's hand – but it was a perfect submarine in every way and even had its own tiny Ocean Squid Explorers' Club waterproof flag. Max had created different attachments too, and this one had a little robotic arm that was able to take the shell from the dolphin and return to the submarine with it in no time at all. Max pressed another button and the next moment the midget sub had shot through an internal pipe to arrive with them on the bridge.

'It looks like it's for you,' Max said to Ursula, taking the shell from the submarine and handing it over.

She had a brief impression of her name written across the shell in sparkling gold letters before her mother's angry voice began to speak. Normally, you had to press your ear right up to the shell to hear the message, but this was a voice loud enough for everyone on the deck to hear.

'Ursula Jellyfin, I am extremely disappointed in you – actually, no, more than that, I'm furious! In the last message I sent with the firebird, I ordered you to come to Mercadia, and yet I have still had no word back from you.'

Ursula winced. The firebird had been recalled by Scarlett shortly afterwards because she wanted it to communicate with more promising inventors. Ursula had had no way of replying to her mother's message, even if she'd wanted to.

'Explorer blood may well run in your veins,' her mother's voice went on, 'but I am still your mother, young lady, and I won't have you ignore me, even if it means I have to spend a ridiculous amount of money sending a message by dolphin. The purple sea flowers can create a bubble around any object, no matter how big or fast, and won't release it until the message has been delivered – so it's no use trying to pretend this didn't reach you. What's more, I've instructed the dolphin to wait for you to return the shell to him. You will be able to give your message once mine comes to an end. And I'm warning you, Ursula, I don't want to hear any excuses or explorers' nonsense about rescue missions. All I want to hear is that you're coming to Mercadia, like I told you. And for goodness' sake, be careful and take care of yourself. Lots of love from Mum.'

The shell in Ursula's hand finally went quiet and a few moments passed before Max sniggered. Ursula looked up and saw that the others were hiding grins too, while shuffling their feet and avoiding her eye. Like all children, they found it a strange mixture of awkward and funny to be present whilst a friend was being told off. Even Zara was grinning.

'Sounds like you've properly annoyed your mum,' the fairy said.

Ursula sighed. She could feel a blush warming her cheeks and very much wished her mother had chosen a quieter shell that would not have broadcast her telling-off to her friends.

'I'd better send a message back,' she said, glancing out of the porthole to the dolphin. 'We won't get going again otherwise.'

She raised the shell to her mouth and gave a very brief message.

'Hold your horses, Mum. We're actually on our way to Mercadia now and should be there in a couple of days. I couldn't reply to your message because we no longer have the firebird and I didn't know you could send a speedy one by dolphin because you never told me.'

Ursula heard the accusatory tone that crept into her voice and felt a little bit guilty. After all, her mother had tried to tell her about mermaid life every time she came to visit, but Ursula had always shied away from it. She had wanted to be an explorer more than anything in the world, and nothing jeopardised that as much as being a mermaid.

'I'll see you soon,' she ended shortly.

After they'd used the midget submarine to return the shell to the dolphin, Ursula felt bad about not telling her mum she loved her, as she normally did. She had felt cross and embarrassed by her mum's message, but even though she'd been told off she realised that her mum had still sent her love at the end. It was too late to change the message now, though. The second the dolphin had the shell, it thrust it back in its bag, flipped its tail once in farewell and then took off into the ocean, taking the glowing bubble of flowers with it.

The submarine continued on its way and the explorers returned to their various pursuits. The next couple of days passed by uneventfully, and Ursula became more and more excited at the prospect of seeing a real mermaid city for the first time. However, she was nervous too, because her mother had always told her that the mermaids might not accept her because of her human father. As far as she was aware, there'd never been a girl who was half human and half mermaid before. And it didn't help that her mother was cross before she even arrived. Ursula knew she would have an argument on her hands and that it would be difficult to persuade her mother to let her leave with her friends on the *Blowfish*. But she would just have to figure that out once she got there.

The day came soon enough. The explorers were all on the bridge when they first saw the lights of Mercadia shining through the water up ahead.

They had finally reached the mermaid city.

Chapter Four

For several long moments, the explorers simply stared. The submarine floated slightly above Mercadia, so they had a wonderful view of it sprawled out below. Sunshine jellyfish drifted about, casting their warm, golden glow. There were pearls everywhere they looked, in every colour – creamy ivory, pale pink and powder grey – studded into the sides of buildings, and gathered in piles upon sandy beaches. And dozens and dozens of beautiful mermaid gardens filled with glowing sea flowers, and elegant coral, and bright sea sponges.

There were no roads or pavements, but twisting tunnels of waterways wound up and around the various buildings, many of which took the form of giant, spiralled shells. Striking statues of dolphins made from blue sea glass gazed down from their plinths and multicoloured mosaic tiles depicted whales and waterfalls and walruses.

They could see mermaids swimming to and fro, all

with different-coloured tails and hair. And there was a great deal of animal life too. Seahorses zipped between the flowers, turtles drifted lazily along the currents, and to Ursula's delight water horses frolicked in the dark water at the edge of the city. There were even some grand-looking chariots pulled by dolphins, which elderly or disabled mermaids were using to travel around.

But best and most wondrous of all was the castle. Made entirely from sea crystal, it rose up from the centre of the city and shed sparkling ripples of blue light over everything around. Its slim turrets stretched up high into the sea above and the walls were covered in dozens of shining silver starfish, while the pointed roofs were crusted in barnacles and pearls. The many balconies were carved into the shape of giant shells, and golden statues of majestic narwhals peered over the railings down at the city.

Ursula was speechless. She thought it one of the loveliest sights she could have imagined, and the mermaid half of her ached to be a part of it all. She wanted to swim through those shimmering streets, and play with the turtles, and take mermaid picnics in the sea gardens. Her explorer friends were equally impressed.

'It's ... it's just magical,' Genie breathed. 'Wonderful.

Oh, Ursula! You must be so thrilled to finally get to see it!'

'It's amazing,' Ursula agreed.

'Who lives in the castle?' Max asked.

'I don't know,' she admitted.

'Do mermaids have a royal family?' Genie said. 'It looks like the type of castle a king and queen would live in.'

'I don't know,' Ursula repeated.

Jai looked surprised. 'Didn't your mother tell you?'

'I didn't ask,' Ursula said, feeling uncomfortable. 'I didn't want to know too much about mermaid life.'

'Why not?' Jai asked.

'Well … the Ocean Squid Explorers' Club thinks mermaids are monsters. So that part of me just always felt like a secret … a burden.'

Genie reached for Ursula's hand. 'I'm sorry you felt that way,' she said, squeezing her fingers. 'Once we rescue the club, maybe things will improve. Perhaps the club will change its mind about mermaids.'

'And girls being explorers,' Jai said.

'They'd better,' Max agreed. 'If we manage to rescue the club we should all get big, shiny medals. I bet you'd like another one to add to your collection wouldn't you, Jai?'

He gave his friend a nudge. Jai was something of a poster boy for the club and had been awarded more medals than any other young explorer in history, a fact of which he was immensely proud. Max liked to tease him because he often wore his medals on his cloak and spent many hours polishing and cleaning them, when he wasn't working on his biographical tribute to Biscuit.

'The medals are beside the point,' Jai said, a little pompously. 'All that matters is doing what's right.'

'It's still nice to get a medal, though,' Max said, grinning. 'Some nights I lie awake thinking about it.'

They all knew this wasn't true. In fact, there probably wasn't a single rule in the Ocean Squid Club rule book that Max hadn't broken at some point, and he'd made it quite plain that he didn't give two hoots about medals or accolades or awards of any kind. Indeed, sometimes he quite enjoyed breaking rules just for the thrill of it.

Sensing that he was about to be made fun of, Jai hurriedly took control of the conversation. 'We need to go into the city and introduce ourselves.' He glanced at Ursula. 'Any thoughts on how we should proceed? Obviously we hope we'll be welcomed, but we can't be sure.'

Ursula shook her head. 'I don't know any more than you do,' she said. 'I'm sorry. I'm not much use.'

Jai gave her shoulder a quick squeeze. 'Not to worry,' he said. 'We'll figure it out together.'

'I guess we'll have to swim down there,' Max said. 'There isn't room for the submarine.'

'We'll have to go through the gates,' Ursula said, pleased to have something useful to add. 'Mum told me once that there's a magical force field around the city that keeps out any unauthorised visitors.'

'Should we go in diving suits, or eat some of the Ocean Discovery ice cream?' Genie asked.

'Best go with the ice cream,' Jai said. 'We can talk then too.'

The ice cream had been given to them by Selina as a thank-you present. It was bright blue in colour, with chocolate dolphins, candy starfish and sugar shells, but best of all it was magical. Just one bite could allow a human to breathe and speak underwater as easily as if they were mermaids themselves. Its effect would last for a full twenty-four hours, but after that a person needed to breathe air for twenty-four hours before the ice cream would work again.

Humans were still awkward in the water compared to mermaids, though. Without flippers and fins they couldn't swim as well or as fast, and their movements tended to be somewhat slow and cumbersome. Max had been working on some small robot dolphins to help them, and they decided this would be the perfect time to test them out.

Zara did not trust the mermaid ice cream, nor did she have any interest in going to a mermaid city. 'There's even more bad blood between pirates and mermaids than there is between pirates and explorers.' She looked at Ursula. 'No offence, but me and Ollie will stay on the submarine, thanks very much.'

Ursula could see that this gave Jai something of a dilemma. The *Blowfish* was utterly precious to him, especially as it was one of the few surviving subs from the Ocean Squid Explorers' Club. Most of the others had been swept up into a snow globe when Scarlett captured the club. Normally, Jai would not allow an unknown guest to remain behind unattended, but clearly he could not force the fairy into the sea against her will either.

Something of these concerns must have shown on his face, because Zara rolled her eyes and said, 'I'm not going to steal the submarine, if that's what you're thinking.'

'One little fairy wouldn't be able to do that by herself,' Ursula said. 'This submarine requires a four-person crew, minimum.'

'You could still damage it, though, if you had a mind to,' Max pointed out.

'I don't,' Zara said shortly. 'But I guess you're never going to trust me, no matter what I do, so if it'll make you feel any better, you can lock me and Ollie up in the brig until you get back.'

'Capital idea,' Max said at once.

Ursula didn't like the thought of the little fairy being confined to a prison cell when she hadn't done anything wrong, and was about to say so when Jai shook his head.

'No,' he said. 'You don't have to do that. You can have the run of the submarine.'

'Look, I know I voted for Zara to join the crew, but I'm not so sure about leaving her on the *Blowfish* by herself,' Max said. 'Pirates are rule breakers and it's dangerous to trust one of those. I should know.'

'Well, sometimes it's dangerous not to trust people too,' Jai said. 'We've all seen it with the adult explorers, haven't we? If anyone's different, or doesn't fit into their mould, they get shunned and pushed to one side. We know the Ocean Squid Explorers' Club thinks that only a certain type of man should be an explorer and we've seen how that makes the club less than what it could be.' He began ticking points off on his fingers.

53

'They don't want mermaids, or kraken whisperers, or fairies, or . . .' He looked at Max. 'Well, you're always breaking the rules and getting into trouble, so you kind of bring that on yourself, but you get my point. When it's my turn to take command and captain a submarine, I don't want to be pointing fingers, and putting people in boxes, and distrusting everyone all the time. As far as I'm concerned, all are welcome if they act fairly and honestly, and it seems to me that Zara has been completely fair and honest with us since we met.' He turned to the pirate fairy. 'So, yes, I will trust you alone on the submarine, and if that turns out to be a mistake then I guess it's on me.'

'I think you're right,' Ursula said at once.

'Yes,' Genie said quietly. 'Everyone should have the chance to prove themselves.'

They all looked at Max. Typically, a submarine captain had the final word on all such things and it didn't much matter whether the crew agreed with him or not, but the junior explorers preferred to discuss things as a team. They liked to be in agreement where possible and hoped that Max would see things their way too.

'I'm still not sure,' he said with a shrug. 'But you're right about the adult explorers. They're a bunch of fussy old fusspots, that's for sure. Perhaps we should try things a different way. I suppose this means you're against the idea of taking weapons into Mercadia with us too?'

'I am,' Jai replied. 'Explorers and mermaids have been enemies for years. If we want that to change, then someone has to be the first to extend the hand of friendship. It wouldn't look good if we went in armed.'

Max sighed. 'It's a risk.'

It was one they all decided to take, however, so Max went to the lab to fetch the robot dolphins, Genie got some Ocean Discovery ice cream from the kitchen, and then they all changed into their swimwear before meeting back at the swim-out hatch. This was a big metal room that sealed them off from the rest of the submarine and then slowly filled with water so they could open a hatch and swim straight out into the ocean.

'Here are the dolphins,' Max said, handing one to Genie and Jai, while keeping the last one for himself.

They were quite small, only about the size of a cat, but Max said they had powerful motors inside them. 'Just hold on to their fins and point the nose to steer,' he said. 'They ought to pull you through the water as fast as a real dolphin would.' He looked at Jai and said, 'Yours is adapted slightly so you can steer it with one arm – you just hold on to that handle there rather than the fins.'

Jai nodded. 'Got it.'

'How do you control the speed?' Genie asked.

'Why would you want to?' Max asked with a grin. 'Fast is always best. Just squeeze the fins to go faster and relax your grip a bit if you want to be boring and dawdle along slowly like some old granny.'

They all took a bite of ice cream, apart from Ursula, then closed the door to seal themselves into the room. Ursula flicked the lever and sat down on the floor as seawater immediately began to rush up through the grates in the floor. It swirled about their feet in salt-scented foam and Ursula's legs immediately turned into a mermaid's fin. She took off the swim skirt she'd been wearing and tied it around a hook on the floor. A few minutes later, the swim-out hatch was almost entirely full.

'It feels so strange being here without a diving suit,' Jai said, and even though they were now all underwater, his voice came out normally and they could all hear and understand him perfectly. Genie and Max could breathe as easily as Ursula too.

'I wonder what other magical things mermaid ice cream can do?' Genie wondered.

It was yet another question Ursula would like to know the answer to. Her hand went to her clam locket – a gift her mother had given to her on her last birthday to help channel her mermaid magic. She promised herself that there would be no more shying away from the mermaid side of herself. From now on, she intended to find out everything there was to know, and to embrace this part of who she was as best she could.

Jai pressed the button to open the hatch and they all swam out into the ocean. As always, Ursula delighted in the cool feel of the silky waves sliding over her tail fin, especially as she hadn't been in the water for a couple of days.

Bess was there to greet them, but Genie gently asked her to stay back with the submarine for now. After all, the mermaids might not realise she was a shadow animal, and they did not want to get things off on the wrong foot by appearing as if they'd brought a sea monster along to attack the city.

Max, Genie and Jai spent a few moments experimenting with the robot dolphins. Ursula saw at once that they were extremely powerful by the way Max went shooting around the *Blowfish*, leaving a trail of bubbles behind him. Jai and Genie were a little more cautious, but when they set off towards Mercadia, the human explorers were easily able to keep up with Ursula, and they approached the city gates together, fear and excitement bubbling up inside them in equal measure.

Chapter Five

Ursula kept her eyes peeled for her mother, half expecting to be accosted by her the moment she entered the city, but there were no civilian merfolk at the gates, only a pair of guards. One was a blue-tailed female and the other a red-tailed male, and the explorers could tell they were guards because they had a fierce look in their eyes and both carried gleaming silver tridents.

The explorers stopped in front of the guards, eyeing the tridents nervously.

Jai cleared his throat. 'Good morning. We are explorers from the Ocean Squid Explorers' Club, and we would like to—'

'We know who you are,' the female guard said. 'And we've been expecting you. You have come to discuss the Collector. We have orders to take you to the princess as soon as you arrive.'

'Princess?' Ursula asked.

So there was a mermaid royal family after all!

'Princess Coral,' the male guard said. Both merfolk were looking at Ursula intently and she guessed they must know who she was. She hoped they were only curious about her heritage and not hostile to it, but their guarded expressions made it quite hard to tell what they were thinking.

'Come,' the merman said. 'We will escort you to the palace.'

Without waiting for the explorers' agreement, the guards ushered them through the gates. Everywhere they went, mermaids stopped what they were doing to stare at them. They were not altogether friendly stares and Ursula began to worry that perhaps they weren't going to get a very warm welcome here after all.

Before long, they had reached the castle and were shown into a large entrance hall. It was a double-height room, with large pillars reaching up to the ceiling. A vast stained-glass window depicted a pair of crowned narwhals, and the rippling green and blue light gave the space something of a church-like feel. Every tile on the floor contained paintings of bubbles and there were more dolphin statues on marble plinths around the room. The palace smelled of seaweed and shells and sand.

The mermaid guards handed the explorers over to

a member of the palace staff – a pretty mermaid with a tail as green as Ursula's. She smiled at them shyly and said, 'The princess will receive you in the Throne Room. Follow me.'

They went down several long hallways, all decorated in a similar fashion to the entrance hall. Ursula noticed that there were no doors, only open archways, some of which had curtains of seaweed or strings of pearls hung over them. She had a brief impression of paintings on the walls depicting serious-looking mermaids that she guessed must be previous members of the royal family, because they all wore crowns or tiaras, along with other fine sea jewels.

At last, they reached the Throne Room, although Ursula thought that Throne *Hall* would have been a better description. It was a huge space, easily large enough to accommodate two or three hundred mermaids. A host of mermaid guards stood to attention along both sides of the room, all holding silver tridents. A great chandelier of pink coral hung from the ceiling and slabs of pale marble made up the floor. More stained-glass windows lined the room, depicting various sea creatures, such as turtles and seals, and bestowing the same church-like feel that the lobby had had. There must have been sunshine jellyfish

drifting by outside because light poured in through the coloured glass.

But the most impressive thing in the room was certainly the throne. It was a gigantic seat made entirely from different-coloured shells. Ursula thought it was hopelessly lovely, but nothing could compare with the beauty of the mermaid sitting in it.

She was small and young – Ursula guessed she was only a few years older than they were. And her tail was a colour Ursula had never seen before. Of course, growing up at the club she hadn't seen many mermaids in real life. At Jaffles Hotel and Selina's ice-cream parlour, she had seen mermaids with green, blue, red and white tails, and the Mercadia mermaids had seemed much the same as they passed through the streets. But Ursula had never ever seen a mermaid with a golden tail before. It looked like the brightest gold there could be in the world – the shining sort that dragons hoarded, or talented imps spun into magical cloaks.

And her hair was different too. Most mermaids had green, blue or purple hair, or a mixture of all those colours, but Princess Coral's was the same golden colour as her tail. She wore it piled on top of her head, arranged with silver starfish combs, while long strings of pale pearls adorned her neck and wrists.

Tucked up close to the base of the throne, Ursula was astonished to see a water horse – only this wasn't a powerful adult one like those she'd seen before, but a foal, with gangly long legs, huge eyes and very long lashes.

'Greetings, Your Majesty,' Jai said. He tried to bow, but it was a little awkward in the water, especially as he was still hanging on to his robot dolphin. 'We are very pleased to—'

'Silence.' Princess Coral's voice was cold and hard. She did not even look at Jai, but focused her gaze on Ursula. She had extraordinary eyes which were the same shade of gold as her tail. They should have been beautiful, yet somehow they were unnerving and otherworldly, reminding Ursula of the pictures of snow queens she had seen in the pages of storybooks, and bringing to mind images of wickedness, stepmothers and spinning wheels.

The mermaid princess raised a hand and made a beckoning gesture. 'Come here.'

Ursula frowned, feeling her doubt about Princess Coral deepen into dislike. Surely it would not kill her to be polite, and to acknowledge Jai, and to say please? But then she'd heard that human kings and queens could be this way too. She swam closer to the throne and gave a bow. The little water foal was so close that Ursula could see each individual eyelash as it gazed at her with beautiful liquid eyes. She wished she could reach out to touch it and wondered where its mother was.

'Thank you for receiving us, Your Majesty.'

'Is it true that you are half mermaid and half human?' Princess Coral asked abruptly.

Ursula felt a wave of nerves wash over her but swallowed them down. 'Yes,' she said. 'I am.'

The golden gaze had no warmth in it as it lingered on Ursula. 'That is forbidden,' she said. 'Your very existence is forbidden.'

Ursula wasn't sure what a person was supposed to say to that, so she said nothing. Suddenly, she wondered whether coming to Mercadia had been a mistake. Perhaps the mermaid princess was going to put her in prison. Perhaps her mother was already there and that was why there'd been no sign of her since they arrived.

Nervously, she glanced back at the others and saw that they looked wary too. Perhaps Max had been right – perhaps they should have brought some means of defending themselves. And yet … they were vastly outnumbered. There must have been fifty mermaid guards in this room alone, so it wouldn't have made any difference.

'Well?' Princess Coral said. 'What have you got to say in your defence?'

Ursula suddenly thought of Miss Soames, the teacher who had been in charge of her care back at the Ocean Squid Explorers' Club. She was a mean-spirited, miserable woman who clearly disliked all children and had never once done anything to make Ursula's life any easier. Instead she constantly berated her for the most trivial offences, and tried to make her feel like a burden and a nuisance, and a thoroughly bad child. Ursula disliked her intensely but in that moment she was almost grateful to her because her horrible ways meant that Ursula had had experience of standing up to bullies. The thought gave her strength now and stiffened her spine. She raised her chin a little and spoke calmly.

'I won't apologise for something that isn't my fault. Yes, I am half human and half mermaid, but my parents loved each other and me, and I don't believe they did anything wrong.' The princess's eyes widened slightly, and Ursula hurried on before she could be stopped. 'Also, I don't see why humans and mermaids can't work together and be allies, especially now when we have a common enemy. When we spoke to the mermaids at Jaffles, they said that—'

Princess Coral suddenly looked angry. 'Those mermaids had no authority to forge an alliance with explorers.'

Ursula swallowed hard. 'We understood that they couldn't talk on behalf of all mermaids,' she said. 'Just like my friends and I couldn't talk for all explorers. But we hoped it might be the start of something – of better relations between us.'

'You are four children alone.' The princess's eyes ran over Ursula and her friends behind her. 'Is that correct?'

'Not entirely,' Max said. 'We've got a pirate fairy and some robot ducks back on the submarine.'

Genie nudged Max sharply in the ribs. Now was not the time to be glib, but he didn't seem to get the message.

'We've got some plankton too,' he went on. 'Jai, why don't you tell the princess about your plankton and how important they are for the ocean?'

Jai owned four pet plankton, which he had named Brian, Jessop, Sofia and Clyde, and indeed plankton were his favourite sea creatures – a fact that Max found endlessly amusing.

'Shh!' Jai hissed at him.

But the princess had not picked up on Max's sarcasm and said, 'Yes, plankton are very important for the health of the ocean, and the world. It's refreshing to hear of someone who appreciates that, for a change.' She looked back at Ursula. 'I am not convinced by the idea of mermaids and humans working together, especially if those humans are explorers. The Ocean Squid Club has been a menace to us ever since it first began, hunting us down and treating us like monsters. But I accept that the four of you are not to blame for that, and I won't waste time lecturing you on the crimes committed by your ancestors. You are right that the Collector and the Phantom Atlas Society are a grave threat to us all.'

Her hand drifted down to the water foal at her feet and she stroked him gently behind the ears. He immediately looked up at her with an adoring expression and pressed his wet muzzle into her palm. 'News of the world on land can be slow to reach us beneath the sea,' Princess Coral went on, 'but it sounds as if the explorers' clubs are dithering about in their usual incompetent fashion. At least you are here and attempting to do something useful. So, yes, we will aid you. The question is how?'

'We're making our way to Pirate Island,' Ursula said.

'That's where the Collector has her headquarters. One of her prisoners managed to get a message to us, but Scarlett doesn't know we've found her. With the help of a pirate fairy we're hoping to disguise ourselves as pirates and sneak on to the island.'

'And then?' Princess Coral asked.

'Then we'll try to rescue the prisoners and capture Scarlett so that she can be brought to justice.' Ursula swallowed hard and forced herself to go on. 'We hoped that perhaps some of your mermaids might agree to come with us as back-up in the water around the island in case Scarlett tries to escape that way?'

'I would be happy to grant your request,' Princess Coral said. 'But there are no mermaid colonies near Pirate Island. Our kind stays as far away from that place as we do from the Ocean Squid Explorers' Club. And since mermaids cannot swim as fast as a submarine, they would not be able to keep up with you on your journey.'

'Oh.' Ursula couldn't help feeling a little crestfallen, even though the princess's words made sense. She wondered briefly whether they could take mermaids with them on board, but she knew at once that wouldn't work. They would not fare well out of seawater, the pirate galleon took up most of the swimming pool and, even if it didn't, mermaids needed the cool, blue ocean around them – a pool couldn't compare with that, even if it did have a flume slide. Perhaps their visit to Mercadia had been a waste of time after all.

'There is one other thing I can offer you, though,' Princess Coral said.

Ursula looked up eagerly. 'Yes?'

Princess Coral gave the water foal one final pat before leaving her throne of shells and swimming to the doorway, her golden tail flashing in the light coming through the stained-glass windows. She spoke to someone in the corridor beyond and then returned to the throne with a trident in her hands. Unlike the ones held by the guards, this one wasn't silver, but golden from end to tip.

'Here.' Princess Coral held it out to Ursula. 'For the purposes of such a vitally important mission, you may borrow it.'

'Thanks.' Ursula took hold of the trident uncertainly. It was surprisingly warm beneath her touch and seemed to glow with a light of its own. 'What, er ... what does it do?'

Princess Coral looked scandalised. 'You do not know?'

Ursula felt a wave of embarrassment and squirmed.

'I don't know much about mermaid life,' she admitted. 'But I would like to learn.'

Princess Coral looked so annoyed that for a moment Ursula feared she would take the trident straight back, but finally she said, 'It's the Crown Trident, of course. I expect you to return it in one piece the moment your mission is achieved. Now I suggest you depart. There is no time to lose.'

The princess turned back towards her throne and Ursula made to join her friends, but then hesitated. The meeting had been a success, and she knew she ought to quit while she was ahead and leave quietly with the others, but she simply could not bear to go without asking one final question.

'Excuse me, Your Majesty,' she said. 'I was wondering what has happened to the water foal's mother?'

She could feel her heart beating a little faster in her chest as she waited for Princess Coral's answer. What if the water foal had been taken from its mother against its will? Ursula could suddenly sympathise even more with Genie's comments earlier about the captive kraken on Smugglers' Isle. It would be a tricky thing to steal a mermaid princess's pet and reunite it with its mother in the ocean, but Ursula knew she would set herself to that task if the baby horse was a prisoner.

Princess Coral turned her golden gaze on her. 'Why do you ask?'

For a moment Ursula thought of attempting to think up some lie, but then decided against it. 'I'm worried that the foal ought to be with its mum and keeping it here by itself is cruel.'

Princess Coral smiled at Ursula then, the first time she had done so. 'You are right,' the princess replied. 'The foal should be with his mother, but she is lost. Snatched up in one of the Collector's snow globes. The foal is too young to survive in the sea alone so I am keeping him safe until we can get her back. You need not worry about him, but I am pleased you did. It shows you are worthy of carrying that trident, despite being part human.'

Ursula sighed with relief. 'Well, perhaps we can rescue his mother from Scarlett too.'

'That would be wonderful,' Princess Coral said. 'Oh, and speaking of mothers, yours is waiting outside. I agreed she could spend a few moments talking with you. I recommend you keep it brief, though. There are important things to be done right now. Reunions will have to wait.'

So the princess did know who Ursula's mother was! And they were going to see each other after all. Ursula felt feelings of excitement and dread mix together as she and the other explorers thanked the mermaid princess and were shown out of the Throne Room. Ursula glanced over her shoulder as she left and saw that Princess Coral had coaxed the foal to his feet and was playing with him, frolicking about in the water around the shell throne. Seeing the princess this way made her look younger and Ursula thought that despite her cold manner she couldn't be so bad if she was caring for an orphaned water foal. Then the guard closed the door, cutting them off from view. At the same time, an angry voice spoke behind them.

'Ursula Jellyfin! You have some serious explaining to do, young lady!'

Ursula winced and turned around to see her furious mother bearing down on them.

CHAPTER SIX

When they realised that an argument was going to ensue, the guards ushered the explorers and Ursula's mother into a little side room full of seahorse statuettes.

'Mum, these are my friends,' Ursula said, trying to forestall the row. 'Genie, Jai and Max.'

'I'm glad to meet you,' her mother said, still looking annoyed. 'I'm Calista, Ursula's mother.'

Calista had an emerald-green tail, like her daughter, but her long green and blue hair was tied back from her face and arranged with shell combs, whereas Ursula's hair was chin-length and black, except for the blue and purple streak she had recently acquired.

'Mum, I know you're cross,' Ursula said. 'But I really don't think I've done anything wrong.'

'Not done anything wrong?' Calista exclaimed. 'How about stealing a submarine, for a start?'

'Who have we stolen it *from*?' Ursula exclaimed.

She was getting pretty tired of people accusing them of stealing the *Blowfish*. After all, if it belonged to anyone, it rightfully belonged to them. 'Our entire club has been snatched away by Scarlett Sauvage,' she went on. 'The four of us are all that's left of the Ocean Squid Explorers' Club.'

She carefully neglected to mention the fact that Ethan Edward Rook and his explorer father had also escaped the attack and there were probably other submarines that had been out on expeditions at the time. It seemed more information than her mother needed to know and besides, those explorers weren't here and so they couldn't help. It was up to Ursula and her friends.

'Ursula, you are all too young to go tearing off into danger—' her mother began.

'No, we're not,' Ursula cut her off. 'We're explorers, Mum. Tearing off into danger is what we *do*. It's all part of exploring. If we wanted safe, comfortable lives then we never would have joined the club.'

Calista narrowed her eyes. 'I didn't think you *had* joined the club. It doesn't permit female members.'

Ursula frowned, annoyed that her mother had recalled this detail.

'We very much hope that will soon change, Ms

Jellyfin,' Jai volunteered. 'The other clubs have all recently updated their policy. The Ocean Squid Club is just a little behind them, that's all.'

'Besides, I'm still an engineer and the club is my home, like it was Dad's,' Ursula said. 'And Princess Coral has approved our mission too. She even gave me this trident, look.'

She held it up and Calista's eyes widened as she took it in for the first time. 'She gave you the Crown Trident?'

'Yes, and she said we shouldn't waste too much time talking to you. I wasn't sure if she would even know about you – how did she find out? She seemed pretty disapproving about the half human, half mermaid thing. Did you get into trouble?'

'I went to her and confessed the truth,' Calista replied. 'When I knew you were coming here, what else could I do? She wasn't happy, but it wasn't too bad in the end. You earned yourselves a lot of goodwill when you helped save that mermaid ice-cream parlour; Selina used to work at the palace and Coral is fond of her. I am still astonished she gave you the Crown Trident, though. It's the most powerful weapon in the mermaid armoury, and has been passed down through generations of royalty, alongside the Crown Jewels and the Shell Throne.'

'Oh.' Ursula looked at the trident. 'Well, that's good, I guess. It might come in handy against the Collector. How does it work?'

'Ursula, the fact you're even asking that question shows that it's not suitable or safe for you to have it. You have to focus your mind while holding it and it'll shoot bolts of lightning.'

'Cool,' Max said. 'Perhaps if I study it I'll finally learn how to make a robot that can shoot laser beams from its eyes.'

'We really have to go now, Mum,' Ursula said. 'But please don't worry. We'll be careful. I'll practise with the trident so I know how to use it properly. And we'll be straight back here as soon as we've found the Collector.' Her mother still didn't look convinced, so Ursula said, 'I *have* to do this. Remember Dad. I'm like him when it comes to exploring. It's something I need to do, just like you need to be in the water. Please.'

Calista shook her head. 'Your father died,' she said sadly. 'And now you want me to let you go off into danger too.'

'I can't sit on the sidelines and let my friends go without me,' Ursula insisted. 'It wouldn't be right. And I can make a difference to the mission with my mermaid magic. Please, Mum. Scarlett has kidnapped some children, including Max's sister. If we don't go to help them, no one else will.'

They all waited with bated breath while Ursula's mother ran her hands through her hair, clearly going through an internal struggle. Finally, she said, 'It seems like I don't have much choice.' Her face crumpled. 'It's just that I've missed you so much. It always seemed like it was too dangerous for you to come to Mercadia, but now you've been accepted by the princess and you're still not going to stay. I've so longed to share it all with you, darling. I want you to see the shell house where I live, and meet my terrapin Ambrose, and see the seahorse races and—'

Ursula darted forwards to give her mother a hug, taking care not to poke her with the trident. 'I want all that too, Mum,' she said. 'As soon as our expedition is over, I'll come back, I promise. Even if I can't live here with you, I bet I could still visit for a while before I had to return to the surface. We'll do all those things you said, but I need to stop the Collector first. Otherwise she could steal Mercadia away next. No part of the world is safe while she's out there.'

And so Calista reluctantly accepted that her daughter was leaving with the explorers, but before they went she wanted to give them a magic sea flower, like the one they'd seen the dolphin messenger use to stop the submarine.

'It might come in handy,' she said. 'Can you wait while I go to get it? The bubble tide office is on the other side of the city.'

'Would you mind very much if we returned to the *Blowfish* and you brought it to us there?' Jai asked apologetically. 'It's just that we've left a member of our crew on board and she might start to worry if we don't return soon.'

Ursula suspected Jai was probably more concerned with checking up on Zara to make sure his trust in her hadn't been a mistake, but she thought it was about time they went back to the submarine too, so they agreed to meet Calista back there shortly.

A guard escorted the explorers from the palace and they made their way through the mermaid streets towards the *Blowfish*. And it seemed they were returning not a moment too soon. Jai gave a shout of dismay as they passed through the city gates, and Ursula looked up to see Bess waving her tentacles frantically as the submarine's distress beacon flashed a bright red light through the water.

CHAPTER SEVEN

The explorers raced back as fast as they could. Ursula was glad that Max had made the robot dolphins because it meant that her friends could keep up with her and they all arrived at the swim-out hatch together. As soon as the water drained out through the floor, they threw open the door and Jai and Genie ran into the corridor together. Max stayed behind to help Ursula dry off her tail to get her legs back and put on her swim skirt before they followed.

As soon as they left the chamber, they could smell smoke – the worst scent you could possibly get on board a submarine. They followed it to the engine room, bursting in just a few minutes behind the others. Wisps of smoke still hung about the room, but they saw at once that the fire had already been extinguished. It looked like Jai and Genie had arrived just in time to help put it out because they both had fire extinguishers clasped in their hands. Zara crouched on one of the control panels, breathing hard. Her curly hair was damp with sweat and the feather in her hat was wilting slightly. Ollie was all puffed up and irritated on her shoulder and kept squawking over and over again, 'Fire in the hole! Fire in the hole!'

'What happened?' Jai gasped, turning to the pirate fairy. 'Are you OK? There's blood on your arm!'

'She bit me!' Zara panted, putting her hands on her knees to steady herself.

'What? Who?'

'That sea gremlin.'

Zara pointed and they all turned to see a sea gremlin on the floor of the control room. Gremlins were impish creatures with enormous bat-like ears, webbed feet and golfball-sized eyes. They had been the scourge of the Ocean Squid Explorers' Club for years, getting into engines and meddling with the machinery in order to sabotage their submarines. Many explorers had died or injured themselves as a result, but they had only recently learned that the gremlins were working with the Phantom Atlas Society and acting on Scarlett's orders.

They were extremely fast, but this gremlin clearly hadn't expected there to be a pirate fairy on board and Zara had managed to tie her up. She lay on the floor, bound tight in silver fairy rope, but they could see she wore a smart little jacket with gold braid and the Phantom Atlas insignia on it. Her huge eyes blinked up at them furiously.

'Somehow Scarlett knew where we were,' Zara said.

'But how?' Max asked. 'We didn't tell anyone we were coming here.'

Zara shrugged. 'I haven't got round to interrogating her,' she said. 'In case you hadn't noticed, I was too busy turning on the distress beacon and putting out the fire she started.'

Jai strode over to the gremlin and carefully propped her up against the wall. 'You'd best start talking,' he said sternly. 'How did Scarlett know we were here?'

The gremlin glared at him, then spat noisily on to the floor. 'If I had my hands free, I'd pelt the lot of you nasty explorers with bogies!'

'You know, that's not exactly giving us much incentive to release you,' Max said. 'Besides, being tied up is the least of your problems. If you don't start talking I'm going to fetch my robot penguin, and you won't like what happens next.'

Jai frowned up at him. 'That's enough of talk like that,' he said. 'This gremlin is our prisoner, which means she's under our protection and we have certain obligations and responsibilities towards her and—'

'Obligations and responsibilities, my foot!' Zara cried. 'She almost burned me to a crisp! I say we interrogate her with pistols and parrot poo!'

'Now you're talking!' Max looked down at the angry little fairy approvingly and reached out his palm to give her a high five. 'It's great to have another rule-breaker on board.'

'No,' Jai said firmly. 'There'll be no interrogations like that. I won't have that sort of thing on my submarine. The captain's rule book specifically and categorically states that all prisoners are to be treated with the utmost courtesy and respect, and that they're to be allowed three rations of ship's biscuits a day and—'

'Three rations!' Max exclaimed. 'That's more than I get!'

Jai shrugged. 'I don't make up the rules,' he said.

'Do gremlins even eat ship's biscuits?' Ursula wondered. 'I thought they just ate bogies?'

'You stupid explorers!' the gremlin jeered. 'Ship's biscuits taste like poo! The Pacificans were right. You're nothing but a bunch of—'

'Pacificans!' Genie exclaimed. 'What have they got to do with it? Don't say they're helping Scarlett too?'

The gremlin snapped her jaw closed and shook her head vehemently. 'I'm not saying anything.'

'You already have,' Ursula said. She looked at the others. 'And I bet that's how Scarlett knew where we were. The Pacificans have psychic abilities, don't they?'

They all looked glum. This had been one of the reasons to free the Sunken City of Pacifica in the first place. They'd hoped the inhabitants might show their gratitude by using their psychic abilities to tell them where Scarlett's headquarters were. Instead it had all gone horribly wrong and now they were working *with* the Collector instead.

'Oh, that's just great!' Max exclaimed, looking cross. 'How can we have the element of surprise when she has a psychic spyglass to watch our every move?'

'There must be something we can do,' Genie said quietly. 'Some way to shield ourselves from the Pacificans. Perhaps if we—'

Jai held up his hand to quieten her. 'We should discuss this in private,' he said, with a meaningful look at the gremlin. 'And Zara needs medical attention.'

They agreed that the gremlin – who told them her name was Jubba, but refused to say anything further – would be confined to the brig for the time being. After seeing her safely installed there with food and water, Jai untied her ropes and they all narrowly missed being pelted with gremlin bogies as they hurriedly retreated. They went straight to the sick bay, where Genie cleaned Zara's arm wound and Max fetched her a jellyfish plaster.

'There you go,' he said, sticking it carefully over her skin. 'Good as new.'

'Thank you for your quick actions,' Jai said. 'They probably saved the submarine.' He sighed and ran his hand through his hair. 'Now what are we going to do? Scarlett obviously knows we're at Mercadia. There's no reason to think she realises we're on our way to Pirate Island, but if she's using the Pacificans to spy on us then she'll find out soon enough. We've got very little advantage as it is. We can't lose the element of surprise. Does anyone have any ideas?'

Ursula felt a frustrated sense of helplessness rise up in her because the truth was she had no ideas at all. Jai was right – it was vital that they sneak on to Pirate Island undetected, but how could they possibly defend themselves against psychic spying from people who were miles and miles away?

Before they could discuss it, however, a rapping on the porthole window made them jump. They turned to see Ursula's mother outside, peering in at them and gesturing with a blue flower. In all the commotion, they had forgotten she was coming.

Feeling guilty, Ursula hurried to the swim-out hatch and transformed into a mermaid to meet her mother. Calista began to scold her for the fact that she'd had to peer into dozens of the submarine's portholes before she found them, and had had a terrible shock when she'd seen Bess, but Ursula interrupted to explain about the sea gremlin and the Pacificans.

'So perhaps you'll get your wish,' she finished glumly. 'And we won't be able to go on our expedition after all. Not unless we can think of some way to hide ourselves and the submarine.'

Calista was silent for a moment. She glanced at the *Blowfish*, then looked back at Ursula and held out the blue flower.

'Here,' she sighed. 'Take it. And don't worry – you'll be able to go on your expedition. I know a way you can stay hidden.'

Ursula took the flower and clutched it tight, hope rising suddenly in her chest. 'You do?'

Calista nodded, causing the shell combs in her green and blue hair to sparkle. 'You will need the help of a sea witch.'

Of course! Ursula knew that a sea witch's charm had turned her mother into a human for the five wonderful years they had lived together with her father as a family.

It must have taken immensely powerful magic to achieve such a thing.

'You know a sea witch!' she exclaimed. 'Can you introduce me?'

'She doesn't live in Mercadia,' Calista replied. She looked her daughter in the eye and said, 'You'll find her in Skeleton Cove.'

Ursula gasped. The place was notorious, even as far away as the Ocean Squid Explorers' Club. People said it was a forsaken place, haunted by sea spirits.

'Not all the stories about it are true,' Calista said. 'You ought to be safe enough as long as you don't disturb any of the eels. It took me two weeks to swim there, but I guess it will take you much less time in your submarine. Did you bring the map of the Bubble Ocean I gave you?'

'Yes. We'll be able to find the cove, all right. What's the witch's name?'

'Her name is Thalla and she lives in the largest cave there. You'll know it because it has whale bones hanging in the entranceway. But Ursula, you must be careful. Sea witches are very powerful, and they don't give anything for nothing. Her help will come at a price.'

Ursula nodded. 'We haven't much choice. Thank

you for telling me, Mum. I know you don't want us to do this.'

Calista gave a sad smile. 'There's no use trying to stop an explorer from exploring. I learned that with your father.'

'I need to go now,' Ursula said apologetically. 'We're in a bit of a hurry, and there could be more sea gremlins on the way.'

'I know. I wish there was more I could do.' Calista swam forwards to wrap her arms around Ursula in a hug. 'Be safe,' she whispered into her hair. 'And know that I am very, very proud of you.'

Ursula had to blink sudden tears from her eyes as it occurred to her that she didn't know when she would see her mother again. It seemed they were forever snatching stolen moments and never had the chance to really spend proper quality time together.

'I'll come back as soon as I can,' she promised. 'I want to meet Ambrose and see the seahorse races and all the other things.'

'If you need to use the flower, just pluck off one of its petals and stick it to your letter,' Calista said. 'Then give it to a sea creature to deliver. A dolphin is the fastest method, but if you give it to any passing fish or crab, they'll hand it over to the first dolphin they meet.'

Ursula thanked her and with a final wave goodbye returned to the submarine. When she told the others about Skeleton Cove, a strained look came over their faces and there was a heavy silence.

'Well,' Genie eventually said. 'It's good that we have some sort of plan, at least.'

Genie was adept at looking on the bright side, but the boys and the pirate fairy were less convinced.

'You hear some mighty strange tales about Skeleton Cove,' Zara said nervously. 'All kinds of weird goings-on there.'

'Well, if a sea witch calls the place home then perhaps that explains it,' Max said. 'She's probably always mixing up strange potions and whatnot in her cauldron. Do sea witches have cauldrons, do you think? Or is that just ordinary witches?' He scratched his head and frowned. 'Come to think of it, how exactly is a sea witch different from an ordinary witch?'

Ursula shook her head, cross with herself for lacking the answers once again. This time though, it wasn't really her fault. She had tried to ask her mother about the sea witch over the years, but Calista hadn't liked to talk about her.

'Hardly anything is known about sea witches,' Jai said. He took his battered copy of *Captain Filibuster's*

Guide to Sea Monsters from his cloak pocket and opened it up to the sea witch page to show them. There was only a single paragraph of text beside a sketch of a thin figure in a ragged shawl, their face hidden by a tattered hood.

Genie leaned over Jai's shoulder to read the words out loud. '"There are few things in the world's oceans more nefarious and frightening than sea witches. When enraged, they spit lightning, howl gales and turn people to stone with their gaze."'

'Sounds more like a storm maiden,' Ursula remarked. 'Apart from the turning people to stone part.' She frowned at the book. 'Do you think Captain Filibuster might have got the two muddled up?'

'Not Captain Filibuster, surely?' Max exclaimed in mock horror. 'Why, he's the fount of all knowledge! The oracle!'

He grinned at Jai. Max had made no secret of the fact that he didn't think much of Captain Filibuster and thought it was fun to tease Jai for possessing all the famous explorer's books. Jai wasn't looking at him, however, but frowning down at the page instead.

'Well, whether this is accurate or not, we don't intend to enrage the witch, so hopefully we won't need to find out if she spits lightning or not.'

'Mum said there'd be a price,' Ursula said. 'For helping us. Sea witches don't give their magic away for free.'

'I wonder what a sea witch would like?' Genie wondered. 'Perhaps I could make her a hat?'

The others carefully avoided her eye and shuffled their feet. Genie's hats were strange and elaborate creations but the truth was that she was the only person bold enough to wear such odd headgear.

'Maybe a robot?' Max suggested. 'I wouldn't want to part with my robot shark, but perhaps I could make her a present of my robot duck?'

'There isn't much point in speculating,' Jai said. 'The sea witch will tell us her price. We just need to concentrate on getting there. It looks as if Skeleton Cove is a day's journey away.'

'I don't like it,' Zara said. She sat on the control panel, using a dagger to clean her nails. 'Skeleton Cove is a haunted place, and we've got no business going there.'

'It can't be that dangerous,' Ursula said. 'I mean, my mum went there to see the witch all by herself. She lived to tell the tale and was happy to send us there too. She said we should be all right as long as we don't disturb the eels.'

'No eel-disturbing,' Max said. 'Got it. I've never much cared for eels anyway.'

They usually avoided contacting the other explorers' clubs because the adults only ever told them off, or forbade them from continuing with their expedition, or issued strict orders that they must return at once. But this time Ursula suggested that perhaps they should radio them to let them know about the Pacificans.

'I think Stella ought to know about it at least,' she said. 'Scarlett Sauvage has declared her to be her mortal enemy, hasn't she? And she needs her to help make more snow globes too. She might use the Pacificans to try to find her.'

And so they made radio contact with the Polar Bear Explorers' Club and spoke to the president there, Algernon Augustus Fogg. Unsurprisingly, he wasn't at all helpful, and mostly issued instructions for them to return home at once. He refused point blank to fetch Stella for them to speak to or even pass on a message. When Ursula tried to insist that it was important, he finally lost patience and told them Stella wasn't even at the club.

'She's supposed to be back home with her father, but I happen to know they've launched an expedition to Pirate Island to try to stop the Collector, thanks to you lot, despite the fact that it's quite forbidden! Pirate

Island, indeed! Pah! I bet Scarlett Sauvage isn't even there. Probably nothing but a bunch of pirates.'

It was no use trying to talk sense to President Fogg and the explorers finally ended the call. The explorers weren't surprised to hear that Stella was also on her way to Pirate Island. The last time they'd spoken to her on the radio she'd made it quite clear that she had no patience with the adult explorers' dithering. Still, it was reassuring to know for certain that they were headed to the same place.

'I say we use the mermaid flower to send Stella a message,' Ursula said, taking out the blue bloom her mother had given her. 'I would have preferred to speak to her directly, but this is better than nothing.'

'We can't be sure it will reach her,' Jai said, frowning. 'They're Polar Bear explorers after all – what if they're travelling overland? The dolphin wouldn't be able to deliver the message. We'll have no way of knowing whether Stella has received it or not.'

'I know, but it's better than nothing,' Ursula said. 'And anyway, they're not all Polar Bear explorers. Ethan Edward Rook is from Ocean Squid, isn't he? And he and his father still have their submarine. If they're heading to Pirate Island, then they're probably travelling by sea.'

'Isn't that flower meant to help *us* in an emergency?' Max pointed out. 'If we use it to warn Stella, we won't have it if we need it later ourselves.'

'True, but I still think we ought to,' Ursula said.

'I think we should try to help Stella too,' Genie said. 'She'd do the same for us.'

'Yes.' Jai nodded. 'We're all explorers. We ought to be working together and looking out for one another, even if we are from different clubs.'

'All right,' Max said. 'Let's give it a go.'

And so Ursula composed a message on waterproof mermaid paper, then attached the flower. She transformed into a mermaid and swam out of the submarine to pass it to the first marine animal she found – a turtle slowly drifting towards the mermaid city. She could only hope that the turtle would pass it to a very fast dolphin, who would travel along the bubble tide to deliver the message to Stella as quickly as possible.

In the meantime, with some trepidation, the explorers entered Skeleton Cove into the navigation system and the *Blowfish* moved silently through the dark water, leaving the shining lights of the mermaid city behind them.

CHAPTER EIGHT

They arrived at Skeleton Cove early evening the next day. The explorers gathered on the bridge as Jai raised the submarine to the surface. Evening light filtered through the portholes, but it wasn't the usual pinkish tint of a sunset over the sea. Instead it was a washed-out, yellow sort of light – like an old bruise – and the ocean lapping around them had a green, almost swampy look about it. Skeleton Cove did not look hospitable at all, and their hearts sank at the sight.

The sheltered bay formed an oval shape with cliffs looming up on either side. There was a sandy beach directly ahead, and the explorers saw at once how the cove had come by its name. The beach was littered with skeletons. Some were lying down, others were propped up against the cliffs and several were slumped inside the wrecks of rotting rowing boats. Dozens and dozens of sun-bleached skulls grinned at the explorers across the water, making them shiver.

'What could have happened here?' Genie wondered. 'How did this many people die on the beach at the same time?'

'Let's hope it wasn't anything to do with the sea witch,' Max said grimly. He glanced at Jai. 'I don't care what you say this time – I'm taking my robot duck. I think we need all the weapons at our disposal in a place like this.'

For once, Jai agreed with him. 'Just make sure it doesn't shoot any stink pellets at us by accident,' he said.

'We're going to have to take one of the rowing boats,' Ursula pointed out. 'The water is too shallow for the *Blowfish*.'

'Perhaps we should wait until morning?' Genie suggested, looking worried. 'I wouldn't like to be stuck on that beach with those skeletons after dark.'

'You could be right,' Jai replied. 'Maybe we should—'

'No,' Max said, in a quiet but firm voice. 'I don't want to wait until sunrise. In fact, I don't want to wait one more minute. All of this is taking far too long as it is. Jada needs me *now*.'

It was unlike Max to speak openly about his sister and the worry he had for her. Normally he preferred to cover these feelings up with jokes and poking fun at Jai, but Ursula knew he was terribly concerned about Jada, and she didn't blame him.

'I don't expect any of you to come,' Max said. 'You can stay here, but I'm going to find this sea witch.'

'Don't be daft,' Ursula said at once. 'Of course we'll come with you.'

Genie nodded. 'You're right. We shouldn't wait. The kidnapped children are relying on us.'

'Well, I'm not staying behind,' Zara said, tipping back her hat. 'It sticks in a pirate's craw, having to stay behind. It was bad enough at Mercadia.'

'What's a craw?' Genie asked.

'Not sure,' Zara replied with a frown. 'Some sort of fish, I think. Perhaps the bony one with the weird eyes?'

'It's only right that we should go together,' Jai said.

Ursula could tell Max was glad not to have to venture into the sea witch's cave by himself, but it still wasn't quite enough to prevent him from grinning when Jai began pinning medals on to the front of his cloak.

'Good idea,' Max said. 'The sea witch will know not to mess with us when she sees those. Don't forget to show her your plankton medal.'

Jai sighed. 'You promised you wouldn't make fun of my medals any more.'

'But I'm not making fun of them,' Max said, keeping a completely straight face. 'I think the sea witch will be very impressed with your plankton medal. Who wouldn't be?'

Genie rolled her eyes at Max.

'We should go and get ready,' she said firmly. 'There's no time to lose.'

They separated to fetch their various things, and then met back on the outside deck of the submarine. Max had brought his robot duck, Jai had a harpoon gun, Zara had her duelling pistols and although Genie did not technically have a weapon, she had the protection of Bess's monstrous form looming in the water below. She'd also worn one of her favourite hats – with a shaggy sea mammoth perched on top – just in case the sea witch might accept it as payment for her help. For the first time, Ursula had more than a heavy spanner in her pocket – she had her gleaming golden trident.

'Are you sure that's a good idea?' Jai asked, frowning at the mermaid weapon. 'You don't know how to use it.'

'That's because you wouldn't let me practise with it,' Ursula replied.

She had been a little miffed when Jai had forbidden her from trying out the trident inside the *Blowfish* in case she started a fire.

'It could act as a deterrent, even if I don't use it,' Ursula pointed out.

'Might it not put the sea witch's back up if we go walking into her cave armed to the teeth like this?' Max wondered. 'My duck could just be an eccentric pet choice, but you two are pretty conspicuous.' He gestured at Jai and Ursula.

'That may be,' Jai replied. 'But I'm not venturing into Skeleton Cove unarmed. Better to have the weapons and not need them.'

'Hear, hear!' Zara said, patting her duelling pistols affectionately.

And so they piled into one of the rowing boats and let it down on ropes. When they reached the water, they saw that the greenish shade of the waves came from electric lights beneath the surface. The sea below was writhing with dozens and dozens of eels.

Max grimaced. 'I've never much liked eels,' he said.

The others weren't thrilled at the sight of them either, especially as Ursula's mother had warned that they shouldn't be disturbed.

'Let's just take it nice and steady,' Jai said, picking up an oar. 'If we don't bother the eels then hopefully they won't bother us.'

They rowed slowly towards the cove, taking special care with the oars. Bess drifted along in their wake, her tentacles floating contentedly in the water. As she had no physical substance, she passed straight through the eels and they did not seem to mind her presence.

'There must be hundreds of eels down there!' Genie said, gazing over the side of the boat. 'I wonder how your mother managed to avoid them, Ursula? She would have had to swim straight through them.'

They couldn't help shuddering at the thought.

'Very brave,' Jai said in an approving tone, looking down at the water. 'I guess she must have loved your father very much to do such a thing.'

Ursula felt a sudden burst of pride in her mother then. She was grateful to her for giving them those years on Peekaboo Island as a family, even if it couldn't last. And all that happiness had come from the very same sea witch they were going to visit now, so she couldn't be that terrible. At least, that was what Ursula tried to tell herself, but her heart still beat uncomfortably fast in her chest, especially as they approached the beach.

Up close they could see there weren't just human skeletons there, but also the bones of parrots, fairies and even a mermaid stretched out on the sand. Strangely, there were dozens of keys glinting on the shore as well. Ursula had assumed they were shells to begin with, but now they were closer she saw they were ancient keys, all covered in rust.

'Should we pull up to look for the cave?' Jai asked, frowning at the ghoulish beach.

'You must be able to reach the cave from the water,' Max pointed out. 'Otherwise Ursula's mother wouldn't have been able to get there, would she?'

'Why don't we row around the perimeter?' Genie suggested. 'And hopefully we'll see the cave from the boat?'

'Good idea,' Jai said. 'Everyone keep a sharp eye out. It's been many years since Ursula's mother was here. Things might have changed since then and there could be new dangers that she wasn't aware of.'

It was a sobering thought and they all kept their eyes peeled as they continued on. They saw several caves, but they were quite small and there was no sign of any whale bones. The sun was rapidly setting now and the wind had picked up, blowing a salty breeze across the ocean. And with it seemed to come a sound that was more than the wind – a sort of sad sighing that made the explorers shiver.

'Sea spirits,' Zara said, glancing around with superstitious dread. 'The souls of all the men and women who've drowned in the ocean.'

'Don't be silly,' Jai replied, trying to sound firm. 'It's only the wind.'

'Are you certain?' Zara asked. 'Have you ever stopped to consider how many dead people there are beneath the sea? It's like a giant graveyard.'

'How cheerful,' Max said, frowning at Zara. 'But look, perhaps we ought to steer clear of thinking about things like sea spirits, and graveyards, and dead men under the water and—'

'Ghost ships!' Zara said, with a certain relish. 'There have been sightings of ghost ships around here too.'

'I agree with Max,' Genie said. 'We should think about nice things. Like hats.'

'And water horses,' Ursula added.

'And robot penguins,' Max said. He nudged Jai. 'You can think of your medal collection.'

Jai frowned at him. 'Nonsense. I shall think of Biscuit. He wouldn't be afraid if he was here, so I won't be either.'

'Did that cat actually accompany you on your expeditions?' Max asked, surprised. 'I assumed he just slept on your pillow on the submarine.'

'Oh no!' Jai cried. 'Biscuit came everywhere with me. He was the most brave, intrepid cat ever to . . . well, that I've ever had the honour of knowing.'

A wobble suddenly came into Jai's voice and he blinked rapidly, as if to stave off tears. Genie patted him comfortingly on the back. He could not speak of Biscuit without becoming emotional, and Ursula liked him for the fact that he'd loved his pet so dearly.

'There'll never be another cat like him,' Jai added.

'Look there!' Zara suddenly said. 'What's that? There's a light.' She looked up from her telescope. 'While you lot were all blabbering on about robot penguins in hats and berserk cats, or whatever it was, I've been searching the coastline with my telescope. And look, there are lights coming from that cave over there!'

The pirate fairy was quite right. Now that it was going dark, the flickering lights shone clearly over the inky waves and they saw that there was a large cave mouth straight ahead of them.

'May I?' Max asked, holding out his hand for Zara's telescope.

She handed it over and he peered through with some difficulty, as it was designed for an eye much smaller than his, but nevertheless he managed to get a good look at the cave.

'Well, I'll be a monkey's uncle!' he exclaimed. 'Those are whale bones, all right!'

In fact, an entire whale skeleton hung in the vast entranceway, and soon enough they didn't need a telescope to see it. The lights from the electric eels were particularly bright around the cave and lit up the huge bones. They were suspended from the ceiling by individual ropes that looked thick enough to carry an anchor, and swayed slightly in the breeze, which made it look as if the ghostly whale was still swimming through a vast, black sea.

They had found the sea witch's cave.

CHAPTER NINE

Whales were one of the largest creatures in the ocean, and they had a certain dignity, which made them special to all Ocean Squid explorers. The group fell reverently silent as their little boat entered the cave and glided silently beneath the massive ribs.

Inside, the cave stretched back a long way and fireflies winked and blinked from within its depths. They knew at once that they were in the right place and this really was a sea witch's cave because of the collection of strange things lined up on shelves around the rocky walls. There were bowls of different-coloured sea salts, piles of peculiar-looking shells, and rows and rows of glass jars containing everything from newt's eyes to pickled fairy parrots.

Seeing the parrots, Max tapped Zara on the shoulder, pointed them out and then gestured at Ollie, who was perched on her shoulder.

'I wouldn't take any chances, if I were you,' Max whispered. 'Give the parrot to me – I'll keep him safe.'

With a last frightened look at the horrible jars, Zara gulped and then handed over the tiny parrot. Max quickly slid him into a little compartment inside his robot duck, ignoring the indignant squawk of protest.

'He's in there with the stink berries, I'm afraid,' Max said. 'But it's better than being pickled.'

'Fairy parrots have no sense of smell anyway,' Zara replied. 'He'll be OK. Thanks for looking out for him.'

The boat glided slowly forwards until it came to rest on a little beach filled with purple sand.

'I've never seen purple sand before,' Jai said, frowning at it.

'I've never seen a pickled parrot before either,' Genie added. 'What kind of a place is this?'

They pulled the boat further up the sand so it couldn't accidentally float away and strand them, and then they took their courage into their hands and ventured further into the cave. It was cold and damp and smelled of salt and storms and the vinegary whiff of pickled parrot. There was nothing to illuminate their way except for the glimmering fireflies, and whenever Jai tried to light his lantern, it went out instantly, as if some invisible person had blown out the flame.

'Evil magic, probably,' Zara muttered, looking uneasy. 'I knew we should have waited until morning.'

'It goes so far back that it would still be dark in the cave during the day,' Jai pointed out.

'Ducky has light-up eyes,' Max said. He flicked a switch and his robot duck's eyes were immediately illuminated with a bright red glow. As they picked their way through the cave they saw more evidence of sea witches, including large cauldrons, stuffed eels and a couple of storm cats sneaking about. The explorers had come across these during their last expedition and made sure to give them a wide berth as no one wanted to have a mini tornado hissed at them.

Finally, they reached the back of the cave, where they found the sea witch – only she wasn't what they were expecting at all. For one thing, she didn't have a tattered robe, or a fearsome expression, or long, dirty fingernails. At least, she *might* have had long, dirty fingernails, but it was impossible to tell because she was wearing thick gloves, along with a leather apron and a pair of sturdy leather boots. Her black and green hair was scraped back in an untidy bun and she wore a protective visor over her face. Rather than stirring up some sort of green mixture in a cauldron, or cackling over a spell book, she was – inexplicably – tying purple bows to the tail of a very fluffy-looking duck-billed platypus.

'Ahem.' Jai noisily cleared his throat. 'Pardon me, madam, but we're—'

The witch spared them barely a glance before turning back to her task. 'Just put your platypus down over there.' She indicated a corner of the cave. 'I've got several others to do today, but I'll get to him as soon as I can.'

'We don't have a platypus,' Jai said.

'We've got a robot duck, though,' Max offered.

The witch picked up a brush and began combing it briskly through the platypus's fur. 'Don't do robot ducks,' she said. 'Storm ducks, yes, for an extra fee, but my speciality is platypuses. And puggles.'

'What's a puggle?' Zara wondered.

'A baby platypus, of course,' the witch replied.

'Oh,' Genie breathed. 'There are lots of them – look.'

She pointed to the edge of the cave where they saw there were about twenty platypuses sitting on little stools in front of dressing tables. Each table was covered in an assortment of combs and powders, and faced a mirror on the cave wall, the frame covered in light bulbs. Most of the platypuses had bows on their tails, ribbons around their necks and fur that had been crimped, curled or ruffled. Their expressions ranged from smugly pleased to faintly embarrassed. The explorers felt only confusion. This wasn't what they had been expecting.

'Doolally,' Max announced. 'She's gone doolally living here by herself all these years with only the skeletons and the pickled parrots for company.'

'Pickled parrots!' the witch exclaimed, turning back around. 'For heaven's sake, are those horrible things still there? I told Percie to clear them out weeks ago. And I am not doolally, young man, nor have I lived here for years. In fact, my platypus-grooming business is new – we've only been going for three months, but word has got around and now storm maidens are bringing their hurricane platypuses to be groomed from all around.'

'*Hurricane* platypuses?' Ursula repeated, giving the creatures a nervous look. She had heard them mentioned once before by the tiny old storm keeper they had met on Gilly's Island during their last adventure. They'd come across storm cats on the same island – fearsome beasts that hissed out mini-tornadoes. If those creatures were anything to go by, then the hurricane platypuses probably weren't anything good either.

'Yes, of course,' the witch replied. 'Don't make them sneeze, whatever you do.' She pushed back her visor to stare at the explorers and Ursula realised she wasn't as old as she'd first thought – probably no more than forty. 'Look here, didn't you know this was a platypus-grooming parlour?'

'No, we didn't,' Jai said. 'We're looking for Thalla.'

'Well, you won't find her here,' the woman replied. 'Thalla hasn't lived here for years. She moved west and left all her skeletons and pickled parrots and other junk behind to clutter up the place, even though she promised to clean out the cave once she sold it to me. I'm Jojo. And I'm very busy, so if you haven't got a platypus for me to groom, perhaps you wouldn't mind moving on?'

She turned back to the platypus, picked up a cloth and began polishing its beak.

'Oh dear,' Ursula said. 'But we really need Thalla's help. Do you know where she went?'

'Nope,' Jojo replied. 'Not a clue. If I did, I'd be after her to come and clean out this cave like she promised.'

'Are you a sea witch, Jojo?' Genie asked.

'What? Don't ask stupid questions – of *course* I'm a sea witch,' she said impatiently. 'That old platypus sleeping in his basket over there is my familiar Wilbur. Only a sea witch with a platypus familiar would dare to groom a hurricane platypus. One wrong move – an errant whisker pulled or a claw clipped just a bit too far – then no one knows what's up and what's down because they're all getting swirled about inside a hurricane. That's why Percie is such a bother to me. She was meant to be helping, but she's no help at all – always running about with those pesky sea otters of hers. I tell you, I'd give anything to be free of her, but I can't spare the time to take her home. Sometimes I think her mother tricked me into taking her on purpose, just to get some peace and quiet.'

'Er ... well, sorry to hear that Percie has been a bother, whoever she is,' Jai said. 'But if you're a sea witch too, then perhaps you can still help us? You see, we're looking for a charm to disguise ourselves and our submarine from an enemy's psychic gaze. There's this woman called Scarlett Sauvage and she—'

'Let me stop you right there.' Jojo held up her gloved hand. 'I know all about Scarlett and the Phantom Atlas Society. Terrible business, but I don't want to get mixed up in any of it. All that matters to me is my platypuses and ... hang on a minute! Did you say you've got a submarine?'

'That's right,' Jai said. 'The *Blowfish*. It's one of the finest submarines of the Ocean Squid Explorers' Club.'

Jojo put down the cloth, removed her visor and gave the explorers her full attention for the first time. 'Well, why didn't you say so sooner?' she asked. 'I'll help you all right. I can create a charm that will hide you from any prying gaze, even a psychic one.'

'Oh.' Jai beamed. 'Well, good. That was easy. And what is the price for your help? We haven't much in the way of cash, but we've got various robots, and rare books, and—'

Genie nudged him. 'Don't forget my hats!'

'Yes, a remarkable hat collection,' Jai added. 'And a rather good ice-cream machine, and—'

'Don't offer her the ice-cream machine!' Max hissed, poking him in the side. 'We need it!'

Jojo shook her head. 'I wouldn't dream of depriving you young people. Especially not when you're set on such an important, selfless mission for the good of the entire world.'

'Well, thank you.' Jai looked pleased and puffed up slightly so that the light from the mirrors caught the medals pinned to his chest. 'It *is* rather selfless and important actually. You see, we—'

'Quite so,' Jojo cut him off. 'I will help you, and all I ask in return is that you take Percie back home to Barnacle City on Smugglers' Isle.'

'Oh!' Genie gasped, looking at Zara. 'Isn't that where those captive kraken are?'

The pirate fairy nodded.

Jai frowned. 'We're not going to Smugglers' Isle,' he said. 'It's a dangerous place, full of cut-throats and thieves. And we don't take passengers on board the submarine either. Not unless they've been vetted, and checked, and verified by the Ocean Squid Explorers' Club. That's rule two hundred and six in the captain's rule book.'

'How many rules *are* there in the captain's rule book?' Max asked.

'Four hundred and three,' Jai replied promptly. 'And I know them all by heart, including the additional clauses, exemptions and indexes.'

'Of course you do.' Max rolled his eyes.

'Well, the price is non-negotiable I'm afraid,' Jojo said with a cheerful shrug. 'Take it or leave it.'

'It'll take up valuable time,' Jai said, looking miserable. 'But I suppose we've got no choice.'

'Sensible boy,' Jojo replied, looking approving.

'Wait a moment, who is this Percie?' Ursula asked. It would be just their luck to agree to a passenger only to find out that it was a sea giant, or a toxic squid, or some such ridiculous thing. Her eyes narrowed suspiciously. 'She's not a monster, or a vicious poisonous platypus, or anything like that?'

'Gracious, no!' Jojo replied, although her eyes slid away from them in an evasive way as she spoke. 'Percie is short for Persephone. My little niece, you know. She's just a ten-year-old girl. I'm sure she'll be no trouble to seasoned explorers like yourselves.'

Jai frowned. 'But if she's a ten-year-old girl, why would she live somewhere as dangerous as Smugglers' Isle?'

'Oh, it's not so bad as all that,' Jojo replied. 'Barnacle City has some of the best seafood restaurants in the world, you know. Percie lives there with her parents.'

'But that means they must be—' Ursula began.

'Smugglers.' Jojo nodded. 'At least, her mother is. Her father is my brother and a sea warlock. A bit of an incompetent one, I'm afraid. Doesn't know a winkle from a walrus. Look, it'll be quite all right. They have a place on Scrimshaw Street, near the harbour. You'd best deliver her right to the door or else she'll get into who-knows-what mischief. It'll take you five minutes to drop her off and then you can be on your merry way.'

'We will take our charge of her most seriously,' Jai promised. 'And see that she eats a balanced diet, takes a bath once a day and gets the appropriate amount of sleep while on board our submarine.'

'Huh,' Jojo grunted. 'It'll be more than I've been able to manage if you can. Well, come along. I suppose it's lucky that Thalla left some of her knick-knacks around after all – we'll need some for the spell.'

Jojo gave the platypus a final pat before peeling off her gloves and beckoning the explorers to follow her back through the cave towards the boat. She took them to one of the shelves filled with pickled parrots and picked up a jar containing a bird with bright green feathers. The explorers watched as she turned it upside down three times and spoke a babble of magic words over it. Before their eyes, the parrot's feathers changed colour, from green to a misty silver.

'Here.' Jojo thrust the jar at Jai. 'One by one, the feathers will go back to being green, but the charm will work for as long as there's a single silver feather left on the parrot. Just put it somewhere on your submarine and it will protect the sub itself and any member of its crew, even if they're on land. If anyone tries to find you by psychic means, they'll only see mist.'

'Thank you,' Jai said. 'How long do you think it will last?'

'Hard to say.' Jojo shrugged. 'I'm a little rusty at this type of spell. It could be a month, it could only be a fortnight.'

'A fortnight?' Jai frowned at the pickled parrot. 'But that doesn't give us much time at all.'

'You'd best not waste any then,' Jojo said briskly. She turned away from them and raised her voice. 'Percie? Percie! Wherever you are and whatever mischief you're doing, stop it at once and come here.'

There was no answer and Jojo sighed. 'Oh dear. I suppose she's wreaking havoc again.'

'Where's our boat?' Max said suddenly.

They all looked towards the sandy beach where they'd left it.

The boat had vanished.

'We pulled it right up on to the sand!' Jai exclaimed. 'The tide hasn't come in. Where could it have gone?'

'Some of the pickled parrots have disappeared too,' Zara pointed out. 'Those shelves over there were full when we arrived.'

They saw she was right – two of the shelves were completely empty.

'There's the boat!' Genie cried, pointing to the very end of the beach. 'A little girl's sitting in it!'

The girl had wild black-and-green hair that looked as if it had never been brushed, and which stuck out around her head in something of a bird's nest. She wore a green dress with chunky black lace-up boots and there was a sea otter perched on her shoulder. A second otter scampered about inside the boat, which was full of jars of pickled parrots.

'Percie!' Jojo called crossly. 'Come here at once. Didn't you hear me calling you?'

'I'm leaving, Auntie,' the little girl called back without turning around. 'It's too boring here. Me and the boys are going on an adventure.'

'Percie—'

'No, I mean it! I'm sick of eels and skeletons and biting waves and—!'

'I'm going to count to three, Percie,' Jojo announced.

The explorers realised this must be a serious threat because Percie immediately scrambled from the boat and came trotting along the beach towards them, the otters at her heels.

'Biting *waves*?' Max looked aghast. 'She doesn't mean that the water itself can actually—?'

'Only when the ocean is in a bad mood,' Jojo replied. 'But yes, sometimes.'

Ursula frowned. 'How can the ocean be in a bad mood? Or any kind of mood? It's a big body of water. I mean, it's wonderful and beautiful – but it's not alive.'

'Geez.' Percie skidded to a halt in front of them. 'Is that really what you think? What kind of mermaid are you anyhow?'

The explorers looked at the little witch. She was quite short, although Jojo had said she was only a couple of years younger than they were. Her eyes were the same shade of dark brown as the otters' and practically bubbling over with mischief. A generous dusting of freckles covered the bridge of her upturned nose and there was an eager, curious look in her eyes as she stared up at them.

Ursula was startled. 'How did you know I was a mermaid?'

Percie looked smug. 'Sea witches can see things other people can't. Like the tail inside your legs. It's very pretty, by the way,' she added. 'I wish *I* had a tail like that.' She pointed at Genie. 'And your hat is the best thing I've seen all week.'

'Thanks.' Genie adjusted it slightly on her head. 'I like it. The mammoth is quite heavy, though.'

'Percie, my dear, it's time for you to go home,' Jojo said. 'These nice explorers are going to take you back to Barnacle City.'

Percie narrowed her eyes at her suspiciously. 'I thought I was supposed to stay and help you for another month?'

'Never mind that, dear.' Jojo patted her awkwardly on the head. 'I think I've had enough help for now, and you

were just saying you've had enough of eels and skeletons anyway. It will be a lovely surprise for your parents to have you back early. I'm sure they will be thrilled.'

'But we were going to go for an adventure in that boat.' Percie gestured back along the beach.

'That's *our* boat,' Jai said. 'And I'm afraid we need it for our expedition, but you can ride on our submarine until we reach Barnacle City. That will be fun, won't it?'

'I guess.' Percie shrugged. 'I've never been on a submarine before. And it'd be the perfect way to visit a sea wizard museum. I've got the *Complete Illustrated Encyclopedia of Sea Wizard Museums* back home, you know. I've always wanted to visit one.'

'We won't have time for that, I'm afraid,' Jai said. 'We're taking you directly home.'

Percie rolled her eyes. 'That doesn't sound like much of an adventure.'

'If you were planning to go on an adventure, why did you load the boat with so many pickled parrots?' Genie asked.

Percie stared at her. 'Why wouldn't I? Pickled parrots come in handy for so many different things.'

'That's funny,' Max said, staring at the jars. 'Because I can't think of even one single, sensible use for a pickled parrot.'

Percie raised her eyebrows. 'You must be pretty dumb then.'

'I'm actually rather clever,' Max replied. 'I'm a robot inventor, you see.' He gestured at his robot-duck T-shirt. 'In fact, my little sister is the only person I know who's better at inventing than I am.'

'I bet that annoys you!' Percie said, grinning.

'Sometimes,' Max replied. 'But mostly I just feel so proud I could burst.'

'Perhaps you're not so dumb after all then,' Percie conceded. 'Even if you know diddly squat about pickled parrots.'

'Never mind about the parrots now,' Jojo said hurriedly. 'And Percie, please don't be rude. Go pack your bags and make sure you're back here in five minutes.'

'OK.' Percie turned away but then looked back at the explorers. 'This is Midge, by the way.' She pointed at one of the otters by her feet. 'And the other one is Moe. They're my familiars. The way to tell them apart is that Midge has white hairs on his chest, and Moe doesn't.'

'They're very handsome,' Genie said.

Percie grinned at her, then scampered off.

'Well, that's that.' Jojo brushed her hands together, looking pleased. 'When you get back to the submarine, tell the adult explorers that—'

'There are no adult explorers,' Jai said. 'It's just us.'

Jojo looked disbelieving. 'What, just the four of you children?'

'Ahem!' Zara said.

'And one pirate fairy?' Jojo added.

'That's right,' Max said. 'So whatever you wanted to say to the adults, you'd better say to us.'

'Oh.' Jojo seemed nonplussed for a moment. 'Well, I was just going to offer a word of warning.'

Ursula expected the witch to echo her mother by telling them about the eels, but instead she said, 'Just . . . keep a sharp eye on Percie. She's not a bad child but . . . well . . . sea otters are the cheekiest, naughtiest creatures that live in and around the sea, and there's a reason she has not one, but two of them for familiars.'

'I read once that some witches thrive on mayhem,' Genie said. 'She's not one of those, is she?'

'No, no, of course not!' Jojo said quickly. 'What a ridiculous idea!'

Percie appeared just then, dragging an enormous suitcase behind her. 'We're ready!' she said, panting slightly.

'Do you really need to bring quite so much stuff?' Jai asked. 'That suitcase is as big as you are!'

Percie stared up at him. 'Well, you've plenty of room on the submarine, haven't you?'

'Yes, but the rowing boat isn't that big.' Jai gestured at it on the sand. 'And it's already half full with parrots. Perhaps some of them might stay behind?'

Percie shook her head vigorously. 'Nope. Those are *my* parrots and I think they're the coolest thing I've ever seen.'

Jai sighed. 'Well, I suppose we'll all just about fit.'

'Excellent,' Jojo said. 'Now if you'll excuse me, I really must get back to my platypuses before one of them sneezes out a hurricane.' She gave Percie a quick pat on the head and a peck on the cheek. 'It's been lovely having you to stay with us, dear. Do send your mother my love.'

'Bye, Auntie!'

Percie didn't seem fazed to be leaving so unexpectedly and in fact had already turned away and was skipping along the beach towards the boat.

'Goodbye,' Jojo said to the explorers. 'And good luck.'

'Thank you,' Jai said. 'We'll have a much better chance of defeating the Collector now that we have your charm.'

'Oh yes,' Jojo said. 'Yes, good luck for that too.'

Then she turned and hurried away back to her platypuses.

Ursula frowned. 'What was she wishing us luck for the first time?'

Jai shrugged. 'It doesn't matter. Let's get back to the *Blowfish*. There's no time to lose.'

The explorers walked along the beach to the boat. Percie was already sitting in it with her otters, somehow managing to take up an awful lot of space for such a small girl.

'Can't you budge up a bit?' Max complained as the others squashed in alongside her.

'Witches don't like to be crowded,' Percie said, although she slid along the seat a small way.

Once the explorers had managed to find somewhere to put their feet around the jars of parrots, they picked up their oars and set off, passing beneath the whale bones and out of the cave to the open sea beyond. It had gone dark while they were inside and now the moon painted the beach silver, and the eels shone even brighter beneath the surface.

As they rowed across the water, Percie kept up a constant stream of questions about the submarine. How many rooms did it have? How fast could it go? How big was the swimming pool? How many different desserts were on board?

Jai loved talking about the *Blowfish* and was very

happy to answer her questions. Finally, they rowed around the corner of the rocky outcrop, and the beach came into view once again.

'Those skeletons look even spookier in the moonlight,' Genie said with a shudder. 'I still think it's odd there are so many of them. Um.' She frowned. 'Does it look to anyone else as if some of them have changed position?'

Jai rolled his eyes. 'Skeletons can't move, Genie.'

'Oh.' Percie stared at them, an expression of disbelief on her freckled face. 'Don't you know? But I thought you were explorers?'

Max instantly looked wary. 'Know what?'

'About Skeleton Cove,' said Percie.' What it *is*.'

The explorers gave her blank looks and she grinned. 'It's where the skeletons come to party.'

'Huh.' Max grunted and looked back towards the beach. 'Well, I know a thing or two about parties and it doesn't look like a particularly fun one to me. There ought to be more ... you know ... dancing, and music, and performing fire ducks, and—'

'Performing fire ducks?' Jai frowned at him. 'What kind of parties have you been to?'

'Sounds awesome,' Genie and Ursula said at the same time and then grinned at each other.

Ursula had never really had a female friend before

Genie or, indeed, any proper friend her own age, and it always gave her a little warm glow when they thought and said the same thing at the same moment.

'Well, fire ducks or no fire ducks,' Percie said. 'No one tells skeletons how to party.'

'Whatever.' Max had already lost interest in the conversation as they continued to row past the beach. 'All I know is that a bunch of mouldy old skeletons lying still and silent on a beach sounds like the world's most boring party to me.'

Percie giggled.

'What's funny?' Jai asked.

'They're only still and silent because the moon has gone behind a cloud.' Percie pointed up at the sky. 'They'll come to life as soon as it reappears. Skeletons come to life in the moonlight, you see.'

The explorers all stared at her, wondering if she was trying to amuse them, or perhaps making up stories to frighten them.

'That's codswallop!' Max said.

'You'd better hope we're back at the submarine before the moon comes out,' Percie went on, rubbing her hands together gleefully. 'We'll never get away from them otherwise.'

Genie shuddered and gave the beach a fearful look.

'Pay no attention,' Jai said, although it seemed like he suddenly rowed a little faster. 'She's just making it up to scare us.'

'Um, Jai?' Ursula said. 'What's that floating about on the beach? It looks like ... balloons.'

'I don't remember seeing any balloons when we arrived.' Zara frowned. She took out her telescope and directed it at the beach. 'She's right, there *are* balloons!' she cried. 'They're arranged in big bunches tied to rocks. There's something written on them, but I can't quite make it out ...'

Before anyone could say anything further, the moon slid out from behind the cloud.

And immediately every skeleton on the beach came to life.

CHAPTER TEN

The explorers watched, horrified, as the skeletons all clambered to their feet with a rattling of bleached bones. Some picked up instruments that had been lying on the sand, and the air became full of the sound of accordion music and the swoop of skeleton parrots. The scent of frying fish drifted over to them across the water as the skeletons started cooking, while others began to dance energetically to the music, their bones clicking and clacking together. Some of them even grabbed up bunches of keys and started shaking them around to create a chilly, jingly noise.

'The writing on the balloons says "Skeletons' Beach BBQ",' Zara said, lowering her telescope to look at the others, an expression of relief on her face. 'That doesn't sound so bad.'

Percie laughed. In fact, she laughed so hard that she wrapped both arms around herself and almost doubled over with mirth. 'That's what *you* think!' she cackled.

'But if you set foot on that beach, you'll turn into a skeleton, doomed to repeat the barbecue every night for all eternity. You'll never leave the beach again, except to pluck other victims from the sea. And search for raw material to create keys. I hope you all really, *really* like fried fish!'

There was a moment of silence inside the boat as the explorers all stared at the sea witch. Then hoarsely Jai gasped a single word: 'Row!'

Everyone snatched up oars, but it was too late – the skeletons had already seen them and, to their horror, several plunged into the water in pursuit. They could see the white of their skulls moving shockingly fast through the waves, their bones lit up by the electric eels below. Some of them still had keys looped through their fingers, flashing silver in the water.

'I'm not sure why you're finding this so funny!' Jai snapped at Percie, who was still laughing. 'You're in as much danger as us!'

'No, I'm not,' she replied cheerfully. 'I can just fly away if I want.'

Ursula narrowed her eyes. 'Sea witches can't fly,' she said, although truth be told she wasn't exactly certain what sea witches could do. 'You don't even have a broomstick.'

Percie shrugged. 'I could fly away if I wanted to. There's practically nothing a sea witch can't do.'

'Except repel skeletons, apparently,' Max groaned. 'Why didn't Jojo warn us rather than let us float out here like sitting ducks?'

'There's no need to panic,' Percie said. 'Just use your skeleton repellent.'

'Our what?' Ursula asked.

For the first time the smile on Percie's face faltered and she frowned. 'Is that supposed to be funny? Well, ha ha, congratulations on a rubbish joke.'

'None of us has ever heard of skeleton repellent,' Max said between puffs as he rowed. 'What the heck is it?'

'But *everyone* around these parts has skeleton repellent!' Percie almost wailed. 'It comes in a little can with a picture of a skeleton on it! You just point it at the skeleton and spray them with it, and then they'll leave you alone. Otherwise there's nothing to stop them from dragging you back to their barbecue, or their shindig, or gala, or jamboree, or barn dance, or whatever it is! Most of the coves and caves around here have a skeleton gathering of some kind.' She glared at Zara. 'Surely *you* must have used it before, being a pirate and all?'

The fairy shrugged. 'We don't need to bother with things like that because our ships have magical cannons.'

'Well, too bad there's no magical cannon with us now!' Percie exclaimed.

The skeletons had almost reached their boat, and more were leaving the beach behind them. They were close enough that the explorers could see their grinning faces. Everyone yelled as the first skeleton arrived at the boat and a bony white hand clamped on to the side. Max's robot duck fired a stink berry at it, but this seemed to have no effect on the skeleton at all.

'Ew!' Percie screeched, covering her nose with her hand. 'Skeletons have no sense of smell, you idiot! They haven't got noses, never mind nostrils! Stink berries won't do anything!'

Jai picked up his harpoon gun and brought it down hard on the skeleton's hand, causing it to let go with a yelp.

'I can't believe you were stupid enough to come to Skeleton Cove without skeleton repellent,' Percie said. 'It's like going into the jungle without mosquito spray, or venturing into the Icelands without yeti furs. What kinds of explorers are you people, anyway?'

'Would you shut up?' Max gasped, as he batted another skeleton away with his oar. 'You're not helping!'

Zara took aim and shot at the skeletons with her duelling pistols, but the tiny bullets just ricocheted wildly off the bones, so everyone yelled at her to stop before someone lost an eye.

'What about these pickled parrots?' Genie asked, snatching up one hopefully. 'Is repelling skeletons one of the many uses you spoke of before?'

Taken with the idea, she tossed one over the side, but it only bounced harmlessly against a skull before sinking out of sight.

'Hey, don't throw my things overboard!' Percie protested. 'How would you like it if I started chucking all *your* stuff at them?'

'Well, isn't there something you can do?' Ursula asked, frustrated. 'I mean, you're a sea witch, aren't you?'

Bess had appeared a little way away and was making a good effort at appearing threatening by waving her tentacles around, but it seemed the skeletons could sense she wasn't a physical animal and were paying her no mind at all. Meanwhile, more and more skeletons were swimming across the waves towards them. Pretty soon the boat would be completely surrounded.

'Don't be scared!' one of the skeletons suddenly called across the water in a thin, high voice. 'Why don't we introduce ourselves? My name's Terry. We mean you no harm. We simply want you to join our barbecue. There's nothing frightening about that, is there?'

134

'We've got balloons!' another skeleton called. 'And fried squid!'

'And rum punch!' a third skeleton added. 'And an everlasting moonlight curse!'

'Quiet, Cyril!' Terry said sharply. He bobbed up and down in the waves, his skull grinning up at the explorers. 'These nice people aren't interested in curses. In fact, there is no curse! No curse at all. Just a lovely barbecue with balloons and party whistles for everyone.'

'Stay away from this boat,' Jai warned. 'We don't want your barbecue or your curse.'

Terry didn't stop grinning. In fact, being a skeleton, his expression didn't change at all, and yet there seemed something suddenly malevolent about his skull. 'That's too bad,' he said. 'Because you're all coming to our barbecue whether you want to or not.'

The skeletons surged forwards, their bones painted yellow by the eel-lit sea. Max and Genie attempted to hold them back with their oars, while Jai took aim with his harpoon gun. It had been specially adapted so he could use it with just one arm, and he was an expert shot, firing off dozens of tiny harpoons with such force that they blasted the skeletons' skulls apart. This really seemed to enrage the remaining skeletons and they began to hurl eels into the boat. Unfortunately, they had very painful stings and the explorers were forced to scrabble around to hurl them overboard. Zara spread her wings and took flight, hovering above the boat from where she called out warnings and encouragement to the explorers and shouted curses at the skeletons.

Throughout all this mayhem, Ursula used the trident to hit the skeletons across the head, just as Max and Genie were doing with the oars, but when they began to be pelted with eels as well, she saw that they were fighting a losing battle and that drastic action was needed. She had hoped to have the chance to practise first, but it seemed that she had no choice but to attempt to use the trident.

She took a deep breath, aimed it right at some skeletons a little way from the boat, concentrated her thoughts and, immediately, a bolt of lightning shot from the end, so white and bright that they could barely look at it. It was larger than she had thought it would be, and it was much more difficult to keep the trident pointing in just one place. The power of the surge made it jerk around in her hands so that she struggled to keep hold of it. The lightning sliced through the water in jagged, uneven bursts that blew the sea up in towering, terrifying waves.

'Stop!' Jai cried desperately. 'Ursula, stop!'

She hastily lowered the trident, but it was too late. One of the waves rose right over them, a great wall of water, before crashing on top of their little boat. It flipped over as easily as if it were a toy. Ursula barely had time to suck in a deep breath before the ocean engulfed her. She felt her legs transform into a mermaid's fin and cold, salty water roared past her ears until she couldn't work out what was up and what was down, what was the eel-glowing sea and what was moonlit sky.

Glass jars of pickled parrots bashed and bruised her as they went tumbling past and she cringed as she recalled what her mother had said about not disturbing the eels. They were bound to bite, or sting, or both. Ursula had the grace and speed of a mermaid, but even she would be powerless against so many of them ... Fortunately, though, it seemed that the eels did not like the pickled parrots, and they hurriedly abandoned the cove and fled out to sea. The skeletons had no such qualms, however.

Ursula beat her tail to rise back to the surface and her head broke through the waves. She saw at once that her fellow explorers were all in the water and that the only one of them who had managed to remain inside the boat was Percie. The little witch was soaked but still sitting right where she'd been before, with her otters curled around her shoulders. Ursula would have expected her to be leaning over the side, reaching out a helping hand or an oar to them, a panic-stricken expression on her face, but instead she appeared – inexplicably – to be making some sort of balloon animal.

'Percie!' Ursula bellowed. 'Percie, help us get back in the boat!'

'Quiet!' the witch replied, without looking at her. 'I'm trying to concentrate.'

She pulled another balloon from her pocket and began blowing it up. Ursula turned her attention to her friends, who were all attempting to swim back. Genie had barely moved before a skeleton clamped a bony hand around her arm. The eel light flashed off a bunch of keys tied around its neck.

'Get off!' Genie yelled. 'I don't want to go to a skeleton barbecue!'

'That's too bad.' The skeleton was deaf to her protests and began swimming back to the beach, dragging Genie along with it. She fought as hard as she could, but was slow and clumsy in the water. Bess thrashed her tentacles desperately alongside them and Zara yelled at the skeleton from the sky above, but neither had any effect.

'No!' Ursula gasped, lunging forwards.

This was her fault. If she hadn't used the trident, then the boat would never have capsized. To her dismay, Max and Jai were faring no better than Genie. Both were struggling in the bony grips of two more skeletons, who were already starting to tug them towards the cursed beach. Ursula cast one last desperate glance at Percie, but the witch was intent on her balloon animal, which appeared to be taking shape as a rather plump manatee. Ursula had got her friends into this trouble and it would be up to her to save them. She had absolutely no idea how she was going to manage that yet, but she swam forward, determined to try.

Almost at once, a pale skeleton suddenly burst up out of the water before her and Ursula recoiled in horror. The spectre was even more horrifying close up, with its gaping, dark eye sockets, its rotten teeth, and the salt and barnacles crusted all over its yellow bones. It grinned at Ursula as it clamped one hand over her forearm with an inhuman strength and tore her trident from her grip with the other. Ursula tugged with all her might and thrashed her tail, but was unable to free herself.

'It's barbecue time,' the skeleton leered.

Ursula's terrified eyes found the others and she saw

that the skeleton holding Genie was almost at the beach, with Zara fluttering in helpless panic above them. Any moment now it would surely drag her friend ashore and then she would turn into a cursed skeleton, closely followed by the other explorers . . .

Then all of a sudden, the skeleton grasping Ursula went completely limp, falling face down into the sea and releasing its hold on her and the trident. She saw that the same thing had happened to the others. Their skeletons had collapsed in the ocean, and so had the ones on the beach. The accordion music had abruptly stopped and there was no sound but for the churn of the waves.

'Over here!' Zara yelled across the dark water. 'Genie needs help!'

Ursula saw that her friend was perilously close to the beach and seemed to be struggling to get back. The tide was too strong and the waves were pummelling into her, trying to drag her onto the enchanted sand. Max and Jai both started swimming over to assist, but Ursula was the fastest. She snatched up her trident and shot through the water to Genie.

She reached her just in the nick of time and put an arm round her friend. Genie was breathless and almost sobbing with the effort of battling against the sea; her eyes were red from the salt and she grabbed hold of

Ursula gratefully as the mermaid turned and used her powerful tail fin to swim quickly back to the boys, with Zara following above them.

'Are you lot coming here, or what?' called a bored-sounding voice.

They looked up to see Percie slowly rowing towards them as if she had all the time in the world.

'The moon must have gone behind a cloud again,' Jai gasped, glancing up at the sky. 'To the boat, quick!'

They swam as fast as they could, shuddering as they went past floating bones. Percie made no move to help, so they heaved themselves over the side of the boat and landed sprawling and gasping in the bottom.

'Are you all right?' Ursula asked Genie.

Genie nodded, still panting for breath.

Zara fluttered down to land on her shoulder. 'What's that?' she asked, pointing.

Ursula saw that there was a key sticking out of her friend's pocket and realised she must have torn it from the skeleton in the struggle.

'Is anyone going to help me row, or do I have to do everything around here?' Percie complained.

'You haven't done a darned thing!' Max gasped. 'Fat lot of use you are. I think you'd have been quite happy to see us all turned into skeletons!'

'That's a nice thank you,' Percie said pertly, sticking her upturned nose into the air with a sniff. 'Seeing as I just saved all your useless skins.'

'I suppose you're going to tell us that you were responsible for a cloud coming along at just the right moment?' Jai demanded.

'That's no cloud, you dummy,' Percie replied, rolling her eyes. 'It's a balloon. A balloon manatee.'

Ursula looked up and saw that what they had first mistaken for a cloud was, indeed, a giant inflatable manatee. She could see its flippers and the curve of its muzzle. She recalled the manatee she had seen Percie make in the boat, but this one was much bigger – seeming to fill almost the entire sky.

'Balloon-animal magic is one of the most powerful types of magic there is,' Percie said. 'Not to mention the most fun. It won't be that big forever, though, so I'd help with the rowing if I were you.'

Ursula realised she was right. Already, the manatee floating above them was shrinking rapidly, allowing moonlight to pour down through the space it left and causing the skeletons there to come to life instantly.

As one, the explorers all scrambled hastily upright, snatched up oars and rowed for all they were worth. The boat zipped across the sea, with the ever-decreasing balloon manatee keeping pace above them, and a bunch of very angry-looking skeletons pressing up as close as they could outside the shadow. By the time they reached the *Blowfish*, the shadow only just surrounded the boat.

The explorers had attached the ropes and were starting to rise up the side of the submarine when the manatee shrank back to its original size. The last of its magic seemed to vanish at the same time, because it fell back into the boat to land in Percie's lap, just an ordinary balloon once again.

The skeletons all lunged towards them, and one managed to wrap a bony hand around an oar, hanging on as the boat was lifted on to the submarine and clutching greedily at the explorers with its spare hand. Hastily, Genie kicked the oar free and the skeleton went tumbling into the dark water to join its fellows as the little boat rose upwards to safety.

'Well,' Percie said, grinning over the side of the boat at the angry skeletons. 'It's a jolly good thing I was here. No need to thank me ... Actually, scratch that, I would definitely like you all to thank me in fantastic ways which we can discuss later.' She shook her head and gave another chuckle. 'I still can't believe you didn't bring any skeleton repellent with you.' Her eye fell on Genie, who'd yanked the key from her collar and looked like she was about to hurl it overboard. 'Gosh, I wouldn't do that if I were you!' the sea witch said.

'Why not?'

'Because it's a skeleton key.' Percie gave a long-suffering sigh and spoke slowly, as if talking to idiots. 'They're very valuable. It can open any lock. You could sell it for a lot of money on Smugglers' Isle.'

'*Any* lock?' Max said, with sudden eagerness. 'Even ones in an impenetrable fort?'

'Certainly,' Percie replied. 'They're magic. Only skeletons can create them. Nothing in the world is impenetrable to a skeleton key.'

The explorers all stared down at the small rusty key clasped in Genie's hand. A delighted grin spread over Max's face and Ursula knew they were all thinking the same thing. There was now a real possibility of getting into Scarlett's fort and rescuing Jada and the other children.

CHAPTER ELEVEN

Ursula didn't think she'd ever been so glad to be back on board the *Blowfish*. Nor had she ever been so pleased to leave a place behind. She tried to relax as the skeletons and eels got further and further away, but her entire body felt wound tight as a coiled spring. She apologised to her friends over and over again about the trident. It felt like a mistake she would never be able to make amends for and she felt a terrible sense of shame about it.

'Ursula, would you stop?' Jai finally said. 'It was a desperate situation and I'm sure any of us would have done the same thing in your place. You weren't to know. And everyone is all right. Plus, you wanted to practise with the trident and I wouldn't let you. I was wrong about that – from now on, you can practise whenever you want. Just make sure you have a fire hydrant nearby.'

'Also, we would never have got the skeleton key if the

boat hadn't capsized,' Genie said cheerfully. 'I've tested it out and Percie is quite right. It can open every single door on the *Blowfish*, even the extra-secure locks on the brig. It will make all the difference in our rescue plan. So really it's a *good* thing that skeleton grabbed me.'

But Ursula couldn't shake the memory of how close her friend had come to being dragged on to the beach and turned into a cursed skeleton forever. She wished Princess Coral had never given her the trident, and would have been quite happy to toss it into the sea had it not been for the fact that it was not hers to throw away and she'd promised to return it. She felt that old familiar fear of being a mermaid, and dangerous, rise up inside her once again, so she shoved her trident under her bed.

Ursula spent most of the next couple of days dressed in her engineer's coveralls, crawling around by herself in the submarine vents under the pretence of performing maintenance. It was certainly the case that submarines required endless checks and tinkering to keep them in good working order, but she made up jobs in order to be by herself. She felt ashamed to face her friends. Worse than that, she felt like a bit of a monster. On the afternoon of the second day, Genie had had enough of this and crawled into the vents after her.

'What are you doing here?' Ursula asked, so startled by her friend's sudden appearance that she almost dropped her spanner. No one usually climbed into the vents but her. It was cramped up there, and dirty, and a complicated maze of tunnels and hatches. 'You don't know your way around; you could have got lost,' Ursula added, a little more sharply than she'd meant to.

Genie's skirt and lime-green T-shirt were already covered in grease stains, as was her hat. As usual, she wore one of her own creations and this one was fashioned to look like a giant jellyfish, with long pink tentacles that trailed all the way down to her elbows.

'I just . . . came to see if you needed any help,' she said, looking uncertain.

'Well, I don't,' Ursula replied.

'It seems unfair that you have to do all this work by yourself,' Genie persisted.

'No one else is a trained engineer so I'm the only one who can do these jobs.' Ursula went back to tightening up a loose bolt with her spanner, her hands covered in grease.

'You could teach me?' Genie suggested. 'I'd really like to help.'

'It's quicker if I just do it myself,' Ursula said. 'Thanks, though,' she forced herself to add.

'Oh.' Genie looked rather crestfallen. 'OK, then. I guess I'll see you later?'

Ursula nodded, relieved that this seemed to be the end of the conversation, but rather than crawling back the way she'd come, Genie hesitated. Finally she took a deep breath and said, 'Ursula, have I done something to make you mad at me?'

Ursula froze, surprised. 'What? Of course not. Why would you think that?'

'You're avoiding me,' Genie said. 'Like the kids at school.'

Ursula knew that Genie had had a miserable time at school as a result of being a kraken whisperer. The other children had been frightened of the great shadow kraken always trailing after her, and their fear had caused them to call Genie names and make fun of her.

'I don't have much practice at being a friend,' Genie went on, seeming to choose her words carefully. 'I mean, I'm friends with Jai, but that's different because he's my brother. He kind of has to be my friend. But otherwise I've never really had any ... so perhaps I'm not very good at it yet. I've been trying to work out what it is that I've done to upset you, but I'm not sure, even though I've spent hours and hours thinking about it. So I'd like you to tell me, please, so that I can put right whatever's gone wrong.'

Genie's calm voice finally stopped and she looked at Ursula in patient silence. Ursula felt her heart clench with a new wave of guilt.

'You haven't done anything wrong,' she said, forcing out the words like stones. 'It's me. I'm the one who almost got *you* killed.'

There was more that Ursula wanted to say, but her throat closed up with shame and she couldn't go on. She couldn't even look at her friend and found herself staring at the floor of the tunnel instead. There was a pause, and Ursula wondered whether Genie might simply leave. But instead, her friend scooted closer along the tunnel towards Ursula and wrapped her arms around her in a fiercely tight hug.

'I'm sorry you feel bad,' Genie said. 'But I don't blame you at all. You risked your life to save me from that awful beach – only a really great friend would do something like that. Oh, please don't push me away. You're the best friend I've ever had.'

The warmth in Genie's voice seemed to pop the cold little bubble Ursula had put up around herself and she realised there were tears on her cheeks.

'You're the best friend I've ever had too,' she said,

returning Genie's hug. Her mind went back to all those sad, lonely nights at the Ocean Squid Explorers' Club with only mean Mrs Soames for company. Old Joe had been friendly enough to her while they worked together during the day, but it wasn't the same as having a friend her own age. 'I just ... I feel like I'm dangerous sometimes.'

'And you think I don't?' Genie drew back from Ursula slightly to clasp the kraken pendant and hold it up. 'The kids at school always said that if part of my soul was a sea monster then that must mean I was monstrous too.'

'That's rubbish!' Ursula replied, swept with sudden hot anger. 'There's not a drop of badness in you! How dare they say that?'

Genie shrugged. 'I don't *feel* like a bad person,' she said. 'But I do wonder about it sometimes. I don't think there's another kraken whisperer in the world besides me. The club has got seahorse whisperers and turtle whisperers and dolphin whisperers, but not *kraken* whisperers. And yet ... if I could change this thing about myself, I wouldn't. I *like* being a kraken whisperer and I love Bess.'

As if sensing she was being talked about, the shadow kraken suddenly appeared in the tunnel with them.

Of course, she was far too big to fit her entire body in there, but she wound one of her long, dark tentacles in and curled it affectionately around Genie's shoulders.

'I think kraken are majestic, and beautiful, and magical,' Genie went on. 'And they're frightening to people and they're misunderstood. But I'd much rather be a kraken whisperer than a seahorse whisperer, even if that means people don't always understand or like me.'

Ursula felt a surge of affection for her friend and gave her arm a squeeze. 'I love the fact that you're a kraken whisperer,' she said. 'I think it's cool and amazing.'

Genie smiled. 'I think it's cool and amazing that you're a mermaid. So can we go back to being friends?'

Ursula nodded. 'I'd like that.'

'And will you carry on practising your mermaid magic with me?'

Ursula was more reluctant about this, still worried about causing harm, but Genie's expression was so hopeful and expectant that she found herself nodding.

Genie grinned. 'Shall we celebrate with mermaid sundaes?'

'Definitely!'

They crawled out of the vent, giggling as Bess's tentacle weaved and coiled around them in excitement. Finally, they climbed out of a hatch that took them into a corridor close to the library. When he wasn't on the bridge, Jai spent much of his time in there, either polishing his medals or working on his book about Biscuit. The girls could tell he was there now because Max was talking to him and, from the sounds of it, the robot inventor was feeling quite irate.

'Look here, Jai, you're the acting captain, aren't you?' Max said. 'Well, can't you do something about Percie? That pesky little witch is wreaking havoc everywhere she goes. She took a single bite out of every one of the apples in the galley this morning and then just left them there in the fruit bowl, all covered in saliva – so gross! And she's drawn pictures of otters on the walls of the corridor outside my room. She's filled the swimming pool with so much bubble bath that you can hardly see the masts of Zara's ship. She's—'

'Well, what do you expect me to do?' Jai snapped. 'Trust me, no one is unhappier about this state of affairs than I am.'

'Order her to stop being so naughty,' Max said. 'If you get her to stop being such a nuisance, then I'll … I'll clean out your pet plankton tank for a week. How about that?'

'I've tried to tell her about the captain's rule book.' Jai sighed. 'She just laughs and threatens to turn me into a starfish.'

Max grinned. 'Well, I guess I can understand that. I'd have turned you into a starfish many times if I'd had the power to do so.'

'Thanks,' Jai replied briefly.

Ursula and Genie rolled their eyes at each other. It was nothing new to hear the boys bickering, so they left them to it and made their way to the ice-cream machine.

'Max has a point about Percie, though,' Genie said as they walked along the corridor. 'She's been up to all sorts of mischief. Her otters are very naughty too. Yesterday I caught them making a nest in one of my hats. But speaking of hats,' she went on, 'I've almost finished making our pirate ones. For our disguises.'

'I bet they're wonderful,' Ursula said. 'I can't wait to see them.'

They pushed open the door to the soda-fountain room. The food wasn't that good on board a submarine, since it had to be long-lasting and tended to consist of things like instant chicken dinners and tinned spam. To help compensate, each submarine was fitted with a special room like this one, containing a soda fountain, a candyfloss maker and an ice-cream machine.

Aside from the fantastic treats found inside, it was also one of the most beautiful rooms on board. Pale marble tiles lined the floor, and silver seahorse lamps were attached to the gold-and-cream striped walls. The tables were all covered in crisp, white cloths, gleaming silver cutlery and bunches of sea flowers. Huge glass windows took up much of the wall space, allowing explorers to look out at any interesting underwater landscapes or creatures that the submarine might be passing. There wasn't much to see at the moment – they were very deep underwater and so the view outside was dark as space, with only the occasional glowing jellyfish or electric eel to break it up.

The most splendid thing in the room was undoubtedly the soda-fountain counter. It was incredibly ornate, covered in sparkling green tiles depicting some of the Ocean Squid Explorers' Club's most fantastic finds, including the fluffy lullaby crab, the singing sea cucumber, the ocean mammoth and the snow shark. There were tall stools lined up along the gleaming counter, and behind this was the soda fountain itself, with bright red cherryade, white cream soda and fizzy, dark cola all cascading into a tiled bowl with a mosaic of a mermaid in the bottom.

But it was the ice-cream machine that held the greatest attraction for Genie and Ursula, and they walked straight over to where it sat at one end of the counter. They took bowls from the shelves and pressed the mermaid sundae button, already anticipating the delicious swirls of green, blue and purple ice cream, with silver sprinkles and a chocolate mermaid's tail finishing it off on top.

Except that wasn't quite what they got. Instead, black-and-silver ice cream came out, filling the air with the smell of liquorice and magic. Then came bright green sprinkles in the shape of sea otters. And instead of a chocolate mermaid's tail, there was a sea snail that Ursula hoped was made of candy, but which looked horribly realistic.

'What on earth is this?' Ursula asked, wrinkling her nose and staring down at her sundae.

'Do you like it?' a cheerful voice said behind them. 'I think I've improved it.'

Genie and Ursula turned round and saw for the first time that Percie was sitting under a table near one of the windows. She'd removed the tablecloth and used it to make hammocks for Midge and Moe, who were swinging lazily back and forth and looking very pleased with themselves.

'What do you mean "improved" it?' Ursula asked suspiciously.

'The flavours were awful,' Percie replied. She glanced

at the girls only briefly before turning her attention back to the window. She was staring intently through the glass as if waiting for something.

'What are you talking about?' Ursula frowned. 'The flavours were great! It did mermaid sundaes, dolphin delights, seahorse floats and—'

'Boring!' Percie interrupted.

'Oh dear.' Genie looked down at her ice cream. The sea snail on top was definitely real. She could see a slimy trail where it had moved through her dessert. 'What have you done?'

'Well, that sundae you've got there is sea-witch flavour,' Percie said. 'And the machine also does storm-cat floats and pickled-parrot scoops.

Ursula was aghast. 'Pickled-parrot scoops!' she exclaimed. 'Yuck!'

'Have you ever tasted pickled parrot?' Percie asked.

'Of course not!'

'Then how do you know you won't like it? Gosh, some people are so narrow-minded. Not to mention ungrateful.' She gave a haughty sniff.

'Maybe it won't be so bad,' Genie said, valiantly trying for her usual optimism but unable to keep the doubt from creeping into her voice.

'It'll be terrible!' Ursula exclaimed. She glared at

Percie. 'You'd better change it back before Jai finds out what you've—'

'Can't,' Percie cut her off, sounding quite unconcerned. 'The other ingredients have all melted. Now would you please be quiet so I can enjoy the view?'

'What view?' Ursula said. 'There's nothing out there but dark water.'

Percie shook her head. 'You people are forever wandering into things you have absolutely no idea about.'

'We're explorers,' Genie said, putting her ice cream carefully on the counter. 'That's kind of the point.'

'It's not more skeletons, is it?' Ursula asked, as they joined Percie at the window.

The sea witch shook her head. 'Nope. This is the Museum of Impossible Bottles. I've read all about it in my encyclopedia, but I never expected to visit. What a stroke of luck!'

'Oh.' Ursula was relieved. 'Well, a museum doesn't sound too dangerous. But like Jai said back at Skeleton Cove, I'm afraid we haven't got time to stop and look around.'

Percie giggled and turned her attention back to the window. 'That's what you think,' she said.

'What's that supposed to mean?' Ursula asked, starting to feel uneasy.

'You don't visit the museum,' Percie said. 'The museum visits you. And it should be here any second now.'

Ursula and Genie both looked out of the porthole, straining their eyes through the darkness.

Finally, Ursula shook her head. 'I can't see—' she began.

But that was as far as she got before the sea around them suddenly lit up.

CHAPTER TWELVE

The light was so dazzling that for a moment they couldn't look out of the window at all.

'What is it?' Ursula gasped. 'I don't know any fish or sea creature that can glow as brightly as that!'

'It's not a sea creature,' Percie replied. 'It's magic.'

The intercom on the wall at Ursula's elbow suddenly crackled and Jai's voice came over the line. 'Genie, Ursula, where are you?' he asked urgently.

'We're in the soda-fountain room with Percie,' Ursula said. 'Where are you?'

'On the bridge with Max. Look, what's going on down there? Is Percie making that light? If so, tell her to stop it. The bridge is so bright we can't see where we're going. Zara was almost blinded and Ollie was sick all over the controls.'

'It's not me!' Percie scoffed from her seat under the table. 'I'm powerful, but not *that* powerful. It's the sea wizard who owns the Museum of Impossible Bottles.'

'The museum of *what*?' Max's incredulous voice came over the line.

'Can you come up to the bridge?' Jai asked. 'We can talk more easily if we're all in the same place.'

But Percie wouldn't budge and potentially miss some of the exhibits, so Jai, Max and Zara joined them in the soda-fountain room instead. They came in just as the light outside the portholes suddenly dimmed enough for them to be able to see out again. And the sight before them really was quite astonishing.

The submarine was surrounded by hundreds and hundreds of bottles floating in the sea. Some were as small as a little finger, while others were as big as a tree. Most were just ordinary bottle size but they all contained something impossibly big, something that would not have been able to fit through the narrow neck of the bottle.

Directly outside their porthole was a bottle containing a small, blazing sun. Ursula guessed that this was what had been making the sea so bright a few moments before. Now the glass around it was darkening, causing the sun to fade before their eyes, though it was still bright enough to illuminate the area around them.

The *Blowfish* moved slowly through the water, past more and more bottles.

'Look, there's a volcano in that bottle,' Genie said.

'And an aquatic dinosaur.' Max pointed.

'And a sword!' Zara exclaimed.

They also saw various sea flowers and fruit, some weird-looking skeletons, a clock, a telescope, and a pack of playing cards with the Phantom Atlas Society crest on the back. Many of them had entire model ships inside, with tall masts and miniature cannons, and there were a few submarines, bathyspheres and rafts too.

'Astonishing,' Jai said. 'I wonder how it works? Does the wizard shrink the objects down to get them inside the bottle, like the pirate fairies do? Or does the bottle get bigger to fit around the object?'

'Well, if you don't pay the wizard his fee then I guess you'll find out,' Percie said. 'Because he'll just take the entire submarine.'

'You don't mean he'd put the *Blowfish* inside one of his bottles?' Ursula asked.

The explorers were horrified.

'But that's not fair,' Max said. 'It's not like we had any choice about it – the museum just sprang up around us.'

'What is the fee?' Jai asked, looking panic-stricken. 'We haven't got much money.'

Percie pulled a face. 'He's not interested in money. You just have to give him something interesting to add to his collection. Something he doesn't already have. Oh, look, it's the bottle with the door inside it. That means we've reached the end of the museum.'

Sure enough, there were no more bottles. The light from the sun had almost disappeared but they could see enough to realise that the water around them was empty. Or at least empty of bottles. All of a sudden, there was something else outside the submarine – something so big it filled the entire window. The explorers could see only a huge curtain of white. The next second, the *Blowfish* suddenly came to a halt with a juddering motion.

The floor tilted beneath them and everyone fell to the floor – except Percie, who was already on the floor and seemed to have been expecting the sudden stop because she was hanging on to one of the nailed-down table legs, and her otters were clinging to their hammocks.

'Great Scott!' Jai exclaimed, scrambling to his feet. 'What on earth is going on?'

'It's the wizard,' Percie said from under the table. 'He's grabbed hold of the submarine.'

Jai gaped at her. 'Grabbed *hold* of it? What do you

mean? This submarine has the engine power of a thousand horses! No man has the strength to grab hold of it, not even a wizard!'

Percie grinned. 'He does if he's sixty foot tall.'

The others had got back to their feet now as well.

'Sixty foot?' Ursula repeated. 'But that would make him as big as a storm maiden!'

'Well, obviously,' Percie said. She pointed at the window and said, 'Why else would his beard be so massive?'

'*Beard*?' the explorers and Zara all exclaimed together.

Their eyes slid back towards the window with a sort of horrified fascination. What they had first thought was a white curtain, they now realised was made up of hundreds of individual strands.

'What did you think all that white hair was?' Percie asked, rolling her eyes.

Before they could reply, the submarine suddenly shifted again, causing everyone to topple back on to the floor.

'I'd grab hold of the table legs if I were you,' Percie said. 'Sometimes the wizard shakes you about a bit, trying to see inside. At least, that's what it says in my encyclopedia.'

Sure enough, the next moment they got a glimpse

of blue fabric with a silver star stitched into it, then a gigantic blue eye appeared. It was so large that it filled the entire window.

'What's he doing?' Ursula gasped.

'Sea wizards have X-ray vision,' Percie told them cheerfully. 'He's peering inside to see what stuff we've got and decide what fee he's going to ask.' She looked thoughtful and said, 'Hopefully he won't ask for a member of the crew. I've heard they do that sometimes.'

'He's not taking a member of our crew!' Jai exclaimed. 'Not a chance!'

'You don't have much choice,' Percie replied. 'If you refuse, he'll just take the entire sub.'

'Aren't you worried he might ask for you?' Genie asked. 'Or one of your otters?'

Percie squealed with laughter. 'Gracious, no! Ha, what an idea! Sea wizards can't stand sea witches, or their familiars. Our magic makes them sneeze, you see. He'd never ask for me. Their sneezes are pretty powerful. Trust me, you *really* don't want to be around when a sea wizard sneezes.'

She clapped her hands over her ears and her otters did the same with their paws.

'Now what are you—?' Max began.

But that was as far as he got before the deep, booming

voice of the wizard spoke. It was so loud that everyone copied Percie and put their hands over their ears. His voice seemed to echo through the entire submarine, making the very walls and floor shake.

'THE PRICE IS THE ROBOT SHARK.'

'Oh my gods, is he trying to *deafen* us?' Max groaned.

'That's just a whisper,' Percie said. 'He asks in a whisper the first time but if you don't give him what he wants then he'll start shouting and, trust me, you *really* won't like that! So give him the robot shark, quick!'

'But it's *mine*!' Max almost wailed. 'I've only just finished it and—'

'ROBOT SHARK!' the huge voice boomed even louder.

'For goodness' sake, send it out before he deafens us!' Jai gasped.

'But I've been working on it for weeks! Can't we give him something else?'

'Sea wizards don't negotiate,' Percie said. 'They just name their price and that's that.'

And so Max had no choice but to run down to his robotics lab and press the button to send his beloved shark out into the ocean. The sea wizard snatched it up at once and the eye left the window. The explorers had a brief view of the robot shark suddenly sealed inside a glass bottle before the wizard released his hold on the submarine, allowing the *Blowfish* to continue on its way, leaving the Museum of Impossible Bottles behind them.

Everyone felt rather sorry for Max over the robot shark affair, and so that evening they prepared a special meal for him, doing the best they could with the limited ingredients in the galley. Even Percie seemed to feel some sympathy and magically produced a plate of shark-shaped chocolate-chip ice-cream sandwiches.

After they'd eaten, the explorers took out their maps and asked Percie what she knew about the other sea wizard museums, and where to find them. No one wanted to experience one a second time around.

'Oh, there are hundreds and hundreds of museums,' Percie said cheerfully. 'Like the Museum of Puffed-Up Fish, and the Museum of Old Pipes and the Museum of Poisonous Sea Flowers. I can't possibly remember them all.'

'If only I could take a look at your encyclopedia myself,' Jai groaned. He had a photographic memory and would only need to cast his eye over the pages once to have every word stored in his brain. 'Just tell us about the ones you *can* remember then.'

'It's not as simple as that,' Percie said, carefully balancing a treat on Moe's nose. 'They don't always stay in the same place, you see. The Museum of Puffed-Up Fish, for example, appears around any passing submarine or mermaid. Sometimes they travel about a bit if they decide they're not getting enough customers. Some of them are pretty much always travelling, kind of like a circus. I can show you the locations of the ones I remember, but that doesn't mean they're still there.'

'It's better than nothing, I suppose,' Jai said.

The little witch was agreeable to doing this for a while, but after Jai had made some notes and marked a few spots on the map, Percie became bored, especially once she ran out of otter treats to balance on her familiars' noses.

'We'll be here all night if I tell you about every single one,' she said. 'Especially at the slow rate you're writing everything down in that dusty old book!'

'It's not a dusty old book, it's our Flag Report,' Jai said indignantly. 'Everything we discover during our expedition needs to be reported in it so that when we return the flag to our club there will be documented evidence about it all.'

'I don't care about any of that,' Percie said, standing up and brushing herself off. 'That's explorers' business. Sea witches have more important things to be worrying about. Like otter hammocks and puggle parties.'

'These sea wizard museums can clearly be extremely dangerous,' Jai said. 'Surely you want to help us make future expeditions safer?'

He looked to the others for support, but they could see it was hopeless and that Percie wasn't in a helping mood.

'Not especially,' she said, already skipping towards the door. 'Look, I've told you about the Museum of Silly Trousers and the Museum of Candy Teaspoons. They're rumoured to be the ones with the grumpiest sea wizards. Other than that, just stay away from anywhere with whirlpools. Remember I said sea witches' magic makes wizards sneeze? Well, plenty of other stuff makes them sneeze too and you can bet your life that whenever a sea wizard sneezes, he's bound to create a whirlpool or two.'

'But Percie, we really need your help—' Jai began.

'Tough, I've already helped you loads,' Percie said. 'And if you ask me about it again, I'll turn you into a starfish. And not a pretty one either, but one of those horrible, slimy little grey ones that's always finding its way into your socks.'

And with that she disappeared out the door, her sea otters scampering at her heels.

'What did she mean about socks?' Genie asked, frowning. She looked at Ursula. 'Have *you* ever found a starfish in your socks?'

Ursula shook her head. 'Maybe that's what happens when you stay in a sea cave in Skeleton Cove?'

'Well, I can't say I blame her,' Max said gloomily. 'I'm sick of talking about sea wizards. If anyone needs me, I'll be in the robotics lab working on my new shark.'

Ursula excused herself too. She dug out her trident from where she'd shoved it beneath the bunk beds she shared with Genie. It felt cold to the touch as she wrapped her hand around it. After checking to make sure there was a fire hydrant in the room, she concentrated her thoughts on the trident. Only she wasn't trying to make it shoot lightning this time. Instead, she was gently reaching out her mind towards it – talking to the mermaid relic to see if it would talk back to her. To her pleasure, the trident lit up in her hand, like the prettiest ever nightlight, filling the bedroom with a soft, golden glow.

'Oh!' Genie exclaimed, walking in. 'It's so beautiful, Ursula!'

Ursula looked at her friend. 'Jai said I could practise

on the submarine,' she said. 'Would you still like to help me?'

A big smile spread over Genie's face. 'Yes,' she said. 'I'd be glad to.'

Over the next couple of days, they began spending time in the swim-out chamber so that they could quickly submerge the room if a fire was to break out. And slowly but surely, Ursula became more confident and competent using the trident.

Otherwise, the time passed fairly uneventfully, but for the fact that Percie kept making balloon-animal penguins that waddled up and down the submarine corridors producing a dreadful honking racket that woke everyone up at night.

Not only that, she somehow managed to befriend Jabba the sea gremlin, and persuaded Jabba to give her some of her bogies, which she then used to create a sea-gremlin flavour ice cream in the soda-fountain room. Ursula dared Max to try it, knowing he'd never been able to resist a dare, but this ice cream was so gross he barely managed a spoonful before retching and declaring it the vilest thing he'd ever tasted, and they all knew this must be pretty serious because Max had once accidentally eaten a stink berry.

Percie was a hopelessly naughty child, and her

sea otter familiars were equally mischievous, always burrowing and tumbling their way into places they didn't belong. On one occasion, Midge, who was the greedier of the two, even mistook Zara's parrot for a snack and swallowed him down whole. The pirate fairy and the sea witch almost came to blows over that, but fortunately Percie managed to get Ollie back by turning Midge upside down and shaking him until the little parrot fell out of his mouth, completely soaked in otter spit, but otherwise no worse for wear.

Even so, it was safe to say that everyone was getting rather tired of their sea witch guest, and were looking forward to arriving at Smugglers' Isle where they would finally be able to deliver her into the care of her parents. It was therefore rather a blow to be suddenly and unexpectedly delayed by a ferocious whirlpool.

Chapter Thirteen

The whirlpool seemed to come out of nowhere, and by the time the explorers became aware of it, it was almost too late to avoid getting sucked into its deadly vortex. Fortunately, Jai spotted it just in time and brought the *Blowfish* to an emergency halt.

'All hands to the bridge.' His voice came loud and clear over the intercom. 'Repeat, all hands to the bridge.'

The others hurried to join him. Zara whistled when she looked through the porthole and saw the great whirlpool raging in the sea beyond.

'That's one of the biggest I've ever seen!' she exclaimed. 'Why, it's practically a maelstrom!'

It certainly was gigantic – a great, spinning tornado of water that stretched above and below them. They could see bits of shell and coral flying past in its revolving currents, along with strings of seaweed and flotsam, and the occasional miserable-looking crab.

'Perhaps that sea wizard passed through this way?' Genie suggested. 'Percie said their sneezes cause whirlpools, didn't she?'

'Speaking of Percie, where is she?' Jai asked, looking annoyed. Nobody knew, so he snatched up the intercom and repeated his earlier command. 'I said all hands to the bridge. Repeat, all hands to the bridge! That means you too, Percie!'

He had to repeat the command a couple more times before her voice crackled back over the intercom. 'I'm not a hand, I'm a sea witch and I don't take orders from you. If you want to spend hours poring over your dusty old maps and Flag Reports that's your business, but me and the otters are going for a swim.'

'A *swim*?' Jai looked aghast. 'Percie, wait! Do not go into the sea! I repeat, do *not* go into the—'

'Just a quick one,' Percie's unconcerned voice trilled over the intercom. 'I want to try out one of these cool diving suits.'

To their dismay, the explorers heard the thud of the swim-out hatch door locking closed and the swish of water rushing in before Percie shut off the intercom.

'Oh my gods.' Jai had gone pale. 'She'll be killed for sure.'

He ran over to one of the control panels. 'There

must be some way to override the swim-out hatch from up here?'

'That's the wrong station,' Ursula said. She raced to the bank of machines on the other side of the bridge. 'I think we need one of these.'

Everyone turned their attention to the various dials, knobs and buttons, but there were so many of them and no one could quite remember which one they needed.

'Oh no, it's too late!' Max gasped. He looked sick as he pointed at one of the portholes.

They all turned to see Percie beyond the glass. She wore one of the explorers'-club diving suits. It allowed a person to breathe underwater, but it was also large, cumbersome and awkward. Its great weight meant it would sink to the seabed without the propulsion technology that blasted powerful jets of air from the feet, keeping the diver upright.

An experienced explorer could make it look easy, but in fact swimming in one of these suits was quite a skill and all Ocean Squid explorers went through extensive training back at the club. There was a massive swimming pool there for the junior explorers to practise in, with special controls to make the water choppy as it would be in a storm. Junior explorers had to spend hours and hours in the pool before they were allowed anywhere near the open sea, but even the most experienced and intrepid of explorers wouldn't think of going out in the ocean when there was a whirlpool nearby.

It was immediately apparent to Ursula and the others that Percie was having trouble with her suit. Her movements were jerky and erratic. She would shoot one way before trying to correct herself, but would then overcompensate and go spinning off in the opposite direction. She did not look as if she was in control at all.

To make it worse, her otters were out there with her too. For some reason, they were both wearing little otter-sized flippers, masks and snorkels and seemed entirely oblivious to the danger. In fact, they appeared to think that Percie's erratic swimming was some kind of game rather than panic, and they cheerfully zipped about in the water alongside her. But the whole time, they were getting closer and closer to the edge of the whirlpool.

The explorers all moved at once, scrambling to mount a rescue.

'There's some kind of lifesaving line that goes out from the bridge, isn't there?' Genie asked, running her hands over the controls in search of it. 'Oh, where is it?'

No one could remember. The huge submarine was

designed to have a crew of twenty, and although four people could operate it, the fact was they simply weren't familiar enough with all the many controls to be able to locate them quickly in an emergency. Ursula silently promised herself that she would examine the design manuals from cover to cover after this, and memorise every page.

'I'll send one of my midget subs out,' Max said, running towards the door. 'I just need to attach a rescue line and then it can tow her in.'

'No, no, no.' Jai cast one last glance out of the porthole at the struggling sea witch.

Ursula knew that he was the reigning junior chess champion back at the club, and just as that game required a player to look several moves ahead, so she could almost see Jai's shrewd gaze calculating what was about to happen now.

'This is all taking too long,' he said. 'Percie will be sucked up in the whirlpool by the time you do that.'

Ursula saw at once that Jai was right. There was only one option available. Her eyes met Jai's across the bridge. 'We'll have to go out and get her.'

Jai nodded.

'Well, the subs could still be useful,' Max said, disappearing out the door.

'I'll come with—' Genie began.

'No.' Jai cut her off. 'We need someone to stay on the bridge and carry on trying to find that rescue line,' he said. 'Ursula and I will go.'

It was a submarine rule that if they needed to venture into a dangerous situation outside the sub the crew worked in pairs. As a mermaid, it made most sense for Ursula to go, and Jai had had a lot more experience in diving suits than Genie, since she wasn't technically a member of the club and had learned to dive using their family suits.

'All right. Be careful,' she said, before reluctantly turning back to the controls.

Jai and Ursula raced to the swim-out hatch, where Jai changed into a diving suit in record time, snatched up the robot dolphin Max had given him, and then they both sealed themselves inside the hatch. Ursula's legs turned into a tail the moment the first drop of cold seawater fizzed up through the grate to touch her bare feet. It seemed to take forever for the room to fill with water, and she and Jai looked at each other grimly. They both knew the mission ahead of them would be a difficult one no matter how good at swimming they were, and they both hoped with all their might that Percie hadn't strayed too much closer to the whirlpool.

At long last, they were finally able to open the hatch and swim out into the ocean. Ursula gasped the moment she was clear of the submarine. She hadn't expected the whirlpool to be so very *loud*. They hadn't been able to hear anything through the thick walls of the *Blowfish*, but out in the sea without a helmet, the roar of the whirlpool was almost deafening. Bess's huge form loomed in the water beside the submarine, and she seemed distressed by the noise too; her tentacles were thrashing energetically.

Ursula and Jai quickly located Percie. Her movements were even more panic-stricken and she must have seen the whirlpool by now as she was floating perilously close to the edge of it. She kept trying to propel herself away using the suit, but her lack of control meant she only managed to move herself closer. The otters had both clearly realised something was wrong too and were clinging to her legs, their dark brown eyes wild with fear.

The explorers swam straight towards Percie. Jai's robot dolphin meant he was able to keep pace with Ursula, even in his heavy diving suit. They reached her at the same time and took hold of an arm each. Ursula got a brief glimpse of the relief on the little sea witch's face when she realised she was no longer alone in the water.

Fortunately, she had the sense to stop pressing buttons inside her suit so that the explorers could take control. Ursula could feel the treacherous tug of the whirlpool reaching out for her tail as hundreds of little bubbles raced past them, and she was glad to turn away and start swimming back to the submarine. Bess held out her tentacles, and Ursula wished she was a real kraken.

But then something awful happened. Perhaps he mistakenly thought the danger had passed, or else his little paws just got tired from holding on – either way, Midge suddenly let go of Percie's leg and his small body was instantly swept back into the whirlpool. One moment the otter was there, the next he was gone, leaving only one of his little flippers floating behind him.

It was one of the strangest things about being underwater that so much sound was lost. Ursula could see that Percie was crying and shouting Midge's name inside her helmet, but she wouldn't have been able to hear her even without the whirlpool. The otter's sudden demise was dreadful, but there was nothing they could do about it now and Ursula was horrified when the little witch tried to hurl herself towards the whirlpool after him. Thankfully, Percie still didn't have much control of her suit, so Ursula and Jai were able to tug her back, although it was difficult with the witch struggling against them so hard.

Genie managed to find the rescue line at that moment, and it shot through the sea towards them with a hook at the end. Jai snatched it from the water, clipped it to the loop on Percie's suit, then gestured at Ursula and pointed vigorously at the submarine. She nodded to show she understood, then gripped Percie's arm and began to swim towards the *Blowfish*. Genie must have pressed the button to draw the line in too, which helped drag Percie away from the whirlpool whether she wanted to or not. Ursula felt dreadful about the otter, but Percie getting herself and Moe killed by going after him wouldn't achieve anything.

She assumed Jai felt the same way and glanced over her shoulder, expecting to see him following right behind. Instead, she saw that Jai had moved closer to the whirlpool. Ursula had momentarily forgotten that Jai had highly developed hero instincts, which made it virtually impossible for him to ignore someone or something in peril. Many of his medals had been awarded for pulling off daring rescues that no one else had thought possible, or worth the risk, but when Jai came face to face with danger, his natural response was to dive straight in to see who he could help.

Still, Ursula could hardly believe he was considering that now. No one in their right mind would willingly go into an underwater whirlpool as big as this. Surely he wouldn't do something so foolhardy? She could see him hovering very close to the edge, watching the water swirl round and round, as if looking for something. Then, to Ursula's absolute horror, he suddenly pointed the robot dolphin and used the propulsion in his boots at the same time to send him shooting straight into the outskirts of the whirlpool. In the blink of an eye, the water closed around him like a fist and he was lost from view.

Ursula left Percie to be dragged into the sub by the rescue line and raced back as close as she dared to the whirlpool. Bess rushed to her side too, her tentacles flailing in panic and distress. As Jai was Genie's brother, Bess had known him her whole life and loved him for being one of the few people to always treat her with kindness and respect. What was he thinking?

Even as a mermaid, Ursula didn't believe she was a strong enough swimmer to plunge into a whirlpool and hope to get out again. It was the most ridiculously risky act she had ever seen anyone do. What could have possessed him? She knew he wouldn't be able to hear her, yet she found herself bellowing his name anyway, almost blind with panic.

Of course, there was no answer, and she was desperately trying to summon her courage to go after him when, to her amazement, Jai came flying out of the whirlpool, his hand gripped tight around the fin of the robot dolphin. Her astonishment was even greater when she saw that he had Midge clinging to his arm. The otter's fur was sticking up in all different directions from his journey around the whirlpool, but other than that he seemed unharmed.

Just then, Max's midget submarine arrived near them, with a rescue line and hook attached to the end. Bess flailed her tentacles to draw Ursula's attention to it, and she quickly snatched it up and turned towards Jai. It seemed as though the whirlpool somehow sensed it was about to lose one of its prizes, because the spin of the current suddenly got bigger and tugged at the edges of Jai's diving suit once again. A flash of alarm crossed the explorer's face and he was almost dragged back, but Ursula shot forwards and attached the hook to him in one deft motion. Then she used both hands to cling to the rescue line herself as the midget sub towed them back to the safety of the *Blowfish*, with Bess following in their wake.

Percie had already been taken on board, and the swim-out hatch was empty when Jai, Ursula and

Midge entered it. Ursula banged the door closed and pressed the button to begin draining out the water. Jai struggled out of his helmet once the water level dropped to their waists. Bess was too large to fit inside the hatch with them, but she reached a tentacle through the wall and curled it round Jai's shoulders in a concerned way.

'Thanks, Bess,' Jai said. 'I'm OK.' Then he grinned at Ursula. 'That was some rescue! Nice work with the midget sub's hook – I've never seen anyone clip one on so fast.'

Ursula shook her head, hardly knowing whether to compliment Jai for his bravery or berate him for his stupidity. 'I can't believe you pulled it off,' she said in the end. 'When you went into that whirlpool I thought you were a goner for sure.'

'I've had some experience with whirlpools,' Jai replied. 'I once had to rescue a crew member who got sucked into one. He was quite a big man too, so I figured one little otter would probably be easier to pull out.'

He set his helmet down on the floor and then reached up to stroke Midge, who was clinging to his neck like a rather bedraggled scarf.

'Well, I'm just relieved it's over,' Ursula said.

The last of the water had drained away, but her tail was still wet, so she had no choice but to sit on the hard, metal floor.

'I'll get you a robe,' Jai said, starting for the door.

He pressed the button to open it, but had barely grasped the handle before it burst open so hard that it knocked him flat on his back. Midge leaped in the air only just in time to avoid being squashed. Percie flew through the door like a mini tornado. She was out of her diving suit and had Moe gripped under one arm. With the other she snatched Midge up from the floor and rained kisses down on his wet head for a moment, before turning her attention to Jai.

'Thank you!' she gasped, flinging her arms round his neck. 'You saved his life! Thank you, thank you!'

'I wouldn't have had to save his life if you hadn't gone against my orders,' Jai said sternly.

He struggled to get free, but it was almost impossible with the little witch clinging to him. Fortunately, the others arrived just then. Genie handed Ursula a robe so she could dry her tail and get her legs back, while Max prised Percie away and then helped Jai to his feet.

'How on earth did you do that?' Max stared at the other boy. 'I've never seen anyone dive into a whirlpool before. You ought to be dead right now.'

'Well, your robot dolphin helped,' Jai said. 'I probably wouldn't have managed without it. It's a very strong whirlpool. Speaking of which, we should set a new course. We need to go around it while keeping a safe distance—'

'I've already set a new course,' Genie said. She looked faintly ill as she turned her gaze on Jai. 'I wish you hadn't done that. I almost had a heart attack.'

'Well, *I'm* glad!' Percie said. 'Midge would have been lost otherwise.'

'Yes, and it would have been *your* fault,' Genie said sharply.

Ursula was surprised. She had never heard her friend sound cross before. Bess seemed worried by her tone too, because she reached a tentacle out to curl around Genie protectively.

'Why couldn't you follow the rules just once?' Genie went on.

'You can talk about breaking the rules!' Percie protested. 'Didn't you steal this submarine, and aren't you on an unauthorised expedition, and—'

'Yes, but we're doing all that to *help* other people!' Genie said. 'Whereas you were just thinking about yourself and what *you* wanted. You put us in danger!'

'I know!' Percie hugged her otters closer, suddenly

looking shamefaced. 'I'm sorry. I didn't realise there was a whirlpool out there.'

'That's exactly why you should have listened,' Genie said, exasperated. 'I could have lost my brother because of you!'

To everyone's surprise, Percie started to cry – big fat tears dropped on to the heads of her soggy otters. 'I'm sorry!' she wailed. 'I don't mean to be bad. I just want to have fun.'

All Genie's anger seemed to vanish. She couldn't bear to see someone upset, so she hurried across the room to put her arms round Percie. 'It's OK,' she said. 'I'm sorry I got cross. I was just worried about my friends, that's all. Please don't cry. Look, you're upsetting Bess. She hates it when people argue.'

Ursula saw that the kraken's tentacle had indeed drooped rather sadly.

'I really *am* sorry,' Percie hiccuped. Midge and Moe both nuzzled closer to her.

'Everyone is OK and that's all that matters,' Jai said, trying to smooth things over. 'Bess, please don't be sad, we're not arguing any more.' He turned back to Percie. 'Rules *are* important, though, especially when you're at sea. I'm sure you'll remember that next time, won't you?'

'Oh yes!' Percie nodded emphatically. 'Definitely.'

Ursula wasn't so sure it was in the little witch's nature to follow rules, but she remained silent.

'All's well that ends well,' Max said cheerfully. 'Even the robot dolphin survived.' He picked it up off the floor to inspect it for damage. Then he looked at Percie and said, 'What I don't understand is why you didn't use magic to save yourself?'

'Oh.' The sea witch shuffled her feet and seemed suddenly very interested in the floor. 'Well, I didn't have any balloons with me. And the hands of those diving suits are so big and clumsy that I wouldn't have been able to make balloon animals anyway.'

Ursula frowned. 'So? Why didn't you use a spell that doesn't involve balloon animals?'

'I can't do other spells,' Percie said. 'I can only perform balloon-animal magic. And a little bit of ice-cream magic from time to time. Oh, I made a magic cake once too, but I've never been able to repeat that.'

Jai looked confused. 'But ... but you've been threatening to turn me into a starfish the entire trip!'

Percie gave one of her old cheeky grins before she quickly smothered it and tried to look apologetic instead. 'Sorry about that,' she said, with a shrug. 'Sometimes it's useful to have people think you can do things you can't, but the truth is I'm not able to turn humans into starfish, or anything else.'

'Why, of all the dirty tricks!' Max exclaimed. 'It's against maritime law to make magical threats against another person at sea! Isn't that right, Jai?'

'Strictly forbidden,' he said. 'This is very serious, Percie.'

'She ought to go straight to the brig,' Max suggested. 'Perhaps being bunk mates with Jubba and getting pelted with bogies every night will give her a taste of her own medicine.'

'Not so fast.' Percie held up her hand. 'I can't turn people into starfish, but I *can* make a balloon pelican that will gobble up everything you own, or a balloon sea flower that will just keep growing and growing until it's taken over your entire submarine, or a balloon mermaid that steals voices, or a balloon terrapin that won't stop yodelling until it's taught you how to tap-dance, or—'

'All right, all right, we get the idea.' Jai held up his hand to quieten her as the explorers all gave a collective shudder. No one much fancied being forced to learn tap dancing by a yodelling balloon terrapin.

'You're a little young to be sent to the brig anyway, but you must promise that you absolutely won't make another magical threat against me or anyone else on board this submarine. Do you understand?'

Percie agreed at once. After his daring rescue of Midge, she was happy to do anything Jai asked. That evening, she even sat with him in the bridge for almost five hours to go through all the remaining sea-wizard-museum information she knew. After that, she helped him clean out his pet plankton tank and even listened in a dazed sort of way while Jai told her all about the wonders of plankton, a speech that lasted almost two hours. Nothing was too much trouble. It didn't seem to matter that the others had played their parts too – Percie was grateful to them in a vague kind of way, but she now practically hero-worshipped Jai.

She scrubbed all her chalk drawings from the corridor walls, rounded up her balloon penguins and even changed all the flavours in the ice-cream machine, which everyone was very happy about because they didn't like finding gremlin bogies in their sundaes. Percie had been telling the truth about the melted ingredients, so she wasn't able to change the machine back to its original settings, but she created a new Ocean Squid Explorers' Club flavour which consisted of minty-green ice cream with chocolate submarines and squid sprinkles. She even managed to make a special hero sundae in Jai's honour, consisting of golden butterscotch-flavour ice cream and solid chocolate medals.

The explorers were all relieved that the next couple of days passed by without any further whirlpool dramas or sea-witch disasters, and before they knew it, the *Blowfish* had arrived at Smugglers' Isle.

CHAPTER FOURTEEN

Ursula had heard stories about Barnacle City, but no explorers had ever been there. Ocean Squid members were forbidden from conspiring with smugglers and so they stayed well away from any of their settlements. Smugglers' Isle was the largest of all of them, and in usual times, Ursula and her friends would probably have faced some serious punishments for docking their submarine at such a place. These were not exactly normal times, however, and they could only add it to the long list of things that they hoped the club would understand if they ever managed to rescue it from Scarlett.

For now, Jai brought the *Blowfish* up to the surface and then the explorers made their way to the outside deck. As always after several days spent cooped up underwater, it was a great relief to open the hatch and step out into sunshine and fresh, salty sea air. It was a bright, beautiful morning, and the sky was a blue dome overhead, with not a cloud in sight.

It was pleasantly warm and they barely had need of their cloaks. Genie was glad that she had worn a head bopper, with two plump seals bouncing around on top of the twin springs, instead of one of her warmer hats. Even Percie was starting to look a bit hot with both Midge and Moe draped around her shoulders like a mink stole.

Around them, Barnacle City's pier was crowded with all manner of seafaring crafts, from sloops and sailing ships, to submarines, rowing boats and rafts. Most of them had dark sails, so as to be better disguised at night when moving illegal goods in and out of various ports. Many of the vessels were tattered and patched, and some had marks where they'd been shot at. Smuggling was a dangerous business – the remit of criminals and desperate men and women. The island was rumoured to be a very unsafe place and the explorers weren't too sure what they would find there.

Still, they had to admit that it looked picturesque enough. The buildings were rather wonky and crooked, crowded together all higgledy-piggledy at the water's edge, and they were covered in barnacles that gleamed white in the sun.

'So that's how the city got its name,' Ursula said. 'But how did the barnacles get there?'

The little crustaceans lived in the ocean and could normally be found on piers and the underside of boats. It was rare for them to appear so far above the surface, especially in such numbers.

'A hundred years ago, Smugglers' Isle was a sunken island,' Percie told them. 'For some reason it rose back to the surface one day, and the barnacles came with it.'

'I thought there would be more fog,' Genie remarked.

'The fog comes in when it goes dark,' Percie replied. 'You can't see a foot in front of your face then. That's why they put ropes out, to help you find your way around the streets.'

'Well, we'll be long gone by then,' Jai said. 'The moment we've seen you safely back with your parents, we'll be returning to our expedition.'

'But you'll stay to tea, won't you?' Percie asked.

Jai shook his head. 'I'm sorry, but we don't have time. It's very important that we get on with our—'

'I'll run on ahead, then!' Percie said. 'I'll pick up some witch buns along the way. Don't worry – I'll be super-quick! I'll even push to the front of the queue. Then everything will be ready when you arrive.'

And with that, she pulled a balloon-animal seagull from her pocket and jumped off the submarine. The explorers were horrified and lunged forwards to try to catch her. The *Blowfish* was some ten storeys tall and far too high to jump on to the wooden boardwalk without injury.

But the balloon seagull came to life in Percie's hands, and began flapping its wings energetically while getting bigger and bigger. The sea otters on her shoulders both chirped in excitement and Percie let out a series of loud whoops as the balloon bird swooped along the pier with the sea witch dangling beneath it. After almost colliding with several people, she was quickly lost from sight in the crowd.

'Finally.' Max let out a breath of relief. 'What a pest that witch was. I'm glad to see the back of her.'

'We have to go after her,' Jai said.

'You can't be serious?' Max gawped at him. 'For goodness' sake, let's just leave her. This is Percie's home and we've already seen she can take care of herself.'

But Jai refused to be budged. 'It's a question of honour,' he said. 'We promised her aunt and I'm not leaving this island until I know she's safely back with her parents. The Ocean Squid Club has a poor reputation when it comes to keeping our vows. If we want people to think we're honourable then we've got to start behaving honourably. There are no shortcuts to that.'

Ursula wasn't exactly thrilled about the idea, but she agreed with Jai. 'We did promise,' she said. 'And for all we know, a sea witch may be able to sense if we don't keep up our end of the bargain, then she might remove the charm and the Pacificans will be able to see us again, and all of this will have been for nothing.'

'I think we should go after her too,' Genie said. 'It wouldn't feel right to break our promise, and although Percie has been . . . well, a little bit of a handful, I'd still like to know that she's safe.'

'I say good riddance to her,' Zara drawled, tipping back her hat. She had never forgiven the sea witch's otter for eating Ollie, even if he had spat him back out. 'But if you lot are going on to Smugglers' Isle, I'm not going to miss out on getting a plate of scampi.'

'This isn't a sightseeing trip,' Jai protested. 'We're not here for scampi.'

'*I'd* quite like to be here for scampi,' Max said.

'No one is going to eat scampi,' Jai insisted. 'What are you thinking! We need to get a move on.'

'For all we know, the smugglers won't like a bunch of explorers walking in,' Max pointed out. 'Perhaps we should go in disguise?'

'I think it's a bit late for that,' Ursula said.

She was right. Genie had asked Bess to forgo her usual pastime of sunbathing on top of the submarine, and to stay out of sight beneath the water so as to avoid the inevitable screaming and fleeing, but their group was still attracting a lot of attention. The *Blowfish* was much larger and grander than the other submarines, and several people on the pier had stopped what they were doing to stare up at them.

After a hurried conversation, the explorers decided to take no weapon other than Max's robot duck, since it was less conspicuous than Jai's harpoon gun or Ursula's trident. Then they climbed down the ladder attached to the side of the submarine. They all felt slightly nervous that a smuggler might stop them and demand they leave the island.

Their fears seemed to be realised when a woman approached them almost at once. She had short dark hair, several earrings down the side of one ear and she wore a black leather jacket dusted with a fine layer of salt crystals. She bore down on them with a rather ferocious expression, but instead of forbidding them entry, she opened her leather jacket to reveal the many keys stitched into the lining.

'Treasure chest key?' she asked abruptly. 'Only ten dollars each.'

'No, thank you,' Jai said. 'We're just here to look for a sea witch. Have you seen her? She's—'

But that was as far as he got before the woman closed her jacket and walked off in search of more promising customers.

The explorers quickly realised that the island was bustling with many kinds of different people, from smugglers and pirates to merchants and tourists and even a few aristocrats. The local smugglers didn't care where people were from – all they minded was how much money they had to spend. As they walked down the pier they had people try to sell them everything from rare pufferfish and magic parrot feathers, to pirate treasure maps and carnivorous cabbages.

'Why would anyone want a carnivorous cabbage?' Max asked, staring at the proffered vegetable aghast. 'Dreadful things.'

They reached the end of the pier and headed into a side street, which was full of cafes, restaurants and shrimp shacks. The crooked, ancient-looking buildings were all covered in barnacles. There were even barnacles on the pavement, so their feet crunched with each step. The explorers could see the ropes Percie had mentioned, winding up and down alongside the pavements. The most delicious smells of garlic and butter and lobster wafted from open doors, making their stomachs gurgle, and Ursula couldn't help thinking it would be rather nice if they were here as tourists instead of explorers and could stop to have a good meal and a rest. Staff stood at each doorway, trying to entice customers in, and Jai paused to speak to one.

'Excuse me, did you see a sea witch go past here?' he asked.

'You'll have to be more specific than that, kid,' the man replied. 'Lots of sea witches live in Barnacle City.'

'This one was flying along underneath a giant balloon-animal bird,' Max offered.

'Huh. Doesn't narrow it down much.'

'*Really?*'

'Sea witches are a lazy bunch,' the waiter said. 'They'll always hang on to a bird rather than put those pointy shoes of theirs on the ground and walk like the rest of us.'

'She's a little girl,' Genie said. 'About ten years old, with green and black hair.'

'And she's got two sea otters wrapped around her neck,' Zara said from her perch on Genie's shoulder.

Finally, a look of recognition flashed across the man's face. He groaned and said, 'Not Percie! I thought she'd gone to stay with her aunt? A crab stylist, or something like that?'

'Platypus groomer,' Ursula corrected. 'And she sent her home early.'

The man grunted. 'Well, I'm not surprised. That girl creates mischief and mayhem wherever she goes.'

'She said she was going to a bakery—'

'There are quite a few of those,' the man said.

'Look, why don't we just go on to her house?' Max said. 'We've dithered about so much that she's probably already there.'

'Can you tell us how to get to Scrimshaw Street?' Jai asked, with a sigh.

The waiter jerked his thumb. 'It's a couple of roads over that way.'

'Thanks.' Jai went to move on, but Genie craned over the man's shoulder and said, 'Is this the restaurant with the miniature fighting kraken?'

'Nope. That's the Flying Fish at the end of the street. We've got a fortune-telling octopus, though. Far more entertaining than fighting kraken, if you ask me. Would you kids like a table? I can get you one right next to his tank.'

'No, thank you,' Jai said quickly. 'We're not here to eat.' He gripped Genie's elbow and steered her on. 'Don't get any ideas,' he said. 'We're not here for the kraken.'

'But we're so close,' Genie protested. 'It seems a shame not to at least *try* to rescue them.'

'The kidnapped children come first,' Jai insisted. 'I'm sorry, Genie, but we can't rescue everyone all at the same time, no matter how much we might want to.'

Genie sighed and cast a dark look at the Flying Fish as they passed, but didn't argue any further. The explorers soon found themselves in Scrimshaw Street and saw that it was littered with shipwrecks. They lay sprawled in tattered heaps of shredded sails and warped wooden planks that smelled strongly of dried seaweed and bony fish. Ursula recalled what Percie had said about the island once being underwater and supposed that these wrecks had come up with it when it had returned to the surface.

It seemed that quite a few sea witches had made their homes here in the wrecked ships because the explorers saw several of them travelling about just as Percie had, dangling from beneath a flying balloon animal. There was an interesting variety of familiars running around, from crabs and sea lions to pelicans and otters.

It didn't take them long to find Percie's home – a steamer called the *Lady Luck*. They knew it must be hers because it was the only place that had both a witch's balloon animals and a smuggler's cart tied up outside. The explorers walked up the crooked path and Jai knocked on the front door. A woman with a pelican on her shoulder answered it a moment later. She was quite clearly Percie's mother – they looked very much alike and even had the same green streaks in their hair.

'Are you the ones who brought Percie back?' she asked, before they could say a word.

'Yes,' Jai replied. 'My name is Jai Bartholomew Singh. Percie's aunt asked us to—'

But that was as far as he got before Percie's mother threw her arms round Jai in a suffocating hug. 'Thank you!' she said. 'Percie told me what you did. Rescuing her from the whirlpool like that. How brave of you!'

'He saved the otter too,' Max pointed out, delighted to see Jai being so thoroughly crushed, especially as the hug had startled the pelican, who was pecking at Jai's hair.

'Oh yes,' Percie's mother said. 'Midge is family too, of course. I mean, he's hopelessly daft, but then most otters are.'

'Hopelessly greedy too,' Zara said darkly. Ollie squawked in agreement.

'Oh dear, I hope he didn't eat anything valuable?'

Percie's mother asked. 'Of course, we'll pay for any damage. It would have broken Percie's heart if anything had happened to him. We can never thank you enough.'

'It was my pleasure,' Jai said, extricating himself with some difficulty. 'He seems like a . . . a very nice otter and I'm glad I could be of service.'

'Come in, come in. I'm Percie's mother, by the way. You can all call me Meg.'

Jai started to protest, but she carried on, 'I know you're in a hurry – Percie told me. So we'll just do five courses for tea rather than the usual seven—'

Jai dug his heels in. 'That's very kind, but we absolutely cannot stay,' he said. 'I'm sorry, but we're on a very important mission and have already lost time by stopping here. I'm glad Percie is all right, but we really must be going.'

Meg sighed. 'Oh dear. Well, if you've got to go, then you've got to go. At least let me call Percie to say goodbye?'

The little witch appeared behind her mother, then grabbed Jai's arm and practically dragged him over the threshold, into the sunken ship.

'Percie, I've already told your mother that we can't stay for tea—' Jai began.

'I'm not asking you in for tea!' Percie gasped. 'I'm

trying to hide you from the smugglers. Scarlett Sauvage has put a bounty on your heads. The posters have just gone up. Now every person on this island is looking for you!'

CHAPTER FIFTEEN

The explorers hurried into Percie's house and closed the door firmly behind them. They soon learned that when Percie had nipped out to buy fresh cream for tea, she had seen a man putting up the wanted posters. Scarlett was offering a vast reward for anyone who captured the explorers or their submarine. She was prepared to pay for information too. Ursula supposed that the witch's charm must be working to keep them hidden, so she'd had to turn to more traditional methods to find them.

Percie had taken one of the posters and now held it up for the explorers to see. Although none of them had ever met Scarlett in person, she must have got one of the Pacificans to describe them because the poster featured accurate pencil drawings of all four explorers, as well as their submarine. Not only that, the poster had pictures of Stella Starflake Pearl and her friends Ethan, Shay and Beanie too. Like the Ocean

Squid team, it seemed they had found a way to hide themselves from her gaze.

'Stella must have received our warning letter,' Ursula said happily. 'It was worth using the flower, after all.'

'Never mind that,' Max said impatiently. 'We're the ones in trouble now. What are we going to do?'

'Well, we can't stay here,' Jai said. 'The man at the cafe knows we were going to find Percie. People will know where to look for us.'

'Your submarine will probably be surrounded now too,' Meg said.

'We've got to get the *Blowfish* back,' Jai said. 'We can't continue our expedition without it.'

'Don't worry, we'll help you,' Meg said. 'We'll think of something, but for now we need to get you out of this house and hide you away until nightfall. It'll be easier to move around once the fog comes. Then we can create a diversion to get everyone away from your submarine.'

'What kind of diversion?' Zara asked.

'I don't know yet, but it'll be a good one. Sea witches are excellent at creating diversions.'

Before they could ask any further questions, there came a heavy knock on the door and a man's voice called, 'Open up, Meg. We know you've got those explorers in there!'

'Go, go,' Meg whispered. 'Percie will show you the way.' Then she turned back towards the door and called through the wood, 'You must have been at that rum again, Seamus! There are no explorers here.'

Percie beckoned them urgently and they followed her through her home. It was strange being inside a sunken ship on land. As they hurried along, they saw that the rooms were furnished with ordinary tables and armchairs and lamps so that it almost seemed like a normal house, except for the barnacles clinging to the floorboards, and the lichen-stained portholes, and the anchor rusting in the hallway.

'This way!' Percie ran ahead and scooted down a ladder into the bowels of the ship.

They followed her and soon found themselves in a cavernous space full of old trunks with names monogrammed on them in golden letters.

'The old luggage room,' Percie explained. 'Guests on board the steamer put all their stuff here when they came aboard.'

'I hope your plan doesn't involve us hiding in one of these trunks?' Max asked, casting a doubtful look at the nearest one. 'Because I don't think I'm bendy enough for that.'

'Don't be silly.' Percie scampered ahead, through

the suitcases. 'I'm going to take you out through the secret tunnel.'

'Secret tunnel?' Ursula repeated, hurrying to keep up with the witch.

'Most smugglers' homes have them,' Percie said over her shoulder. 'Ours leads to the Flying Fish.'

Genie's ears pricked up at that and Ursula knew she was thinking about the fighting kraken held captive there.

'Are they your friends?' Jai asked eagerly, hoping they might find shelter until nightfall.

Percie tossed a trunk aside and gave a snort of laughter. 'Oh no. The Flaggerty family who own it hate sea witches.'

'Well, why does your tunnel lead to their restaurant then?' Max asked.

'I wouldn't call it a restaurant,' Percie said. 'It's more of a pub. And our tunnel goes there partly because my mum likes to sneak in to join their karaoke nights – she goes in disguise, of course – and partly because no one would ever suspect that our escape tunnel leads to a place that hates witches. Here we are!'

She stopped in front of a large trunk with the name *Lady Penelope Pepperton* stamped upon its lid. She took a key from her pocket and unlocked it before heaving it open to reveal that the trunk had no bottom, and no floor beneath it either. Instead, there was a dark tunnel leading straight underground.

'Come on,' Percie said, and without waiting for them to reply, she leaped straight into the hole.

The explorers got a brief impression of her black and green skirts flying out around her, then she was gone.

'For goodness' sake,' Max said, peering dubiously at the hole. 'Do we have to jump in? Isn't there a ladder to climb down?'

'It can't be that long a drop if she's just jumped,' Jai said.

'I could fly down and see if it's safe?' Zara suggested.

But then they heard raised voices from out in the corridor. It seemed that Percie's mother hadn't managed to keep the door to their house barred, and the smugglers could burst in looking for them at any moment.

'We're out of time,' Jai whispered. 'Come on, we'll have to trust Percie and hope for the best.'

As the most intrepid of the four of them, Jai leaped in first, closely followed by the others. The fall went on for much longer than Ursula had expected, and her whole body tensed as darkness went racing past. She realised this was far too long a drop to have jumped safely and she tried to ready herself for the sudden impact and the crunch of broken bones ...

But all at once she landed on something soft and bouncy – so bouncy in fact that she came right off it before landing back down in a heap. As her eyes adjusted to the dimness, she could just make out the others beside her – they were all sprawled on an extremely large balloon.

'What on earth?' she gasped.

'Quiet!' Percie hissed. She reached past Ursula to tug on a cord that must have been attached to the lid of the trunk above them because they heard the thud as it fell closed, and whatever small amount of light there had been vanished completely. Ursula was glad of her cloak because it was chilly down here and smelled of damp stone and old fishing nets.

'There, we're safe!' Percie said. Her voice was very close but Ursula couldn't see even a foot in front of her. 'The trunk automatically locks when you shut the lid. Hang on a sec and I'll get us some light.'

From the darkness came the sound of rummaging and then the deep inhales and blowing of a balloon being inflated. Percie said some magic words and a pale blue light filled the cave. The explorers saw that Percie had a balloon-animal starfish in her hand. It emitted a faint blue glow, and this seemed to wake up all the dozens and dozens of tiny starfish embedded in the rocky walls of the tunnel stretching away from them.

'It's so pretty!' Genie exclaimed, delighted by the sparkling blue light.

'Pretty!' Ollie squawked as he and Zara settled themselves on Genie's shoulder.

'These are galaxy starfish,' Percie told them. 'They feed off the darkness and give out their own light whenever they're woken up. This used to be a mermaid school, you see. Some of their things are still lying about, including the starfish lights.'

Ursula frowned. 'But why would mermaids create a school underground?'

'It wasn't underground then, silly!' Percie replied. 'All of this was underwater when the island was sunken – there are doors and windows that used to lead right out to the ocean. When it came back to the surface, rather than getting rid of the old buildings, the smugglers just built on top of them, so now there's pieces of the mermaid town that once existed still hidden underground. There's actually a whole network of tunnels down here. When we found this one, we realised we could extend it to get to the Fighting Fish. Come on, it's not far.'

Ursula and the others hurried to climb down from the giant balloon that had acted as a trampoline, and followed Percie through the hallway of the old abandoned school. There was evidence of its past everywhere they looked, including portraits of the schoolteachers on the walls of the corridor. The light from the galaxy starfish showed their names and the subjects they'd taught on little bronze plaques attached to their paintings. Ursula was fascinated by this glimpse of what life might have been like for her if she'd been a mermaid with no human side and read them as they went past. There was Merida Mint, professor of magical singing, Piper Shingle, teacher of ocean biology, Genevieve Sandstone, lecturer in terrapin history, and so on.

'What happened to all the mermaids?' she asked.

'They left when the island came back to the surface,' Percie replied.

'Why *did* it come back to the surface?' Max asked. 'I thought sunken islands stayed sunken?'

'No one knows.' Percie shrugged. 'One of the teachers at my school said it was something to do with boring tides and currents, but *I* like to think it's because this isn't really an island at all but actually the back of a giant sea monster. Anyway, it came up so quickly that I guess the mermaids didn't have much warning and they just had to leave their stuff where it was.'

'Can we explore it?' Ursula asked eagerly. 'There's several hours until nightfall, isn't there?'

'If you want,' Percie said. 'It's just a boring old school, though. Here, this is the tunnel that goes to the Flying Fish.'

She indicated a narrow corridor leading off from a door. It clearly wasn't part of the mermaid school because they could see that its walls, floor and ceiling were all dug out of rock rather than made from sea stone and coral.

'Only our house and the Flying Fish lead down here, and no one else knows about the Flying Fish entrance except my parents and me, so it should be OK to wander around. Here, take the starfish. I can make another one.' She handed over the balloon animal. 'It goes dark at around six,' she went on, 'so go to the pub then and I'll meet you there to explain the diversion plan.'

'About that,' Genie said. 'Why don't I just call Bess? If she looms up out of the darkness, it should be pretty distracting to everyone, shouldn't it? And the fog would be the perfect way to disguise the fact that she's a shadow animal.'

'Good thinking,' Percie replied. 'You should definitely call her when the time comes. But we'll come up with a diversion of our own too, just to be on the safe side.'

'I would have thought that Bess would be more than sufficient to—' Jai began.

'Don't be so sure,' Percie interrupted. 'These are smugglers, remember? They've all seen their fair share of kraken. Besides, me and the boys *love* creating diversions.' She gave a little giggle as she patted the otters scampering around her heels. 'Daddy said it's what we were born to do. Don't worry. We'll have you back on your submarine in no time.'

'Thanks for helping us, Percie,' Jai said.

The little witch shook her head. 'It's nothing,' she said with sudden fierceness. 'Nothing compared to what you did for me and Midge. Now I'd better go. Diversions can take a while to plan. I'll see you all later.'

And with that she took off down the corridor leading to the Flying Fish, leaving the explorers alone in the underground mermaid school.

CHAPTER SIXTEEN

'This is so frustrating!' Max exclaimed. 'Jada and the other children are waiting to be rescued and we're stuck down here, kicking our heels. We should never have come to Smugglers' Isle.'

'We didn't have much choice,' Ursula pointed out. 'Without the charm from Jojo, the Pacificans would have helped Scarlett find us by now.'

'It's an unfortunate turn of events,' Jai agreed. 'But we might as well make the most of it. I don't think an Ocean Squid explorer has ever visited a mermaid school before, so it's a unique chance to learn more about mermaid life.'

Ursula knew the kidnapped children were depending on them and it was important that they reach Pirate Island as quickly as possible, but she couldn't deny she was pleased to have the opportunity to explore the school, and she practically ran from one room to another. As Percie had said, the mermaids had left in a hurry and many of their possessions were left behind. They had been well preserved underground so it almost felt like the mermaids might come back at any moment. The explorers found classrooms with rows of desks set out, as well as dormitories filled with mermaid beds and hammocks, seaweed science labs, coral kitchens and a sporting hall still set up for mermaid lacrosse.

But by far the most wonderful thing was the library. It was a circular, double-height room, like the turret of a castle, and the bookshelves stretched all the way up to the ceiling. There was no ladder to reach the higher books since mermaids would simply have been able to swim up to the roof when the room was filled with water.

Ursula felt a tugging sense of loss as they explored. She could almost see herself buying candy crabs from the tuck shop and studying mermaid singing in the music room, and best of all having actual mermaid friends to hang out with – merboys and girls who were the same as her and who she could laugh with, and ride water horses with, and share midnight picnics in the dormitories.

It would have been so different from her lonely experience at the Ocean Squid Explorers' Club.

Ursula couldn't help feeling a sudden flash of sadness for all the things she'd missed out on – things most other children took for granted and barely thought twice about. It was confusing sometimes, being half one thing and half another. Sometimes Ursula wanted nothing to do with her mermaid part and wished she'd been born a human, but other times, like this, she longed for underwater life so much it was painful.

'These books don't look as if they were ever in the sea,' Genie said. 'They're in such good condition!'

'They're made from mermaid paper,' Ursula said, pulling a volume from the shelf. 'They're not affected by moisture.'

The book in her hand was an illustrated volume depicting various types of pearl, including some they had never heard of before, like the singing pearl, the magic wish pearl and the ghost ship pearl. The other books in the library covered everything from enchanted singing, to mermaid mechanics, to the history of whales.

'Perhaps you should take some of these books, Ursula,' Jai said. He pulled one from the shelf and held it up for her to see. 'This one is all about mermaid singing. It might help you understand how to use your magic. If we take a look, we might find something about mermaid tridents too.'

Ursula knew this was a sensible suggestion and yet her first instinct was to shy away from it. The longing for mermaid life she'd felt just a moment ago suddenly drained away.

'Wouldn't that be stealing?' she said, trying to find an excuse not to take the books.

'Well . . . the books are just sitting here at the moment and if the island rose up a hundred years ago then the owners must all be dead by now,' Jai said. 'I don't think there's anything wrong with taking some books, especially if they can help you.'

'He's right.' Genie gave Ursula's shoulder a brief squeeze, perhaps guessing the real reason behind her reluctance. 'If it makes you feel better you can always return them to a library in Mercadia once all this is over.'

'You should take them,' Max agreed. 'There might be something in there that can help us when we reach Pirate Island. It's going to be even more difficult now Scarlett has shown everyone what we look like. I'm not sure the pirate disguises will work any more.'

Everyone fell quiet. Ursula hadn't considered this, but she immediately saw that Max was right. They were all a little young to be pirates anyway, and with Scarlett's posters now all over the place, they would surely be recognised, even if they were wearing seafaring hats and had talking parrots.

'We could add eye patches,' Jai suggested after a moment.

But it would only be a small help, and they all knew it.

'No one will be expecting us on Pirate Island,' Genie pointed out. 'Especially if there's a bounty on our heads. So maybe the posters are a good thing? Like hiding in plain sight. No pirate would think we'd be brave enough to walk straight on to their island.'

'Or stupid enough,' Max muttered under his breath.

'It's still the best plan we have,' Jai said.

Ursula could see that they needed every advantage, so she agreed to take a few books – although not too many, because they were going to have to flee from smugglers who were out to get them later, and books were heavy and liable to slow them down.

The library had some cosy reading nooks and they spent a while flicking through the books by the light of glowing turtle lamps. Zara even found a little hammock that must have once belonged to a sea fairy. She promptly climbed into it, pulled her hat over her eyes and fell into a contented snooze. Eventually, though, they packed up their things and went on their way. Exploring the mermaid school had made the afternoon pass quickly, and it was time to meet Percie at the Flying Fish.

'I hope we're not going to have to creep anywhere silently,' Max remarked as they walked along the corridor. 'Because I'm starving and my stomach is bound to rumble and give us away.'

The others were hungry too. They'd missed lunch and hadn't brought any food with them as no one had expected to be on the island so long. Ursula tried not to think about the chicken dinners and ice cream back on the *Blowfish*, but avoiding thoughts of food got harder as they approached the pub. Delicious smells of crispy scampi, salty chips and hot pies wafted down the tunnel and made everyone groan.

When they reached the end, they found Percie waiting for them outside a little door cut into the rock. For a moment they didn't recognise her because she was, inexplicably, dressed as a clown. She wore a white cone-shaped hat with a bright green pom-pom on top, a white jumpsuit with green pom-pom buttons and extremely large blue shoes. She even had bright face paint on and a squeaky red nose. Midge and Moe seemed to be part of the act too. They each wore a pointed clown's hat and a ruff around their neck, which didn't appear to be very comfortable because they kept scratching at it.

'Oh good, you're on time,' the little witch said.

'Why on earth are you dressed like that?' Max asked, staring at her.

'Like what?' Percie asked. Then she grinned and said, 'Only kidding. I'll explain when we get inside. Follow me.'

She opened the door and beckoned them through to a rickety wooden staircase that creaked and groaned most alarmingly as they climbed it. At last, they came out through a secret entrance and found themselves in a low-beamed room with lots of wood panels and a log fire crackling in the inglenook fireplace. They could hear people chattering on the floors below and the smell of fish pies and seaweed ale wafted up.

Guests were clearly expected soon because the little room was crammed with wooden tables, all laid out for dessert. And it was a most impressive dessert too – each table had a three-tiered cake stand, containing dozens of delicacies, all of which were sea-monster themed. The explorers saw candy sharks and fudge octopuses, chocolate whales and mint squids.

In the centre of the room was a fish tank containing two miniature kraken rather than fish. They were both the same blue-grey colour as Bess and no bigger than the size of a hand. They could almost have been small octopuses, but Ursula knew they must be kraken from the way Genie gave a little cry and raced straight over to the tank. The clockwork kraken pendant she wore, that marked her out as a whisperer, opened its eyes, indicating that Genie was talking to the kraken inside her head.

'The guests will be here any minute for dessert and the kraken fight,' Percie said. 'Everyone is still very much on the lookout for you, so you'll have to hide behind the door and then slip out quickly once I give the signal.'

'What signal?' Ursula asked. 'What are you talking about?'

'I said I'd create a diversion for you, didn't I?' Percie grinned and indicated her hat. 'Me and the otters are going to perform a clown dance. That'll give you time to sneak down to the docks and call Bess. And if a giant shadow kraken isn't enough of a diversion, then Mum is waiting down there on a little boat full of fireworks. As soon as she sees you she's going to set them off in order to draw everyone's attention away.'

Jai frowned. 'Look, we're grateful for your help but this sounds like a ... well, a bit of a ramshackle sort of plan.'

Percie beamed. 'Thanks. Sea witches specialise in ramshackle plans.'

'I didn't mean it as a compliment,' Jai said. 'I'm not sure how well it's going to work. Is one little girl doing a clown dance really going to distract an entire room long enough for us to escape?'

'Oh yes.' Percie nodded emphatically. 'You haven't seen my clown dance. It's quite something. And the otters will be dancing too, don't forget. It's a shame you can't stay and watch, actually, because otters dancing around in clown hats is one of the most wonderful things you'll ever see, no matter how much exploring you do. You could literally go to the end of the world without seeing a spectacle like that.'

'Even so—' Jai began dubiously.

Before he could go on, Genie spun around from the fish tank so fast that the fat seals on her head boppers wobbled energetically. 'Scrap all of that,' she said. 'I've got a different plan.' She indicated the kraken behind her. 'Their names are Jodie and Alf and we're going to rescue them.'

Jai groaned. 'Genie, we've been through this—'

'We agreed we weren't going to make a separate trip,' Genie said. 'But as we're right here, there's no reason not to help them. They've been trapped in this tank and forced to fight each other for years. I'm not leaving them and that's that. Besides, if we set them free, they've agreed to create all the diversion we need. The only thing more distracting than a shadow kraken is a pair of *real* kraken. If Zara can return them to their full size, that is.'

Everyone looked at the pirate fairy.

'Are you serious?' Zara looked at the tank dubiously and shook her head. 'You people are nuts. You can't possibly want two enraged full-size kraken on the rampage. They're just as likely to destroy your submarine as they are to save it.'

'That's not true.' Genie spoke calmly but Ursula could tell she didn't like what Zara had said by the frustrated edge that crept into her voice. 'Kraken are gentle creatures. They only seem scary to us because they're so large. And they only attack ships that fire on them first. Mostly, they just want to be left alone.'

'Well, whatever you're going to do, you'd better decide quick,' Percie said. 'I can hear people moving around downstairs. They've finished their dinner and are about to come up here.'

Ursula realised she was right. They could hear chairs scraping back and boots on the stairs. Genie didn't waste any more time discussing the issue, but snatched up a couple of teacups and used these to scoop up both kraken. A few moments later, the door opened and the Flying Fish's clientele came tumbling in – about twenty smugglers, all very much looking forward to their sweet treats and sea-monster fight. They stopped in astonishment at the sight of the explorers in the middle of the room.

'Why, it's those kids!' a bearded man at the front exclaimed. 'The ones everyone's been looking for. They've got a huge reward on their heads.'

'Is the one in the clown suit an explorer too?' asked another man with an earring. 'And what about the pirate fairy?'

'Dunno,' the first man said. 'Best capture them all, just in case. Come on! Even if we split the reward, it'll still be riches!'

The group started forwards but Zara spread her wings and flew in front of the explorers. 'Not so fast,' she said. She pointed over her shoulder at Genie and said, 'You see that girl in the strange head boppers? Well, she's a kraken whisperer. One spell from me, and those sea monsters are full size again. One word from the whisperer, and it's all of *you* who are going to be dessert!'

There was a moment of silence, then the smuggler with the beard let out a guffaw. 'You must think we were born yesterday!' he sneered. 'There's no such thing as a kraken whisperer! No man or woman alive can talk to those monsters of the sea. It would be a warped soul indeed that could do that – those kraken are brutes.'

'You're wrong,' Genie said calmly. 'On both counts. I *am* a kraken whisperer. The only one in the world, probably. And it's not the kraken who are the brutes, it's people like you, keeping them captive and forcing them to fight each other.'

There were jeers of disagreement from the group.

'Doesn't matter,' said a female smuggler with a long braid. 'Even if you *are* a kraken whisperer, you won't risk changing those beasts back to full size. They're just as likely to crush you as they are us.'

'They'll probably destroy half this pub if you force us to do it here,' Genie agreed. 'But they've assured me they can avoid hurting us.'

'Ha!' the female smuggler scorned. 'That's what they would say! But you'd be a fool to believe them.' She glanced at her fellow smugglers. 'Everyone grab hold of a kid and we'll split the reward!'

The group hurried eagerly towards them and then everything happened at once. Genie yelled at her friends to squeeze in as close to her as they could and she told Zara to change back just one of the kraken.

'We'll be all right,' Genie said when Zara hesitated. 'Please trust me.'

The first smuggler had just clamped a hand down on Ursula's arm when Zara pointed a finger at the teacup in Genie's hand and muttered a magic spell under her breath.

CHAPTER SEVENTEEN

The effect was shocking and immediate. It was almost as if a bomb had gone off. For a few confusing moments, Ursula could barely make out what was happening. She was surrounded by thrashing tentacles as thick as a human being, bricks and plaster rained down around them, and the smugglers were yelling as they were hit by the debris or struck by the kraken's flailing tentacles.

The explorers and their friends remained sheltered because the full-size kraken's body was directly above them, shielding them from the destroyed roof. The great sea monster was so big that it had crashed up through the ceiling and destroyed the walls. Cold night air billowed in, along with a fog so thick they could barely see what was happening. All they knew was that people were screaming and racing to get away from the kraken, pouring back out down the staircase before any more of the building could collapse.

Ursula realised she was trembling. She had become used to Bess, but this was different. Bess had no substance, whereas this was a real flesh-and-blood kraken who could tear them all to pieces if it wanted to. She could see that its tentacles were thick with muscle, and a wide mouth revealed glistening teeth. She tried to hold on to Genie's reassurance that the monster wouldn't harm them, but at that moment it was hard to be anything but utterly terrified of the huge sea creature.

'That ought to convince them that we're serious,' Genie gasped. 'You can turn Alf back now, Zara.'

'Turn him *back*?' The pirate fairy fluttered nervously at Ursula's elbow. 'Do you mean shrink him? I can't!'

'Why not?'

Ollie was squawking on Zara's shoulder and she shushed him before saying, 'I've never been very good at that spell. My second mate was in charge of shrinking things and I made them full size again once we reached port. I mean, I could *try* to shrink him, but the honest truth is that I'm just as likely to turn him into a bubble, and if the bubble gets popped then that's that.' She snapped her fingers. 'Goodbye, kraken.'

'Well, why didn't you mention it before?' Genie cried.

The pirate fairy glared at her. 'How was I supposed

to know you'd want me to shrink the kraken too? Why can't you make up your mind about what size you want it to be?'

'He can't get out through the door!' The fog was now too thick to see the exit but Genie waved in its general direction. They could hear smugglers' boots pounding on the staircase but it didn't seem as if there were any still left in the room.

'I'm not leaving Alf here,' Genie went on. 'They'll kill him.'

'We'll have to go out through the roof,' Jai said.

'The roof?' Genie looked horrified. 'But kraken are scared of heights. They're made for the ocean, not rooftops.'

'It doesn't look like we have much choice,' Max said. 'You'll have to . . . I don't know, coax him or something.'

'*Coax* him?' Genie shook her head. 'I'm not sure that I can.'

'It's the only way.' Ursula put her hand on Genie's arm. She wished there was something she could do to help, but Genie was the only one of them who could communicate with kraken, and so it all fell to her.

They watched as she took a deep breath, tilted back her head, causing the fat seal boppers to bounce around, and then spoke to Alf. Of course they couldn't hear what she actually said, but they knew she was speaking to him inside her head because her clockwork pendant's eyes opened and glowed red. Genie must have been right when she'd said the sea monsters were afraid of heights because Alf's tentacles suddenly started to tremble. Ursula could feel the vibrations coming up through the soles of her boots.

'All right,' Genie said. 'He really doesn't want to be left in this place, so let's give it a try.'

It turned out that aside from the phobia, kraken were actually quite good at climbing. The suckers beneath their tentacles meant they could climb walls as well as a spider, and they were immensely strong too. Alf was easily able to make his way up the pub's wall and on to the roof of the neighbouring building.

'Well, that's all very well, but how are *we* going to get up there?' Max asked, eyeing the wall dubiously. There were no hand or footholds, and since they didn't have suckers there didn't appear to be any way for the explorers to climb it. When Max groped his way to the door, he almost got his head blown off with a musket. The smugglers were waiting for them out in the stairwell.

'We're trapped up here,' he said, joining the others.

'I told you we ought to have done my clown dance,'

Percie said, shaking her head. 'That probably would have involved much less destruction.'

'Probably?' Max gave her a funny look before glancing at the crumbling building around them. 'Just what kind of dance was it?'

'Never mind that now,' Genie said. 'Alf will help us up on to the roof. If we go and stand at the wall, he'll lift us up with his tentacles one by one.'

No one was particularly keen on this plan, but it seemed it was the only one they'd got – especially now the smugglers had started firing their muskets through the open door. So they hurried over to the wall and allowed Alf to help them. Ursula had to force herself to hold still as the gigantic sea monster wrapped a tentacle around her. This was the sort of thing most Ocean Squid explorers had nightmares about and Ursula had always imagined that if an actual kraken ever got this close to her, it would be because her ship or submarine had been attacked and the crew were all being eaten alive.

But in fact Alf held them all with extreme gentleness, almost as if they were made of china rather than flesh and blood. He carefully plucked each of them from the top floor of the pub and deposited them on the roof of the adjoining building.

It was cold up there and Ursula shivered. The fog smelled of salt and the sea, and it made her clothes, skin and hair instantly damp. There was such a briny tang in the air that for a moment she feared the fog might count as seawater and she would turn into a mermaid, but fortunately her legs remained as they were and she joined the others in slipping, sliding and scrambling her way across the rooftops towards the harbour.

The problem was that these ancient, crooked little buildings weren't designed to have five children and two otters slithering across them, let alone a kraken's huge weight. Roof tiles and chimney pots cracked and broke beneath them, falling to smash to bits on the barnacled cobbles below. And so even though the fog hid them from sight, the pursuing smugglers knew exactly where they were because of the great racket they were making.

'You people know absolutely nothing about how to make a discreet escape,' Percie gasped, as they hurried along a particularly steep rooftop. 'I mean, you might just as well broadcast your presence to the entire city. You lot are the worst explorers I've ever met!'

'How many *have y*ou met?' Max snapped.

As he spoke he slipped on a tile, almost slid right off the roof and probably would have fallen and broken his neck had it not been for the kraken quickly wrapping a tentacle around his wrist and yanking him back at the last moment.

'Thanks, er ... Alf,' Max said, glancing up at the great beast. In all the fog it was hard to tell where the kraken began and ended. It simply seemed like a mass of endless giant tentacles writhed above them.

Finally, they reached the harbour master's building, right on the edge of the water. They could see their submarine but there was no sign of Bess, who was still following Genie's instructions and staying underwater, out of sight.

Then Percie startled everyone by doing a rather accurate impression of an owl hooting – a piercing sound that carried across the sea and must have been the secret signal she'd agreed with her mother, because moments later the night sky above them filled with fireworks. And not just ordinary fireworks but sea witch ones, which took the form of birds.

The explorers saw bright green seagulls spread their wings against the stars and dive down to the water below. The *Blowfish* was surrounded by dozens and dozens of smuggler boats, their crews all lying in wait with armed muskets. The firework seagulls dived at these vessels aggressively, letting out raucous shrieks that pained the ears. Not only that, but their firework bodies set the sails alight. Soon there were several boats burning like glowing beacons on the water, and most of the smugglers had jumped overboard and were swimming back to shore. One or two determined crews had managed to extinguish the flames and seemed intent on staying to guard the submarine – until Alf happened.

The kraken took one look at the inky ocean lapping at the mooring posts, and with a strange little bellow of joy, he scrambled down the side of the building and dropped straight into the sea with an immense splash that completely soaked the wooden planks of the pier and even capsized a couple of nearby boats. Firework seagulls were one thing, but an immense kraken was something else altogether – the remaining crews let out shrieks of dismay and terror, rowing their boats towards the pier as fast as they could. Alf wasn't much interested in them, however – his sights were fixed on the deep ocean ahead and the explorers knew they had to move quickly.

'Well, I'll say goodbye to you here,' Percie said. 'Good luck on your journey. And for goodness' sake, remember to pack some skeleton repellent next time.'

'We will,' Jai said. 'Thanks for your help. And thank your mother for us too.'

They waved goodbye to the little sea witch and then climbed down the fire escape on the side of the building. They untied one of the sailing boats moored there and used it to travel the short distance to the *Blowfish*. Fortunately, the firework seagulls seemed to know not to attack them, and soon they were finally back on board their submarine, travelling full steam ahead away from Smugglers' Isle.

CHAPTER EIGHTEEN

The explorers were glad to put Smugglers' Isle behind them and finally set a course for Parrot Island. It looked to be about a week's journey if they went at top speed. In the meantime, they were keen to learn as much as they could about the area. As Jai said, forewarned was forearmed.

Frustratingly, they couldn't find much information in their expedition logs and almanacs because most explorers stayed well away from that part of the ocean. There were too many pirates roaming the seas, to say nothing of the savage, fire-breathing octopus that was thought to live there too. The explorers knew now that this was just a story, but there was still a risk of getting dragged into the fearsome Bone Current. It was the strongest current in the world – so powerful, in fact, that even the gigantic bodies of ocean dinosaurs had been swept into it after they'd died.

Fortunately, Zara was there to help. As she had

told them, she'd been there many times and she assured them that – aside from the hazard of the Bone Current – it was actually rather a nice part of the world, with golden beaches and crystal waters.

'Pirates want somewhere pretty to come home to when they're not out pillaging,' she explained. 'That's why they made up that story about the fire-breathing octopus – to keep everyone else away.'

Since there didn't appear to be much to worry about, Ursula used her time going through the mermaid books she'd taken from the school on Smugglers' Isle. As they had hoped, there was information in them about how to use mermaid magic and Ursula spent many hours in her room practising.

The book about mermaid singing was particularly useful. Ursula forced herself to start right at the beginning with her scales, which were rather boring, but the book made her realise that once she mastered those, she would be able to put them together in different combinations to do a whole host of things. It seemed that a mermaid's voice was immensely powerful. Ursula hadn't known there was a song to make a person fall asleep or forget what they were doing, or even change the weather and fall in love.

She shuddered away from some of the spells.

Many seemed cruel or dangerous, but knowing how to use her magic might help save herself or one of her friends. So she put aside her reservations and poured all her effort into learning more about being a mermaid. Genie often joined her for these practice sessions, providing support and suggestions whenever Ursula found a spell particularly difficult. She even offered to let Ursula practise some of the spells on her – such as the forgetting spell – but Ursula refused point-blank.

'I don't know what I'm doing,' she said. 'What if I make you forget something permanently?'

Instead, she focused on perfecting some of the easier spells first, and before long she could make a sandcastle appear and create a little boat in the form of a large shell, and fashion strong golden ropes out of the magical notes of her singing.

'Amazing!' Genie applauded one day when Ursula had managed to sing the thunder song to create a tiny storm.

They had practised this one in the swim-out hatch so it wouldn't matter if everything got wet. They'd just finished when Jai radioed down to let them know they'd reached the edge of the Fire-Breathing Octopus Current.

'You might want to come and take a look,' he said. 'It's quite something. We're on the observation deck.'

Ursula blew the storm cloud to scatter it, and once the last lightning bolts had fizzled away she and Genie left the swim-out hatch to join the others on the observation deck. Even before they arrived, they knew Jai had been right about it being an amazing view. Buttery-yellow light spilled through the portholes as if there was a glorious sunset happening right outside. This wasn't a sight the explorers were used to seeing when they were several fathoms underwater.

When they reached the observation deck, Genie and Ursula both gasped in delight at the sight of the golden, glittery glow beyond the glass walls. The entire ocean seemed to sparkle with it, clearly illuminating a couple of underwater canyons and even a sea forest, whose seaweed trees swayed gracefully in the currents.

'We're going to pass right over the underwater forest,' Jai said.

The observation deck had a glass floor as well as a glass ceiling, so they were able to look straight down and get an excellent view, especially when they used the room's telescopes. None of them had ever seen an underwater forest before, so Jai furiously took notes as they went by.

They saw extraordinary trees with long, elegant seaweed fronds instead of leaves, glinting green and blue and purple in the glow. The rainbow scales of flying fish winked and flashed between the branches, along with the fluttering wings of ocean moths and bubble butterflies. They even spotted a couple of entirely new creatures. There was something that looked a bit like a squirrel, except that it had blue fur and gills. And a sea mouse with webbed feet and scales. And, best of all, a funny-looking water hedgehog with bright pink coral spikes instead of the usual brown spines.

'Oh, look at that darling little hedgepig!' Genie cried, pointing at it. 'There are some babies with it too!'

She pulled her new necklace from beneath her shirt and held it up to the glass. As well as her kraken pendant, Genie now also had a tiny bottle with the second kraken from the Flying Fish floating inside it. Bess was absolutely fascinated by the miniature kraken and had spent hours gazing lovingly into the bottle. Once the explorers had made their escape, Genie had offered to set Jodie free so that she could swim out into the ocean with Alf, but the sea monster had preferred to stay with her for a while.

'Jodie didn't much care for Alf,' Genie had told them. 'I guess it's not surprising, given that they've been fighting each other for years. But now she's free she says she wants to see the world for a bit before she decides where to settle down. She's been in that horrible tank for a really long time.'

And so Genie held the kraken up to the glass so she could appreciate the beauty of the underwater forest gliding slowly beneath them. Bess seemed to be enjoying it too and spent some time peering curiously at the hedgehogs before catching back up with the submarine. It was so pretty that the explorers were rather sad to leave it behind, but eventually the *Blowfish* was out the other side and carried on deeper into the Fire-Breathing Octopus Current.

'We'll have to start a petition to get the current renamed,' Jai said, still furiously scribbling. 'Now that we know there's no such thing as a fire-breathing octopus. I wonder if we'll see the sunset one?'

Up ahead the water glowed so brightly that it was like they were sailing into the middle of a gigantic orange. And before long they were treated to a view of the octopus itself. It drifted peacefully along the ocean floor, its tentacles glowing with a rich golden light that made it seem as if sunshine streamed all around them. It paid them no attention whatsoever and they left it to its lazy swim.

The octopus's light made the ocean glow around them for a while as they travelled on, but eventually the water became dark and mysterious once again, and later that morning they found themselves at Parrot Island.

Chapter Nineteen

The water around Parrot Island was too shallow to dock the submarine, so as usual they dropped anchor a little way out and then climbed into the rowing boat. They couldn't see any pirate galleons moored around the island, but Zara did a quick flyover just in case. When she came back and gave the all-clear, the explorers lowered the boat down the side of the *Blowfish*.

Bess was waiting for them in the water, waving her tentacles in greeting, but Genie asked her to stay with the submarine. They didn't want to risk frightening the parrots away. Genie wondered whether Jodie might like to stay behind with Bess and take a swim while they were gone. After all, the kraken hadn't been in the ocean for ages and must be desperate to get back to it. But after a discussion, they decided it would be too risky for her to go into the water in her miniature form. She was so small she might get gobbled up by a passing fish or carried away by a tidal current, or squashed by a drifting whale. The ocean was a dangerous place when you were tiny and Bess wouldn't be able to protect her.

Instead, Genie carefully removed the kraken from the jar necklace and allowed the tiny monster to wrap her tentacles around her hand. She then dipped her straight in the sea as they sailed along. The cool, salty water washed over Jodie, making her blue-grey skin shine and sparkle in the sunlight. Everyone enjoyed hearing the kraken make happy little humming noises of contentment all the way to the island.

The explorers pulled their little boat on to a beach. Zara was right – it was particularly beautiful, with golden sand, pale pink shells and swaying coconut palms. It looked like someone had been there before them because there were extraordinary sandcastles stretching all the way along the beach. Many of them had turrets, moats, cannons, and even drawbridges.

'These are amazing!' Max exclaimed, inspecting them more closely. 'Look, this one has a sand dragon guarding the castle walls!'

'What made them?' Ursula asked Zara.

The castles looked like something magical to her – too detailed and beautiful to have been built by mere mortal hands.

'Pirate fairies,' Zara replied. 'The castles are where we stay when we visit the island.'

'If they're made of sand, how come they don't get swept away by the tide?' Jai asked.

'It's fairy sand, which isn't affected by water. And they've got charms to protect them too, otherwise the human pirates would come and smash them down when we weren't here.'

'Fascinating.' Max peered closer. 'What kind of charms do they—?'

But that was as far as he got before straying a little too close to the sand dragon. It was about the size of a small dog and the explorers had all assumed it was a lifeless part of the castle's décor. They were startled when it suddenly came to life, rearing up to flap its sandy wings at Max in a threatening manner. He leaped back just in time as the dragon opened its jaws and breathed out a whole load of spiky-looking shells.

'Best stay well clear of him,' Zara advised. 'He'll start breathing poisoned pearls at you next.'

'You could have given me a heads-up,' Max grumbled.

They left the dragon where it was and followed Zara further on to the island. A path wound through the coconut trees and they continued along this until they were deep into a forest of palms. It was immediately apparent how the island had got its name. There were parrots absolutely everywhere, swooping from branch to branch overhead, rustling the leaves and spreading their glorious wings against the sky.

'They're beautiful!' Genie breathed, staring up in wonder.

The parrots had plumage of many different colours – ocean-blue and phoenix-red, emerald-green and banana-yellow. And they were all talking. Their chattering voices filled the air and it was strange to hear human words spoken in such shrill, squawking tones.

'They don't really understand what they're saying,' Zara told them. 'They just repeat what they've heard. Parrots come here from all over the world. Some were kept as pets before they escaped, others were members of pirate crews that have since perished. Some came from travelling circuses. Even those that were born on the island and have never left it have picked up some words from the pirates who visit. I ought to warn you, pirates don't always use very nice language, so you might hear some words that are a bit ... uncivilised.'

'Yo ho, yo ho!' Ollie agreed.

'The parrots seem pretty happy here,' Ursula said, glancing around the island paradise. 'How do we persuade four of them to come with us?'

She couldn't help thinking that if *she* lived on Parrot Island, she'd never want to leave – at least not until the explorer's bug started itching again.

'Oh, that's easy.' Zara waved a hand. 'We just go to the Adventure Bus Stop.'

'The what?' Ursula wondered whether she had misheard.

Zara grinned. 'Come on,' she said. 'I'll show you.'

She spread her green wings and fluttered ahead, leaving the explorers to follow in her wake. As they walked through the coconut palms, Ursula became aware that some of the parrots were following them. A great cloud of feathers seemed to rustle over their heads as the birds swooped and squawked with unmistakeable eagerness.

'They seem excited,' Ursula said to Zara.

The pirate fairy grinned. 'They are. They know we're going to the bus stop.'

'Do buses actually run on this island?' Genie asked. There didn't appear to be any roads and they couldn't hear any traffic noise.

Zara's grin widened. 'Not any more,' she said. 'Come on, we're nearly there.'

Unfortunately, it turned out that Zara's definition of 'nearly there' was quite different to the explorers'. She led them out of the palm grove and to a steep uphill climb. As a fairy, she was able to fly, but the explorers had to pant and slog their way along, sweating in the tropical heat and sometimes slipping on the small stones underfoot. Beautiful flowers dotted the path and they passed several waterfalls. As they rose higher they had a stunning view of the island spread out below. The explorers were too hot and tired to appreciate it, however.

'How much further is it?' Max finally gasped.

'Just through here.' Zara indicated a bend in the path up ahead. The explorers followed her round it and then stopped short in astonishment.

Before them was the tallest waterfall they had seen so far. Foaming white water cascaded over a ledge and poured down to a blue pool far below. And perched precariously, right in the middle of the ledge, was a big double-decker bus. It looked as if it had once been bright yellow, but it had clearly sat there for a long time, and the paint was starting to peel and rust in places. It was covered in dozens of parrots of all different colours and sizes. They perched on the roof, or clung to the window ledges, or pecked around inside, pulling out whatever stuffing remained in the seats. As the explorers stood and looked, more and more parrots flew over their heads to land on the bus, until there must have been a hundred there. They could just about make out the words painted along its side: 'Parrot Island Adventure Tours'.

Max whistled. 'That looks like a little *too* much adventure,' he said.

Ursula thought he was right. The bus was hanging halfway over the waterfall, appearing as if it might tumble off at any moment.

'How did it get there?' she asked.

Zara shrugged. 'Nobody knows,' she said. 'I guess there used to be some kind of adventure tour company operating here. There are signs of it at various other points around the island too, like the picnic tables at the bottom of the waterfall, and some beach huts on the shore, and even a bit of an old funfair. Maybe the pirates chased them away when they claimed the island? Or maybe the bus drivers just weren't very skilled and that put people off?' She indicated the bus. 'Who knows? I mean, that's a stupid place to put a bus stop for a start.'

For the first time, Ursula realised there was a bus stop there – she could now clearly see the sign saying: 'Adventure Stop.'

'The parrots have taken it over,' Zara said. 'Some of the birds on this island are content to live in the

coconut trees and take it easy, but others like to have adventures from time to time. Those parrots come here, to the Adventure Bus Stop, and wait for a passing pirate, explorer or adventurer to pick them up.'

'Excellent.' Jai looked pleased. 'You know, I was afraid it might be complicated to get a parrot, so it's nice to hear that something's straightforward for once.'

Zara gave a snort of laughter. 'I wouldn't call it straightforward. You have to get to the parrots first.'

'What, go into that death trap?' Max looked at the bus dubiously. 'In case you hadn't noticed, we don't have wings. And even if we were mad enough to want to, there's no way across.'

'There are stepping stones in the water,' Zara said. 'You can't see them from here, but they're obvious once you get closer. Though I ought to warn you that some of them are quite small and, er . . . far apart, so you have to sort of leap from one to the other. And it's a strong current. One misstep and you'll get swept right over the edge. But it proves to the parrots that you're really looking for adventure, you see. Otherwise they'd have traders here all the time, pretending to be adventurers when really they just want to take the birds to sell to collectors and bird enthusiasts. But you're all bona fide explorers, so I'm sure you'll be fine.'

'That's easy for you to say!' Max exclaimed. 'You can just fly across!'

'There are some benefits to being a fairy,' Zara agreed. She rubbed her hands together. 'Well, you'd better get a move on, hadn't you? I thought we were in a hurry?'

'Is it *absolutely* necessary that we have talking parrots?' Max asked, turning to the others. 'Perhaps we could just fashion something out of a bunch of feathers and a coconut?'

'Some pirates are dumb, but they're not *that* dumb,' Zara said.

'Well, better still, how about I make us some robot parrots?' Max suggested.

'Pirate Island is less than a week away,' Jai replied. 'That's not enough time for you to create four robot parrots from scratch. And even if it was, Scarlett knows you're a robot inventor, doesn't she? If word gets back to her that a new pirate has turned up with a robot parrot, she's bound to suspect you. We can't afford to tip her off like that.'

It seemed there was nothing for it – they would have to cross the river.

When they scrambled over to the water's edge, Ursula liked the look of it even less than she had before.

It wasn't just fast-moving – it was a raging current with foaming white froth swirling on top and an angry roar of sound as it disappeared over the edge. As Zara had said, the stepping stones were small, but they were also wet and slippery-looking and some of them even had green algae on them. Ursula felt her heart sink.

'I don't like this at all,' Max said. 'Do you know how many explorers have been swept over waterfalls never to be seen or heard of again?'

'No,' Ursula said. 'Do you?'

'No, but I bet it's a lot.'

'It's not so bad,' Jai said. 'I've done worse.'

'Where?' Max asked dubiously.

'There was a river like this on Jerico Island. I had to cross the stepping stones to rescue a teammate who had unwisely tried to raft the rapids and was about to get swept over the waterfall. The trick is to take it nice and steady and just focus on the stone that's right in front of you.'

'I still think a robot parrot would be better,' Max grumbled, but he rolled up his trouser legs, the same as the others.

'At least we can all swim,' Genie said. 'So it could be worse.'

Ursula didn't find Genie's optimism very reassuring

just then. After all, swimming wouldn't help them much if they got swept over the waterfall. It looked like a *very* long way to the pool below. And, besides, this was river water, so Ursula wouldn't turn into a mermaid if she fell, and she wasn't a strong swimmer in her human form. She'd never needed to be as she'd always swum in the sea as a mermaid. Now she found she didn't much like the idea of being human in water.

'Could I go by myself and fetch back four parrots for everyone?' Jai asked Zara.

The fairy shook her head. 'You'll only get a parrot if you go on to the bus yourself.'

'That's what I thought.' Max gave the others a miserable look. 'I'm sorry you're in this position because of me.'

'It's not your fault, it's the Collector,' Ursula said.

'And anyway, it might be fun,' Genie said. There was an eager sort of look in her eyes as she gazed at the river. 'This is the sort of thing explorers do all the time, isn't it?'

'Well said.' Jai looked excited at the prospect too. 'And look, we can fix a rope to that tree over there and then each of us can tie it around our waists, just in case.' He glanced at Zara. 'The parrots won't object to that, I assume?'

'Probably not,' Zara said. 'After all, even with the rope, you wouldn't want to fall in the river. It's still pretty dangerous – you could get your head bashed against a rock, or the rope could come loose, or you could get tangled up in it and eaten by piranhas before you're able to—'

'OK, we get the picture,' Jai said hurriedly.

He went first, followed by the girls and then Max brought up the rear. They had to step into the shallow edge of the river to get to the stepping stones. The water was cold, but it was rather pleasant after their hot climb. Ursula was relieved to find that her boots gripped the wet stone better than she had expected. It seemed that Ocean Squid footwear came with extra-sticky grips on the soles, just in case the wearer should find themselves running about on a slippery ship deck, or scrabbling on a stony beach, or – as they were doing – venturing over treacherous stepping stones. Genie slipped around a little more in her pink cowgirl boots, but managed to avoid tumbling into the water.

Ursula tried to follow Jai's advice by keeping her eyes fixed on the stepping stone directly in front of her and not giving in to the temptation of looking at the bus or glancing back to see how far away the shore was. They were committed now, and the only way out of it was to keep moving forwards. Despite her fear, Ursula found she was also enjoying herself. There was something exciting about leaping from one stone to the next while the water swirled and foamed around them. It was the kind of daring act that one thought of when the topic of exploring came up.

Finally, there were no more stones to navigate and Jai reached the bus, closely followed by the others. They crowded inside, trying to stay as near to the exit as possible. The further into the bus they went, the more likely they were to shift the delicate balance and tip it over the edge of the waterfall. As it was, the floor creaked alarmingly underfoot as they took in the mass of parrots.

Ursula had never seen so many in one place. Their feathers filled the space as they fluttered excitedly from one perch to the other. They were all sizes, colours and types. Ursula recognised the ferocious-looking hawk's head parrot, the blue-winged macaw, the umbrella cockatoo and the lilac-crowned Amazonian parrot, but there were plenty there she'd never seen before, even in books.

'You need to step to the front of the bus one at a time,' Zara said. 'And a parrot will choose you.'

Jai went first, and they all held their breath as the

bus creaked beneath him. Thankfully, it stayed steady, and a moment later a large orange parrot swooped down from the luggage rack to land on his shoulder. He returned to the back of the bus with it and then Genie stepped forward to be chosen by a noisy, very beautiful rainbow parrot. Max was selected by a grey hawk's head parrot, and finally, it was Ursula's turn. Within seconds, a bird had flapped down to settle itself on her shoulder too.

It was smaller than the others, and Ursula was surprised at how heavy it felt. She'd never been so close to a parrot and was delighted that this one had chosen her. It had remarkable plumage, with feathers that were all different shades of blue, from deep cobalt to pale aqua, and they were tipped with white, as if they'd been dipped in salt. Its intelligent eyes were the colour of seaweed and, strangely, there were webs between its clawed feet.

'Oh, it's a sea parrot!' Zara exclaimed. 'You don't see those very often.'

Ursula looked at her. 'Sea parrot?' she repeated.

'Don't you have them back home?' the pirate fairy asked. 'They like the sea and they're the only type of parrot that can swim. They can even breathe underwater – they've got gills hidden beneath their feathers. I guess that makes them the perfect parrot for a mermaid.'

'Great. Well, now we all have our parrots, how about getting off this bus?' Max said.

They were only too glad to do so.

Chapter Twenty

In no time at all, they were back at the *Blowfish*. Bess had been sunbathing on the outside deck but got up to greet them and insisted on peering lovingly at Jodie before they went inside. Jai went straight to the instruments on the bridge and input new coordinates, looking grim but determined.

'Next stop,' he said. 'Pirate Island.'

They set a course, but unfortunately the underwater currents had other ideas. Normally, tides and currents weren't much of a match for the immense engine power of a submarine, but the Poison Tentacle Sea was home to the powerful Bone Current, and this part of the Bubble Ocean passed perilously close to it. As they had feared, it gave a sudden surge and pulled them in.

The explorers knew the currents were strong but short-lived. There was no point in trying to resist the Bone Current – they would only damage the *Blowfish*'s engines if they did. They had no choice but to allow it to pull them in the wrong direction and accept that they wouldn't be able to return to their course until it had ebbed. It was immensely frustrating, but no one was very much surprised.

'It looks like it will probably last about five hours,' Jai said, consulting one of the tidal almanacs. 'After that it should weaken enough for the *Blowfish* to escape. In the meantime, I guess all we can do is look out for obstacles and try to steer with the current.'

The explorers stayed on the bridge together. Nobody felt much like going to the cinema, or the skating rink, or getting ice creams when they were being dragged helplessly into sea-monster-infested waters. They all knew it was very bad for the submarine to be out of their control like this and everybody hated the fact that there was nothing they could do about it. As a shadow animal, Bess wasn't affected by the currents but stayed close to the submarine as it was pulled along, and they occasionally caught flashes of her tentacles through the portholes.

An hour passed before bones started to appear in the water. So many dead sea creatures had been dragged here by the current that this part of the ocean was permanently filled with them. Some were a fresh pale white, others were yellow with age and clearly came from animals that no longer existed. It was a sombre sight, and they all stood to watch for a moment, listening to the disturbing sound of the bones clicking and clacking against the exterior of the submarine.

'Great Scott!' Max said under his breath. 'Look at that one over there!'

He pointed at a gigantic shape in the distance.

'But that *can't* be a bone!' Ursula exclaimed. 'It's too big!'

'Some of the dinosaurs that used to live in the ocean were even larger than kraken,' Genie said.

As it got closer, the submarine's headlights showed that the huge thing was, indeed, a bone. Ursula could barely imagine what kind of dinosaur would have been big enough to own it.

'It looks like the bone's going to miss us, but we'll have to be extra alert about keeping watch,' Jai said. He looked worried but invigorated at the same time. 'If a bone that size were to hit us it could cause serious damage.'

The children agreed that Jai and Genie would remain on the bridge to try to guide the submarine past any obstacles, while Ursula and Max headed to the viewing gallery. With its glass floor and ceiling, they would have a better all-round view, and would radio the bridge if they spotted anything alarming.

Before long, Ursula was very glad she was there because the most extraordinary sight appeared through the bubbles and bones of the current. Max was looking in the other direction, so she nudged him sharply in the ribs.

'Ouch! What is it?' he asked.

Ursula couldn't speak – she just pointed wordlessly. Max peered through the water and gave a long, drawn-out whistle. Spread below them on the ocean floor was an immense dinosaur skeleton. Ursula tried to imagine the creature as it would once have been – majestic, gigantic, extraordinary. Its massive flippers rested on the ocean floor, and shoals of fish swam in and out of its dark eye sockets and in between its towering ribs.

The radio beeped at Ursula's elbow and she picked it up without tearing her eyes from the dinosaur.

Jai's voice crackled over the line. 'Are you two seeing this?'

'We're seeing it,' Ursula replied. 'It's ... amazing.'

'Amazing!' her sea parrot squawked with enthusiasm.

'I feel like we ought to take our hats off,' Max said at her side. 'If we were wearing hats, that is. Out of respect or something.'

'I know exactly what you mean,' Ursula replied.

It wasn't the only skeleton. The explorers soon realised they had found the edge of a dinosaur graveyard. For the next three hours they travelled through a spectacle of dinosaur bones, showcasing the entire range of creatures that had once roamed the sea. There were dinosaurs with great, long spines, and others with flippers; some had the ferociously sharp teeth of carnivores, while others looked more like crocodiles that would have been large enough to consume an entire shark in one gulp. Bess inspected them all curiously and the explorers were impressed to see that some of the dinosaurs would indeed have been even larger than the kraken.

After a total of four hours, the tide finally released them. It happened so abruptly that no one had quite been expecting it. The bones suddenly stopped flying past in the water and the *Blowfish* slowed right down to a gentle drift. Max and Ursula joined their friends on the bridge, and their parrots swooped about above their heads, happy to be reunited. The explorers paused for a moment to look at the dinosaur skeleton directly in front of them. It was a massive shark-like creature, but the most striking thing about it was what it had clasped in its jaws.

The explorers gazed down at the wreck of an Ocean Squid submarine. And not just any submarine, but one of the most famous ones in their club. It was the *Silent Eel*, and they all knew its story. It had ventured down into the deep to study the dinosaurs but had got caught up in one of the currents and become trapped within the jaws of the shark dinosaur. Fortunately, another submarine had been able to mount a daring rescue and all the crew had been saved. There was nothing they could do to free the submarine itself, however. It was stuck fast, and they had had to leave it behind on the ocean floor. It was badly rusted now and studded with barnacles.

Jai broke the silence first. 'That was . . .' He trailed off and shook his head, but the others understood what he meant, because they all felt the same sense of awe. 'But now we should get going before the current returns. I'll set a new course.'

The group had all turned their attention to the instruments. Ursula alone remained looking down at the dinosaur. For a moment she thought she had seen something impossible. It must have been a trick of the light, or perhaps she was just getting tired . . . But then she saw exactly the same thing happen again, and almost jumped out of her skin.

'The crew of the *Silent Eel* were all rescued, weren't they?' she said.

'Every last one,' Jai replied, without looking up. 'Even the cat.'

'Then how come I've just seen a distress signal flashing from the submarine?'

CHAPTER TWENTY-ONE

The explorers hurried to join Ursula at the porthole.

'You must be mistaken,' Jai said. 'That submarine sank twenty years ago.'

But even as he spoke, the red light flashed again, clear as day.

'There can't possibly be anyone down there after all this time,' Max said. He looked nervously at the others. 'Can there?'

'Drowned men!' his grey parrot squawked unhelpfully.

To their dismay, the other parrots began shrieking about drowned men too.

Ursula raised her voice above the birds. 'Well, someone must be operating the light.'

There was something uncanny about seeing it wink through the darkness at them like that, lighting up the shark's great jaws.

'Perhaps it's just malfunctioning?' Max suggested.

Genie walked over to the control station. 'Let's try radioing them.'

She picked up the handset and signalled the other submarine but nothing came back to them over the line except static.

'The radio could be broken,' Ursula said. 'Or perhaps the person on board is injured or something and isn't able to reach the controls.'

Genie looked suddenly troubled. 'There's another explanation,' she said. 'Perhaps the submarine is haunted.'

Zara shuddered. 'I don't like this,' she muttered. 'I don't like it at all.'

'There's nothing to be afraid of,' Jai said dismissively. 'I already told you the crew were rescued. Ill-fated though it was, nobody died on the mission.'

'Nobody that we know about,' Genie pressed on. 'What if there was a stowaway on board? Or what if the crew picked up someone along the way, like we did with Percie?'

'Then there would have been a record of that person in the Flag Report,' Jai replied.

'Just because you always do everything by the book doesn't mean the same is true for everyone else,' Genie said. 'There might have been foul play.'

Jai shook his head impatiently. 'No,' he said. 'I won't believe it. Look, I know the Ocean Squid Explorers' Club isn't perfect, but the *Silent Eel* was captained by Sir Kelsey Paddington Porter. He was a brave explorer and a fair leader. He wouldn't have been party to leaving someone behind in the submarine.'

'If there was a stowaway then he might not have known anyone else was on board,' Ursula pointed out.

They were all quiet for a moment.

'If there was anyone on board they would have died by now,' Max eventually said.

'So I could be right about it being a ghost then,' Genie said.

'Ghost!' her rainbow parrot shrieked. 'Ghost!'

'Would you and your parrot please stop talking about ghosts?' Max asked with a shiver. 'You're giving me the creeps. A sunken, abandoned submarine is bad enough without that kind of talk. Besides, why would a ghost signal for help? There's not much we can do if he's already dead.'

'Look, if someone got left behind on the submarine, he could have found some way to survive,' Ursula said. 'It's not very likely, but it's not impossible either.'

'I could ask Bess to go and look through the portholes,' Genie suggested. Her shadow kraken had appeared outside the submarine and was waving her tentacles around gently.

'That's not enough,' Ursula said. 'The person could be in one of the rooms without portholes. Or if they're injured they could be lying on the floor and Bess would miss them.' She took a deep breath, realising she was going to be the first to say it. 'I think we should check it out. I think we have to.'

Perhaps it was because she was the one to have seen the distress beacon, she felt they had an obligation to go, despite their time pressures.

'If there really is someone down there, then we're the only chance they've got of rescue – a once in a lifetime chance,' she went on. 'Explorer submarines don't come this way any more.' She glanced back at the old submarine, firmly clamped inside the dinosaur's jaws. There was something gloomy and melancholy about it that made her shiver. 'If we don't check then I'll never be able to get that submarine out of my mind,' she insisted. 'I'll have nightmares about it every night, wondering if we really did leave someone behind, trapped inside to die alone.'

'Well, geez, when you put it like that, I don't think we have any choice about it either,' Max said with a groan.

Jai nodded. 'You're right. We can't ignore a distress beacon from another Ocean Squid submarine, no matter the circumstances. We must check it out. Two of us will stay here and the other two will go on to the *Silent Eel*. Hopefully we'll conduct a quick search and find that the light is simply malfunctioning. Then we can disable it and return to the *Blowfish*.'

They had a brief discussion about who was going to stay behind and who would venture on to the submarine. Since forming the rescue party was the most dangerous option, everyone was keen to put themselves forward, but it was finally agreed that Ursula and Max would be the ones to take it on. Ursula because her engineering knowledge meant she'd be able to work on the hatches if they had fused shut, and Max because he was the most skilled at operating his robot penguin. The robot was immensely strong and might come in handy if there was any heavy lifting to be done.

'Be as quick as you possibly can,' Jai urged. 'There's no telling when another current will come through and if you're in the water then you'll be swept away.'

It was a sobering thought. Deep in the dark ocean, it would be almost impossible for the submarine to find them. They would be completely alone with the dinosaur skeletons. Max's suit would eventually run out of air, and Ursula would struggle to swim free of the currents. She had the disturbing image of trying to escape the Bone Current, only to keep getting dragged back over and over again.

Still, she joined Max to get ready in the swim-out hatch. He had left his parrot in the lab, but Ursula's sea parrot could breathe underwater and didn't want to be left behind. After all, he had come for adventure and what could be more adventurous than venturing on to the wreck of an abandoned submarine?

'Best keep your wits about you, Jellyfin,' Max said as he prepared to put on his helmet. 'Who knows what we're going to find in there.'

Ursula nodded as she put the strap of her waterproof bag over her head.

'You're not bringing the parrot, are you?' Max asked, staring.

She shrugged. 'He seems determined to come.'

'Salty,' the parrot said in his shrill voice. 'Salty!'

'It looks like that's the only word he knows,' Ursula said. 'So I've decided it's his name.'

'Fitting.'

Max pressed a button, and the next moment seawater rushed into the chamber. Despite what Zara had said about sea parrots being able to breathe underwater, Ursula still felt a flash of alarm when Salty became submerged. It was so unnatural to see a parrot underwater like that, but the pirate fairy was quite correct. Salty used his webbed feet to kick and, up close, Ursula saw that he had webs between his feathers too – he appeared perfectly content in the chamber. She grinned. He was certainly the perfect parrot for a mermaid.

Once the chamber was full, the explorers opened the door and swam out into the ocean. The massive dinosaur skeleton loomed before them in the gloom. There were no glowing jellyfish or phosphorescent plankton to illuminate the water here, and the only light came from the beam of the *Blowfish*'s torch. It lit up a narrow section of the sea very well, but this also had the effect of making the surrounding water seem even darker. There was no noise either. The sea was often quiet underwater but the silence seemed somehow even deeper here in the dinosaur graveyard.

Although Salty was able to swim, he wasn't particularly fast, so he clamped his feet to Ursula's shoulder and allowed her to tug him along. As they approached the trapped submarine, Ursula wondered whether some unseen person was watching them from behind the dark portholes. She tried very hard not to think about ghosts as they got closer, but the dinosaur skeleton alone was enough to send shivers down her spine. When they reached the swim-out hatch, Ursula expected the door to be rusted shut, but in fact it opened easily beneath her hands. It looked as if it had been maintained and oiled, which made her think that perhaps there was someone on board after all.

Max and Ursula swam into the hatch and pressed the buttons to drain the water. They were unsure whether or not it would work after all this time, but it operated perfectly and the room was soon dry. Salty shook ocean droplets from his feathers and Ursula towelled off her tail to get her legs back and took a long scarf from her bag to tie around her waist as a skirt. Max kept his helmet on while Ursula opened the door because there was a chance that the submarine was waterlogged – but when the door swung open, it revealed a dry corridor and Max removed his helmet.

'The quiet is really strange, isn't it?' he said.

She nodded.

'Salty!' the parrot squawked, sending a shrill echo down the corridor.

The submarine felt odd without a background hum of engines, although they could see that the lights were on in the corridor. A damp, dank smell hung about the place and Ursula couldn't shake the thought that the submarine felt like a tomb, still and silent and cold. But the lights were another indicator that someone might be aboard, so they continued on.

They headed towards the bridge, as this seemed the most likely place for someone to operate the distress beacon. And if it turned out that no one was there, Ursula would still be able to inspect the equipment and see if a malfunction was causing the beacon to light up.

The design and layout of the *Silent Eel* was similar to that of the *Blowfish* and Ursula and Max made quick progress through the corridors. Aside from the lights, the place seemed utterly deserted. They could see no signs of life whatsoever and the very air felt thin, as if the generator was no longer functioning as well as it should.

'We'll probably find that some crab got into the control boards and messed everything up,' Max said, sounding hopeful. 'I bet that's why the lights are on too.'

'Maybe,' Ursula replied doubtfully.

They were almost at the bridge when they discovered a problem. The hatch they needed to pass through had fused shut and couldn't be opened. When Ursula climbed up into the pipes to take a look, she discovered that a large part of the submarine had become flooded with water. When she returned to tell Max the bad news, he said they ought to return to the *Blowfish*.

'I can't get up into the pipes in my diving suit, and from what you've said, there's too much flooding for me to be able to make it to the bridge by holding my breath.'

'You won't be able to get there,' Ursula agreed. 'But I can. If I crawl up into the pipes I can come into the flooded room through the ceiling and then turn into a mermaid to swim the rest of the way to the bridge.'

Max shook his head. 'I don't like it,' he said. 'I don't think we should split up.'

'What choice do we have?' Ursula asked. 'We'll have to abandon the mission otherwise. Look, we're almost there. It won't take very long to reach the bridge – probably ten minutes or so. We can't get this close and not at least see what's happening there.'

And so Max reluctantly agreed to Ursula's plan and she found herself swimming through the flooded submarine, with Salty at her side. She was glad of the sea parrot's company. Seeing the rooms and corridors filled with water only made the wreck feel even more melancholy and she was grateful to have a companion, even if it was a parrot rather than a fellow explorer.

There were little fish that had got in from somewhere, as well as coral starting to form on the walls and barnacles clinging to the portholes. Eventually, the sea would reclaim the submarine altogether.

When Ursula finally got to the corridor outside the bridge, she found that this door was fused shut too. She knew there were engineering tunnels that ran beneath the room so she opened the grate and swam into one of them, followed by Salty. She expected the tunnel to come up into the bridge, but when she arrived she discovered that part of the floor had crumbled away, so that half the room was flooded and the other half was dry.

When Ursula broke the surface and pushed the hair back from her face, she saw at once that the room wasn't empty. There was a young man standing on the dry half of the bridge. He had pale blond hair that had grown long and dishevelled, his body was thin inside his tattered Ocean Squid robes and he was staring at her with a look of exhausted, yet quiet, despair. A faint scar stretched from beside his right eye down to his ear, and the eyelid on that side drooped slightly. He seemed remarkably familiar, and for a wild moment Ursula thought she was looking at Ethan Edward Rook – except this boy was clearly older, probably about sixteen or seventeen.

'A mermaid,' he said, in a hoarse rasp of a voice, appearing to speak more to himself than to her. 'I should have known an explorer crew was too good to be true. Well, so be it. I suppose you've come to drown me.' He spoke quietly and calmly. 'Is there, by any chance, something I might say to persuade you otherwise?'

Salty erupted from beneath the surface just then with a squawk, and settled himself upon Ursula's shoulder.

'I haven't come to drown you,' she hurried to reassure him. 'I've come to rescue you.'

CHAPTER TWENTY-TWO

The boy stared at her. '*Rescue* me? But ... you're a mermaid. And ... is that a parrot on your shoulder?' He rubbed his eyes and stared at Salty. 'I'm hallucinating again.' He nodded to himself. 'Yes, that must be it.' He gave Ursula a sudden smile. 'Well, a friendly mermaid and her parrot is much nicer than the last hallucination I had. My brother Ethan was here but he wasn't very good company. He kept complaining about the seaweed in his hair. He'd drowned, you see.'

'Ethan?' Ursula gave a start. All of a sudden, she knew exactly why the boy in front of her was so familiar, and her breath caught in her throat. 'Oh my goodness! You're ... you're Julian Elijah Rook! Aren't you?'

The boy frowned. 'Do I know you?' Then he shook his head and said, 'I suppose it makes sense that you would know all about me, since you're from inside my head.'

'I'm not from inside your head, I'm from the Ocean

Squid Explorers' Club. I'm an engineer there. And I know your brother.'

A flash of hope crossed Julian's face, but then quickly vanished. 'The club would never employ a mermaid,' he said.

'They don't know that's what I am,' Ursula replied. 'I'm half human. I have legs on land and a tail in the water.' She reached out a hand. 'You can touch me, I'm real.'

When Julian made no move towards her, Ursula grabbed the edge of the floor impatiently and hauled herself up to sit on the side. Her green tail sparkled with tiny drops of water and Julian shrank back from her. Ursula reminded herself that, to him, she was a sea monster in the same category as giant jellyfish and the screeching red-devil squid that had attacked his family's ship. He'd been taught to fear her, so perhaps it wasn't his fault, but Ursula felt a flash of hurt just the same. She allowed herself to feel it for a moment before, slowly and deliberately, reaching out her hand.

'I'm real,' she said quietly. 'And I'm not here to hurt you. I only want to help. I'm a mermaid, but I'm also an explorer like you are. Your own brother encouraged me to join the club.'

'That doesn't sound like Ethan,' Julian replied.

Ursula was about to point out that one of his own teammates was herself a girl, but then she realised that Julian wouldn't know anything about Stella either. He'd been missing for a year, so he wouldn't know about the Collector, or the Phantom Atlas Society, or the fact that the Ocean Squid Explorers' Club itself had been stolen away. Slowly, she lowered her hand.

'Ethan told me that girls can be good explorers,' Ursula said. 'We talked about it in the lobby of the club.' She looked Julian right in the eye. 'There's a tentacle hanging there now, from a screeching red-devil squid. Everyone knows that you cut it off saving your brother's life. Whenever Ethan comes to the club he goes to look at the tentacle. I've seen him scowling at it like there's nothing he hates more in the world.'

Julian's eyes widened slightly. He looked at her more closely, and when she offered her hand again, this time he took it, his long fingers wrapping firmly around her palm. Ursula returned his grasp with a gentle squeeze.

'Great Scott,' Julian breathed. 'You really *are* here. So Ethan survived? He's all right?'

Ursula nodded. 'He's fine.'

Julian closed his eyes briefly. 'Oh, thank the gods. I wasn't sure what had happened, but if he's OK then it was all worth it.' A sudden smile lit up his pale face as he looked at Ursula. 'Thank you for telling me,' he said. 'I'm so very relieved and glad.'

'Everyone thinks you're dead,' Ursula said. 'How did you get here?'

'It's a long story, and I'm afraid I won't have time to tell it to you.' He glanced back at the control panels. 'The oxygen on the submarine is running out. It won't be habitable for humans for much longer. That's why I sent the distress signal.' He gestured at the submerged floor. 'This part flooded and the floor collapsed two days ago. I've been living off the protein bars I had in my bag. I tried to get back to the main part of the submarine but the tunnel is too far for me to hold my breath.' His face clouded over. 'The last time I tried it, I feared I would drown and only just made it back in time. Even if I had a diving suit, it wouldn't be able to fit through the pipe. I'm trapped.'

Ursula smiled. 'No, you're not,' she said. 'Have you ever heard of Ocean Discovery flavour mermaid ice cream?'

When Ursula returned to where Max was waiting for her in the corridor, he could hardly believe who she had found, but he wasted no time getting back to the *Blowfish* and returning with some of the mermaid ice cream. Julian was sceptical at first but as soon as he slipped into the water beside Ursula and put his head beneath the surface he realised she'd been telling the truth. The ice cream would enable him to breathe underwater for twenty-four hours, and they only needed about fifteen minutes to get through the submerged pipes and join Max.

'It really is Ethan's brother!' Max exclaimed the moment he saw Julian. 'I'd recognise that profile anywhere! There are going to be lots of people very happy to see you! I think your brother is a conceited pain in the butt, by the way, but I'm delighted you're not dead.' He held out his hand. 'Maxwell Xavier Clark, robot inventor.'

'Julian Elijah Rook,' Julian said, accepting the handshake. 'Oceanographer.'

'You don't look so good,' Max said, echoing Ursula's earlier thoughts. 'Come on, let's get you back to the *Blowfish*.'

As well as being undernourished, Julian was also clearly very tired and it seemed to take all his willpower to keep up with Max and Ursula as they retraced their steps back to the swim-out hatch. Once they were in the ocean, Julian swam so slowly that they made only very gradual progress. Finally, Ursula offered him her hand, hoping that he wouldn't be too proud to accept her help. To her relief, he held on to her arm and they were soon back in the *Blowfish*'s swim-out hatch.

When the water had drained away, Julian leaned forward, resting his hands on his knees, and took deep, gulping breaths.

'I hadn't realised how thin the air had got on the *Silent Eel*,' he explained between gasps. 'This is like . . . the best, purest air I ever breathed.'

Max diplomatically paused to allow Julian to catch his breath a little before pressing the button to open the door to the corridor. He had brought Jai and Genie up to date when he'd returned for the ice cream, and they were waiting eagerly just on the other side.

Jai's eyes widened slightly when he saw Julian, as if he hadn't really believed it was true until that moment. 'I'm Jai Bartholomew Singh,' he said. 'Acting captain of the *Blowfish*.' He walked right up to the older boy and gripped his arm. 'You can tell us your story later. Once you've rested and recovered a little. But for now, just know that you're safe, that you made it against all the odds, and that you have other explorers here to help you. You don't have to do it by yourself any more.' His grip tightened slightly and his voice was full of warmth. 'Welcome home, Julian.'

Julian couldn't speak. He tried a couple of times but it seemed no words would come. Finally, he just shook his head, with tears glistening in his eyes, and raised his hand to squeeze Jai's shoulder. The explorers didn't need him to say anything. They knew how he felt and they could see the gratitude written all over his face.

'You're safe,' Jai said again, because they all knew that sometimes, when an explorer had been in danger for a very long time, it could be hard for them to really believe they had actually been rescued.

'Safe.' Julian rasped out the word and then shook his head in wonder.

It seemed to Ursula that he was suddenly unsteady on his feet.

Genie noticed too and said, 'We've got a hot meal ready for you, and a bath and a bedroom.'

Ursula was absolutely burning to know what had happened to Julian since the squid attack a year ago, how he had got away from the sea monster and survived since. But she could also see that now wasn't the time for answers and she was proud of her friends for realising this too and for putting Julian's needs before their own desire to hear his story. Once he had had a hot meal and a bath, they showed Julian to a spare bubble and he practically fell on to the bed, asleep before his head touched the pillow.

Jai had set the *Blowfish* on a course out of the Bone Current. Everyone was keen to leave this part of the ocean before the current could tug them in again. So they said goodbye to the dinosaur graveyard and went full steam ahead back to their intended route. Soon they had left the Poison Tentacle Sea behind them, and were in the clear blue waters of the Bubble Ocean once again, on course for Pirate Island.

Julian was still sleeping soundly in the morning, so Ursula left a note in his room telling him he'd find them on the bridge when he woke up. When he finally appeared at noon the next day, all four explorers were gathered there together, taking lessons from Zara about how best to speak to their parrots. They were glad to take a break and accompany Julian to the galley for some lunch.

'I didn't get the chance to introduce myself yesterday, but I'm Genie Delilah Singh,' Genie said, holding out her hand.

'Pleased to meet you,' Julian replied, clasping it. 'And, er ... what a remarkable hat.'

'Thank you.' Genie beamed. 'I made it myself.'

Today's headgear featured a fluffy lullaby crab perched on the brim. Max had even made a robotic voice box for it so that it sang a little tune if you tapped it on the shell. Genie demonstrated this for Julian now.

'Enchanting,' he said, although he looked rather puzzled by the hat, as well as Genie's sparkly pink cowgirl boots, which weren't exactly club regulation.

'Thanks,' Genie said again. 'I can make one for you too if you like?'

Everyone tensed. Most people had no wish to wear the outrageous hats Genie favoured and they were all a little nervous in case Julian should make a cruel remark. But thankfully, he just smiled and said, 'How kind. Thank you. Are you a mermaid too?'

'No, I'm a whisperer.'

'Fascinating,' Julian replied. He indicated the hat. 'And is the lullaby crab your shadow animal?'

'No.' Genie took a deep breath. 'Actually, I'm a kraken whisperer. Don't be alarmed, but my shadow kraken, Bess, is just outside the window. I promise she's not a monster and neither am I.'

Julian glanced out the porthole and everyone stiffened again, waiting for his reaction, afraid that it might not be good. But fortunately he did not appear in the least afraid of Bess.

'What a beautiful creature,' he said quietly. He looked back at Genie. 'You must have many fascinating insights about kraken. I'd love to hear them one day.'

'If you think *that's* good,' Max said. 'Just wait until Jai shows you his pet plankton.'

'I'm sure you'll be interested as an oceanographer,' Jai said. 'They're quite extraordinary. The smallest plankton in the world is only two micrometres long,' he announced. 'That's smaller than a human red blood cell. Plankton are the main food source for most fish, and a blue whale can eat more than four tons a day. They're the most vital organisms on our planet. If that's not extraordinary then I don't know what is.'

'Perhaps you could show Julian your plankton later?' Ursula suggested diplomatically. She knew how long Jai's plankton lectures could last. 'Right now he's probably starving.'

'I *am* hungry,' Julian admitted. 'And looking forward to eating something that isn't a protein bar.'

The explorers hurried to set out some food and as they ate, they learned Julian's remarkable story. All Ocean Squid explorers knew that he had been dragged beneath the water by a screeching red-devil squid while saving his brother Ethan's life. He'd still been holding the axe he'd used to cut off one of its tentacles and explained that he'd managed to blind the sea monster with it, thus escaping its flailing grasp.

'I got this in the process,' he said, touching the scar on his face. 'The problem was it had dragged me right down to the seabed by the time I slipped away. I knew I wouldn't have enough air to get back to the surface before I drowned.'

'So what did you do?' Ursula asked.

'Well, fortunately, there were some bubble crabs scuttling over the sand nearby,' Julian said, taking a gulp of coffee. 'You're familiar with them?'

Jai nodded. 'They release large bubbles of oxygen whenever they snap their pincers together. Nobody knows why.'

Julian nodded. 'That's right.' He looked suddenly morose. 'I was so happy when I saw those crabs. I thought I'd be able to use one of their bubbles to get back to the surface and join my family. I even managed to catch one of the bubbles fairly easily. It fitted around my head perfectly, like a helmet, and gave me the air I needed to breathe.'

'But then something went wrong?' Max guessed.

'I got caught in the Bone Current, same as you,' Julian said. 'It probably affected my family's boat too, but it was much stronger underwater. I was dragged straight into it. It was awful – there were shells and bones flying everywhere and I was terrified that one would smash into me, but luckily they all passed by. When the current died down I was all alone in the dinosaur graveyard, and my bubble was running out of air. I was even further underwater by this point and there were no more bubble crabs. I knew I'd never be able to reach the surface.'

Ursula shivered even though it was warm in the galley. Julian's story was enough to make her blood run cold. Everyone was silent, waiting for him to continue.

He poured himself another cup of coffee. 'The worst thing was the darkness,' he said quietly, stirring in two packets of sugar. 'It was darker than anything I've ever imagined. Even darker than when you close your eyes and see inside your head.'

'You were very brave to face that,' Genie said.

Julian lifted his thin shoulders in a shrug and gave a rueful smile. 'I didn't have any choice,' he said. 'I thought for sure I would die there. But then a glowing terrapin lit up nearby. Finally, I could see a little bit of my surroundings. When I saw the *Silent Eel* in the distance I knew it was my only chance. I had about enough air left in the bubble to get to it. The bubble popped just as I reached the swim-out hatch.' He shook his head, recalling the dreadful moments. 'It had rusted and was difficult to open, but I managed to get inside in the nick of time. Luckily there were still plenty of air pockets inside the submarine.'

'So you've been living there alone all these months?' Ursula asked.

'It wasn't easy,' Julian said. 'The submarine was in bad condition, and I'm an oceanographer, not an engineer. But I figured out how to get the air system up and running. And once I'd eaten all the tinned food, I found a diving suit that was in pretty good condition and I managed to set traps for lobster and catch fish in nets.' He grimaced. 'I don't think I ever want to eat seafood again, but it kept me from starving.'

'And what did you drink?' Ursula asked.

It was one of the most inconvenient things about submarine travel – you had to keep stopping to pick up fresh water. Ursula had been trying to find a way to somehow purify seawater for drinking, but all her experiments so far had been unsuccessful.

'Soda, mostly,' Julian said. 'But about four months ago I ran out of drinks on the submarine. Then I had no choice but to collect seawater and boil it. It was drinkable once it cooled down, but it didn't taste very good. That's why I kept adding coffee to it.' He eyed his mug. 'It's quite a nice drink once you get used to it. Anyway, the distress beacon was broken but I repaired it before I did anything else, just in case any submarine should pass by.'

'It's a lucky thing you did,' Jai said.

Julian nodded. 'I ventured out of the submarine on many occasions too, looking for help or some means of escape. I knew that everyone would believe me dead and that I'd have to find some way to get myself out. I even tried taking some tools to chip away at the dinosaur teeth, but the submarine was stuck fast. And if I'd freed it, I'm not sure it would have been in good enough condition to reach land anyway. Since then, I fell back on my oceanographer training and have been studying the currents, trying to work out whether there was some way to hijack one and use it to reach the surface with an inflatable raft tied to my back.'

Ursula knew that oceanography was a highly specialised subject, using science and maths to study the relationship between seawater, polar ice caps, the atmosphere and the biosphere. She thought it was fascinating – almost as interesting as engineering – and she often perused the textbooks back at the club when no one was looking.

'What an ingenious idea,' she said.

Julian gave her a rueful smile. 'Well, I never quite managed to make it work. My calculations showed that I would run out of air before I reached the surface. My only hope was to try to capture a bubble crab. I'd cultivated a seaweed garden near the submarine, hoping to attract one, but then the *Silent Eel* began to flood and I became trapped on the bridge. If you hadn't turned up when you did, I'd have died.'

'We almost missed your signal,' Jai said. 'We were so eager to escape the Bone Current. Fortunately, Ursula spotted it.'

Julian looked at her. 'Well, thank you,' he said. 'I'm in your debt, all of you. I can't wait to get back to the club and see my family.'

'Ah. Well, about that.' Jai cleared his throat. 'A lot has happened while you've been gone.'

They filled Julian in on what he'd missed with the Phantom Atlas Society as quickly as they could. The older boy looked appalled by their tale.

'So the club is just ... gone?' he asked.

'It's trapped inside one of Scarlett's enchanted snow globes,' Ursula said. 'But we'll get it back somehow.'

'And my brother Ethan,' Julian said, frowning as he tried to piece everything together. 'Where is he now?'

'He's with Stella and his other teammates. We think

they're going after the Collector too, but we don't know where they are now,' Ursula replied. 'You understand what radio communication is like under the sea. We've kind of lost touch with everyone.'

'There's no point radioing the other clubs anyhow,' Max cut in, 'because all they ever do is tell us off for mounting the expedition in the first place and order us to come home.' He looked at Julian. 'I hope you're not about to suggest the same, because it will fall on deaf ears, and if you make trouble then we'll have no choice but to lock you up in the brig with the sea gremlin. And I should warn you, she's got terrible manners. She's forever flicking bogies through the bars of her cell, and she's got excellent aim too.'

'Max!' Jai snapped. 'You can't threaten to put another explorer in the brig when they've done nothing wrong.'

Max shrugged. 'Better that than have him try to take command and hand the submarine over to the Sky Phoenix Explorers' Club.'

Ursula felt her heart sink. It hadn't occurred to her that this was a possibility, but as the oldest, she supposed Julian was the ranking explorer on board and could technically try to take command from Jai.

'I don't want to give the submarine to the Sky Phoenix Explorers' Club,' Julian said. He shook his head and added, 'I still can't get my head around the fact that there even *is* such a club. Astonishing. And to think my brother was part of the expedition that discovered it! You're absolutely right, we must find the Collector and rescue the Ocean Squid club.' He looked at Jai. 'It seems to me that you've been doing an excellent job of being captain, and believe me I've no interest in taking your place. I want to study the ocean, not lead men. I'll happily work under your command if you'll have me.'

'Wonderful!' Genie said, beaming at him. 'You might even see your brother along the way.'

Julian grinned. 'I never dreamed Ethan would be mature enough to put aside club competitiveness and work alongside Polar Bear explorers! He must have grown up while I've been gone.'

Max started to laugh, but Ursula shushed him.

'We've very glad to have you aboard,' Jai said. 'We need all the help we can get. In just two more days we'll reach Pirate Island.'

They checked the pickled parrot charm Jojo had given them and found that it still had plenty of silver feathers, with only one or two having reverted to their original green. With any luck, the sea witch charm would provide them with a magical cloak long enough for them to reach their destination.

CHAPTER TWENTY-THREE

Over the next couple of days, Ursula continued to practise her mermaid magic with Genie at every opportunity.

'You're definitely getting better at controlling it,' Genie said, applauding after Ursula managed to hit one of the three plastic bottles they'd put there as targets. 'You've done that three times in a row now!'

'But I missed the other two!' Ursula snapped. 'So I don't know why you're clapping. That's not a success, it's a failure!'

Genie immediately stopped and Ursula felt remorse, especially when she looked up and saw her friend's crestfallen expression.

'I'm sorry,' Ursula said, although she still felt angry and frustrated. 'I didn't mean to snap at you. It's not your fault I can't do it.'

'But you *are* doing it,' Genie said quietly but firmly.

Ursula made an impatient noise, but Genie wasn't

finished. 'You can get cross with me again if it helps,' she said. 'Although I expect it will just make you feel worse. But you *are* doing it, Ursula. It's just that you're new and you're learning, and you can't expect to be really good at it straightaway. That's not how acquiring a new skill works.'

Ursula sighed. 'I suppose. But we don't have time for me to keep getting it wrong like this. I wish I was better.'

Genie smiled. 'Well,' she said, 'that's the first step to *being* better, isn't it?'

Ursula felt a confusing mix of admiration and exasperation for her friend. 'How do you do it?' she blurted out.

Genie looked puzzled. 'Do what?'

'How do you manage to be so optimistic all the time? Always seeing the bright side of things? I wish I was like that. I wish it was that easy for me.'

Genie was silent for a moment. 'But it isn't,' she finally said.

'Isn't what?'

'Easy. It's not easy at all.' Genie took a tentacle from her jellyfish hat and twirled it around her finger.

'Oh.' Ursula was surprised. 'You always make it seem like it is.'

'Do I?' Genie fixed her brown eyes on Ursula thoughtfully. 'Well, I expect that's because I've had a lot of practice. At trying to see the bright side, I mean. Like when I was bullied at school, and when I wasn't allowed to be an explorer, and when Dad left us. But the way I see it, life's never going to be perfect and easy, especially if you're an explorer. So you can choose to focus on the bad, hurtful, horrible things, going over and over them inside your head, making yourself feel even worse all the time. Or you can try to concentrate your attention on the things you *do* have, all the amazing, wonderful gifts you take for granted every day. They just become invisible because we're so used to them, but we'd miss them so much if they were gone – things like having people we love, who love us back, and being healthy enough to go on adventures, and sharing secrets with kraken.' She smiled at Ursula. 'Or being a mermaid and having amazing mermaid magic.'

'That's all very well,' Ursula said. 'But it doesn't really help if you're feeling angry or hurt or worried, does it? You can't help how you feel.'

'No.' Genie tugged on a jellyfish tentacle again. 'You know, when Dad left I thought I'd never feel happy again. It hurt so much that he didn't love Jai and me enough to stay, didn't even love us enough to visit, or ask us to visit him, or to write a single letter. I was so envious of all the other kids at school who were lucky enough to have dads who loved them and who ate dinner with them every night, and played with them at the weekends and things like that. It's so horrible feeling jealousy like that. It's a monster that will eat up everything that's good about you if you let it.'

'So what did you do to get it to stop hurting then?' Ursula asked. She was hoping for some kind of magic answer from Genie, some mysterious kraken secret perhaps that would make everything easier.

'Oh, there's no way to get it to stop hurting,' Genie replied. She looked surprised that Ursula would even suggest such a thing. 'I think it will always hurt whenever I think of Dad. That's not the point. The point is that you can almost always find something good out of a bad thing. Sometimes you just have to try really, really hard to see it. For example, when Dad left, it made me see for the first time how strong and amazing my mum is. It made me see that Jai is basically made out of loyalty and love and I know I can rely on him no matter what. And it made me a stronger person. It's so easy to feel sorrow for a thing you never got to have. But it's silly too, because no one ever has everything, and maybe if you had that one thing you think you want so much, you wouldn't have got something else that matters even more to you.'

Ursula sighed. 'I want to be able to do that,' she said. 'To think about things like that and see the world that way. I know it's better. But I'm not sure I can. It's too hard.'

'I can't do it all the time either,' Genie admitted. 'Sometimes I try and try, and it doesn't work and I don't manage to feel any better, and that's OK. That's just how it is some days. If a hurt is too raw or powerful then it can be tricky to get a handle on it straightaway, but I won't give up,' she said with sudden fierceness. 'I won't overlook everything that's wonderful simply because I can only see the things I don't have, or the mistakes I've made, or the wrongs that have been done to me. So when it's hard to see the bright side, I accept that it's hard, but I keep trying anyway. Have you ever heard of crying shrimps?'

Ursula frowned. 'Maybe? Isn't there a stuffed one in a case back at the Ocean Squid Explorers' Club?'

'I don't know,' Genie said. 'I've never been allowed into the club. But anyway, crying shrimps got their name because every evening when the sun goes down, they come out on to the beach and they cry and cry and cry. They miss the sun and they're sad that it's dark. It doesn't matter that it's only temporary and that the sun will soon come back – the shrimps still cry for hours. And do you want to know the *really* daft thing about crying shrimps? Guess what happens if they go to Sunshine Island? It's in the Golden Sea, and at certain times of the year it's light there all the time, even at night. So you'd think the shrimps would be happy, right? But no. On Sunshine Island they cry because it's too bright and their eyes get tired from the sunshine. So it doesn't really matter where the crying shrimps are, they'll always be crying and upset over something. That's just the way their brains work. They're always looking for something to be sad about, and if it's not one thing, it'll be another.'

'But crying shrimps are just being stupid,' Ursula protested. 'The sun setting isn't a real problem.'

Genie shrugged. 'It is to them, and that's all that matters. No one can control what makes them feel sad, can they? But I think you can help yourself a bit by not looking for things to be upset about, and looking for the good things in your life instead. I don't want to be a crying shrimp, wailing because the sun has set. I want to be a kraken falling in love with the stars. And that doesn't mean I don't ever have any problems or really difficult days. I can't control how other people treat me, but I *can* control the way I treat myself. And I want to raise myself up, not drag myself down.'

Ursula thought of the way she'd felt at the mermaid school – the sense that she'd missed out on something other children took for granted. And Genie's words suddenly allowed her to see it in a different light. She hadn't gone to mermaid school or had many friends, but she *had* been lucky enough to call the Ocean Squid Explorers' Club her home. She knew every inch of the place, whereas Genie had never even been allowed to set foot inside its doors. And Ursula had loved the hours she'd spent wearing greasy coveralls and working with Old Joe on the submarines, learning everything there was to know about engineering. And she had been best friends with a dolphin and gone out for secret midnight swims with him.

It might not have been the childhood she would have chosen for herself, but there were parts of it that had been very special indeed. And there were parts of it that she could feel proud of, and important lessons she had learned, like how to be self-reliant, and to work hard, and to stand up for herself. So perhaps she wouldn't change it after all. Especially as it had all led to her being right here, right now, going on an amazing adventure in a fantastic submarine with three children she was pleased and proud to call her friends. It would be terrible not to have Genie and Max and Jai in her life.

Ursula smiled, and this time it felt genuine rather than forced. 'I want to be more like you,' she said, 'so I'll keep trying too. I'm a bit disappointed, though. I hoped you were going to say that Bess had shared some sort of secret with you about how to cope when you're upset.'

Genie cocked her head to one side. 'There is *one* kraken secret she shared with me once,' she said. 'I don't think she'd mind if I told you too.'

'What is it?' Ursula asked eagerly.

'You remember how I told you that kraken are in love with the stars and they come up to the surface of the ocean at night sometimes to look at them? Well, one of the things they love so much about stars is that they make them feel a little bit sad. And kraken think that sadness can be kind of beautiful sometimes. Not something to avoid or hide from. Kraken think that sadness can sweeten and strengthen the soul. It makes us think more deeply about things and helps us to understand other people who are suffering too. So when I'm *really* not able to see the bright side of something, I can at least take comfort from the fact that I'm making my soul a little bit more beautiful. And sometimes that just has to be enough.'

Ursula felt a sudden surge of affection for Genie and put her arms round her friend in a hug. 'I'm so glad I met you,' she said, her words muffled slightly by the long tentacles of Genie's jellyfish hat. 'I think being friends with you makes me a better person.'

Genie squeezed her back tightly. 'I'm glad I met you too,' she said. 'A real friend is such a precious, wonderful thing.'

Ursula nodded vehemently. 'Yes, it is,' she agreed.

She was just about to suggest that they take a break and go get Ocean Squid Explorers' Club flavour sundaes – she couldn't get enough of the chocolate submarines – when the intercom crackled beside them and Jai's voice came over the line. 'I thought you'd like to know,' he said. 'Pirate Island has just come into view.'

CHAPTER TWENTY-FOUR

The explorers stood on the bridge of the *Blowfish* and gazed down at the radar. Most islands showed as misshapen blobs on the screen, but Pirate Island formed the shape of a skull and crossbones.

'It's not actually shaped like that in real life,' Zara said, peering at the radar. 'Goodness knows why it takes that form on the radar.'

'Well, we're almost there,' Jai said. He looked at the pirate fairy. 'Surprise is one of the only advantages we've got. You said you know a secret way on to the island?'

Zara tipped back her hat and nodded. 'That's right. It's through a waterfall on the north shore. It's quite hard to find, so probably the simplest thing is if you put my galleon back in the water and follow me.'

'But we can't raise the submarine,' Jai protested. 'Someone on the island is bound to spot us.'

'You won't have to,' Zara assured him. 'You can stay

submerged the whole time. Just follow my path on the radar.'

'We won't have radio contact with your ship,' Ursula pointed out. 'So how will we know when to come to the surface?'

'Don't worry about that.' Zara grinned. 'You'll know.'

'But—'

'Look, it'd take too long to explain,' the pirate fairy said. 'Just come to the surface when you see the gold. Are we in a hurry, or not?'

'Let's just get on with it,' Max said. Now that they were within sight of Pirate Island, he found he was absolutely desperate to see his sister. It had been hard to cope with when they were miles and miles away and had no idea where she was, but now he was so close, he was more impatient than ever to rescue her from Scarlett Sauvage.

Zara told them she could put a charm on her ship to make it waterproof for long enough to reach the surface once they released it from the submarine, but suggested they all change into their pirate disguises first.

The explorers hurried below deck to do so. Of course, there was no costume prepared for Julian, but the others all had plain trousers tucked into sturdy engineering boots. Genie had dug out some shirts from their father's wardrobe and dirtied them up a bit so that they would look suitably worn. She'd also fashioned them eye patches to help disguise their faces. But it was the hats and the parrots that finished the look. The parrots looked right at home on their shoulders and Genie had done a magnificent job on their headgear. They even had ostrich plumes sticking out from the hatbands.

'I think I look rather dashing,' Max said, examining himself in the mirror. He grinned. 'I could get used to being a pirate.'

'I don't like it.' Jai shuddered. He fiercely disliked anything that even hinted at breaking the rules, and wearing a pirate outfit felt highly unnatural to him.

Ursula was pleased with her outfit, especially as it had lots of pockets, which she always appreciated for storing spanners and other engineering equipment. Once Zara had looked them over and given her approval to their disguises, she returned to her galleon, which they then released into the open sea. As planned, it shot quickly up to the surface and began sailing directly towards Pirate Island.

The explorers followed her on the radar and once they got close, they raised the periscope to take a look and saw a place that appeared very similar to Parrot

Island. It had the same waving palms and golden beaches. The main difference was that there were Jolly Roger flags flying everywhere, as well as threatening signs warning that the island was not open to visitors and any trespassers would be made to walk the plank.

And, of course, there was the fort.

It was just as Zara had described it – a squat, hulking stone building overlooking the island from the tallest hill. Pirate flags fluttered from its turrets, alongside Phantom Atlas Society ones. Ursula felt her heart sink as soon as she saw it. The fort was the picture-book definition of the word 'impenetrable'. The walls were so thick and solid-looking that she doubted even a cannonball would be able to blast its way through.

'At least we know Scarlett is here,' Genie pointed out, trying to find a bright side. 'Because of the Phantom Atlas Society flags.'

Ursula tried to feel happy about that, but it was hard not to be unnerved by the sight of the fort. It looked like the sort of place that once someone went in, they would never see the light of day again.

Even worse, there were pirate ships everywhere. Some were docked at sea a little way out, others were moored in harbours built around the shore. They were formidable, majestic-looking craft, with an awful lot of cannons. The explorers all felt on edge, sailing silently beneath them, and quiet fell upon the bridge with everyone too nervous to talk. Even Bess seemed to adopt a stealthy swimming style as she silently drifted beside the *Blowfish*.

Finally, they'd passed the fleet of pirate galleons and found themselves on the quieter north shore of the island, where they followed Zara right up to a large waterfall that gushed over a clifftop straight into the sea. It looked like a powerful torrent and they expected Zara to go around it, but instead her little ship went straight through. The foaming white water swallowed the galleon, like a curtain sweeping across their view.

'Well, I guess we'd better follow,' Jai said.

They sailed through the water to discover an underwater cave. The pirate fairy had told them to bring the submarine to the surface when they saw the gold, and Ursula had her eyes peeled ready to see sunken pirate treasure. She wasn't disappointed – the cave was full of it. Some trunks were so laden that they'd burst open on the cave floor, and there were piles of gems and precious jewels. But the gold was more than that – it flashed in the water all around them. Ursula thought they were seeing fish at first, but then she realised they fluttered rather than darted, and that these were actually butterflies.

'Treasure butterflies!' Max exclaimed. 'I've read about these back at the club. They gather wherever there's an abundance of gold.'

One of the creatures suddenly came right through the submarine's porthole, making Ursula jump.

'How did it do that?' she gasped.

'They don't have a physical form,' Max said, raising his hand and passing it straight through the butterfly to demonstrate. 'They're made of light. Some entomologists think they're formed of the glint and glow of the treasure itself.'

'They're beautiful!' Julian said, beaming in delight as more and more butterflies fluttered through to the bridge, covering them in a delicate, sparkling glow.

'Extraordinary,' Jai agreed.

'Well, come on,' Max said. 'Let's raise the sub.'

They brought the *Blowfish* to the surface and then hurried to the outside deck, where they stepped out to find that the cave above the water was just as full of treasure and butterflies as it had been below. It extended back a long way, but was only just large enough for a vessel as huge as an explorer submarine. Zara's pirate galleon had risen up on top of the submarine and the pirate fairy was grinning at them expectantly from its deck.

'You see?' she said. 'It's the perfect hiding place. Only fairies know about it. The treasure butterflies disguise themselves as poisonous lizards if any human pirates approach. They know they'd take the treasure, you see, whereas fairies will leave it be, so they let us see them in their natural form. There's a tunnel that leads to the island. I'll show you the way.' Her gaze lingered on Julian suddenly. 'You'd better stay here.'

Ursula thought this was a good idea. Despite his time on the *Blowfish*, Julian still looked very thin and pale. After all, he'd been underwater for a long time, eating a poor diet and breathing low-quality air. Ursula had seen him get breathless and clammy a few times just walking to the brig. It was clear he needed proper rest and some decent recovery time.

'Not a chance,' Julian said, calmly but swiftly. 'This is a highly dangerous mission and I want to help.'

'But—' Ursula began.

'My brother might be on the island,' Julian said. 'I have no intention of being left behind.'

'But you don't have a parrot,' Zara pointed out. 'Or a pirate disguise. No one will ever believe you're one of us.'

'I have an idea,' Julian said. 'I can be your prisoner. You can turn me over to the guards in your pirate disguises.'

They all stared at him.

'Why would we do that?' Ursula asked.

'I saw Scarlett's posters, putting the bounty on my brother and all of you,' Julian said. 'It's only a drawing, so I might be able to pass for Ethan, despite the age difference. That way one of us would be taken straight to the prison and then the diversion would only need to give us time to get back out again.'

'It *could* work,' Zara agreed. 'Pirates are a lazy bunch so you can guarantee they'll put all the prisoners together in nearby cells.'

But Jai was shaking his head. 'Scarlett's no idiot,' he said. 'She'll have made sure that all the pirates are familiar with those posters. It's not a good idea to try to pass Julian off as Ethan. He's clearly older and taller, to say nothing of the scar and drooping eyelid. Distinguishing features like that are exactly the sort of thing that always appear on a wanted poster.'

'Well, what do you think we should do then?' Max asked.

'I think Julian can be helpful, but in a different way,' Jai said. 'No one knows him and he's the only one of us not featured on the poster. So it makes the most sense for *him* to be the pirate and one of us to be his prisoner.'

'I'll do it,' Max said at once. 'Jada's my sister and—'

'No,' Jai said. *'I'll* be the prisoner.'

Genie heaved an exasperated sigh. 'Why do you always have to be the hero, Jai?'

He gave her a hurt look. 'What's that supposed to mean? But in this case, there's one very obvious reason why it should be me.'

'And what's that?' Max asked.

Jai held up his prosthetic arm. 'This,' he said, 'is the perfect place to hide the skeleton key. Even if the pirates search me, they'll never find it, whereas if one of you tries to hide it in a pocket or a boot then it'll probably be discovered. And then the entire plan will be jeopardised. Trust me, I've hidden things in the prosthetic many times before and it's the best hiding place there is. No one ever finds them. No one knows how to get it off for a start, and it never occurs to them that there could be anything hidden inside. It's perfect.'

Ursula felt uneasy about the plan and she could tell that the others did too, but it was hard to argue with Jai's logic. This appeared to be a way they could get into the prison but also, more importantly, get out again. And so Jai gave his pirate disguise to Julian and changed back into his explorer's cloak. There was a small moment of concern when they were unsure whether Jai's orange parrot would deem Julian a suitably brave alternative, but he settled himself on the other boy's shoulder without too much bother.

'Scarlett has taken up residence in the fort's living quarters,' Zara told them. 'So a pirate will likely rush to inform her the moment they lock you up. She'll want to see you for herself and it won't take her long to reach the cells.'

'We'll have to create a diversion almost as soon as Jai's been taken inside then,' Genie said, looking worried. 'We don't want to risk Scarlett seeing through Julian's disguise.'

'Could you use your cannon to turn the pirates into hamsters, like you did to the ones back at Starfish Island?' Max asked Zara.

The pirate fairy shook her head. 'Fairy magic is powered by all of us. We're only strong like that when multiple ships travel together. By myself I *might* be able to turn one guard into a hamster, but not all of them.'

'Bess could create a diversion,' Genie said. 'The guards won't know she's a shadow kraken if she appears from a distance, and even if they've been told to stay at their posts they probably won't if they think their lives are in danger.'

Zara shook her head. 'They'd raise the alarm if they thought there was a kraken attack, and then we'd have all the pirates on the island after us. Besides, a shadow kraken would frighten the captured children and then they'd start screaming and raise the alarm. Why don't you use your rainbow parrot?'

Genie looked confused. 'What do you mean?'

'The golden feather,' Zara said. When the others continued to look blank, she said, 'Aren't you familiar with rainbow parrots? Their feathers are all the colours of the rainbow, except for one, which is golden. If you pull it out, the parrot will make the area around her go temporarily dark. It will allow you to sneak past the pirates. And it'll freak them out too, which is always fun!'

Genie didn't particularly like the idea of pulling out one of her parrot's beautiful feathers, but it seemed the best chance they had. She thought Zara probably had a point about Bess frightening the children too, so she asked the shadow kraken to stay behind and guard the submarine.

'Well, then,' Max said. 'Now that we have a plan, let's get this show on the road.'

CHAPTER TWENTY-FIVE

The explorers followed Zara down a tunnel that led out of the cave and into a forest of palms. Parrots and other colourful birds flitted between the branches, emitting their shrill calls. The air smelled of sunshine and warm sand, and sea spray, and coconuts. Ursula couldn't help thinking that if it weren't for all the bloodthirsty pirates, this would actually be a very nice island indeed.

'The pirates normally stay on the beaches,' Zara told them. 'They've got hammocks there, you see, and water sports. They come here to relax. We're not likely to come across any in the trees. Too many mosquitoes.'

Unfortunately, Zara was right about the mosquitoes. The explorers suffered multiple bites as they made their way through the palms.

'It's too bad we don't have anyone from the Jungle Cat Explorers' Club with us,' Genie remarked. 'They always carry expedition-strength bug spray, don't they?'

'We're almost there,' Zara said, flitting ahead of them.

Ursula was relieved to hear it. The climb was steep and hot and they were all dripping with sweat by the time they reached the treeline. From here, they could peer through the large leaves and see the fort a short distance away, hunkering low to the ground. Even the windows had bars on them and so did the front entrance gates. Again, Ursula couldn't shake the feeling that once a person went inside, they might never come out.

There were two pirates standing guard, as Zara had said. Or rather they were sitting down – slouched on a rum barrel each and using a third as a table to play cards on.

'I guess Julian and I will take it from here,' Jai said.

There was no cover for the last part of the walk, so anyone who stepped out from the trees would be spotted by the guards immediately. The explorers didn't like to be separated but it seemed it was their best chance of getting inside.

'Thank you for doing this,' Max said, squeezing Jai's shoulder. 'I promise never to make fun of your pet plankton again. Or your medal collection. Or your rule books.'

Jai gave him a brief smile. 'We both know you can't help yourself,' he said. He looked at Genie. 'Don't worry. I'll come back.'

Genie nodded. 'I know you will.'

They said their goodbyes and then there was nothing for it but to move on with the plan. Julian hoisted the harpoon gun he'd brought from the *Blowfish* and pointed it at Jai.

'Ready?' he asked.

Jai nodded. 'Ready.'

They emerged from the treeline together. The pirates were so engrossed in their card game that they barely glanced up as the explorers approached, and didn't speak at all until Julian's shadow fell across their table.

'No visitors,' one of the pirate guards grunted.

'I've come to claim the reward offered by Scarlett Sauvage,' Julian said in a firm, clear voice.

The pirates still didn't look up. 'Yeah?' the second one said.

'I have a prisoner for her. This is Jai Bartholomew Singh from the Ocean Squid Explorers' Club.'

At last, he had the pirates' attention. Their eyes widened and they almost fell off their barrels. 'Not another explorer!' one of them gasped, staring at Jai.

Ursula frowned. *Another* explorer? What did he mean by that?

One of the guards grabbed hold of Jai and bundled him into the fort. The other took Julian by the arm and said, 'Come on. The Collector will want to see you straightaway.'

'Oh.' Julian paused. 'I'd rather not go into the fort, if it's all the same, old chap. Things to do and, er, ports to plunder and all that. In fact, no need to bother Miss Sauvage at all – I'm sure she's very busy. Can't you just bring the reward out to me?'

Ursula winced. The plan was going wrong already. The last thing they needed was for Julian to be taken inside. They were supposed to create a diversion and get the prisoners out quickly so he'd never have to come face to face with the Collector.

'He sounds nothing like a pirate!' Zara hissed. 'He won't fool Scarlett for a second. What are we going to do?'

But it was already too late. The pirate guard told Julian that the Collector needed to see him in person, and the next moment he was being ushered round the side of the fort to the main entrance.

'Well, that's gone and torn it,' Max muttered. 'The idiot! He should have refused to go.'

'It didn't look like he had much choice,' Genie said. 'Perhaps he'll give the guard the slip once they're inside?'

They waited in tense silence. Zara glanced at Genie. 'Are you ready with that parrot?'

Before she could reply, the pirate guard who'd taken Jai away suddenly came charging out of the gates at full pelt, yelling about prisoners having escaped.

Max frowned. 'What the—? Surely Jai wasn't daft enough to use the skeleton key right in front of him?'

When the pirate saw that his colleague was gone and that he was yelling at no one, he tore off round the side of the fort, presumably to the entrance Julian had been taken through.

The explorers all looked at each other. 'What shall we do now?' Genie said. 'Try to get inside after Jai or—'

But that was as far as she got before Jai emerged from the fort, running as fast as he could.

'Why is he alone?' Max demanded. 'Where's my sister and the other children?'

They discovered the reason soon enough when Jai crashed through the trees to join them.

'Gone,' he gasped, leaning forwards to catch his breath. 'Everyone's gone. The children have already escaped.'

Max stared at him. '*Escaped?*' he said. 'But *we're* here to rescue them!'

'Well, they found a way out on their own,' Jai said. 'The guard walked me down to one of the cells, obviously expecting it to be occupied, but when we arrived we saw that they'd dug a tunnel. He shoved me into another cell and I used the skeleton key to get out as soon as he left.'

'They can't possibly have dug their way out,' Zara said. She gestured back at the fort. 'There's no human alive strong enough to dig through all that rock.'

'It wasn't a human,' Jai said. 'It was a robot crab.'

'Robot crab?' Max groaned. 'That'll be Jada!'

'Yes. She left a note for the pirates. It was, er . . . quite rude actually, saying they could keep the robot crab and stuff it up their—'

'Why didn't she *wait*?' Max said. 'She knew I was coming!'

'I guess she got fed up waiting,' Ursula said. 'It's taken us a while to get here.'

'Well, if she was going to rescue herself why couldn't she have done it earlier and saved us all a lot of bother?' Max grumbled. 'That's typical Jada.'

'What about the pirate fairies?' Zara asked eagerly. 'Were they there too?'

'I don't know,' Jai said. 'The guard didn't say anything about fairies.'

'At least they're out of the prison,' Genie pointed out.

'Yes, but we've no clue where they are!' Max said. 'All we've achieved is to raise the alarm sooner than it would have been, and lose Julian in the process.'

'Lose Julian?' Jai realised that the oceanographer was missing. 'How?'

'The other guard marched him in to see Scarlett,' Ursula said.

'He'll never be able to pass himself off as a pirate with her!' Jai groaned. 'Max is right, this is a heck of a mess! What are we going to do?'

'You can start by putting your hands up,' a female voice said behind them. 'And if you don't want to be frozen solid then I suggest you turn around very, very slowly.'

The explorers almost leaped out of their skins. They'd been so engrossed in their conversation that they'd failed to keep a lookout and now they'd been discovered. Ursula's stomach seemed to plunge, making her feel sick. It was all going so wrong! They turned around, expecting to see a pirate standing there pointing her pistol straight at them, but a completely different sight met their eyes.

They'd been discovered by two children their own age. One was a boy with brown skin and collar-length black hair, wearing trousers and a pale blue T-shirt with a tiny polar bear emblem stitched on to it. The same polar bear was sewn on to the satchel he carried over one shoulder. A clockwork pendant around his throat marked him out as a wolf whisperer, as did the gigantic shadow wolf at his side.

The other child was a girl with extremely pale skin, ice-blue eyes and long white hair tied back in a plait. She wore the same outfit as the boy. The only difference was the beautiful tiara that sparkled in her hair. Ursula gasped, hardly able to believe it. In the pictures printed in the newspapers, the girl always looked like a princess because she wore dresses and petticoats, but Ursula would recognise her pale face and white hair anywhere.

Standing before them was Stella Starflake Pearl, the ice princess and first female member of the Polar Bear Explorers' Club.

CHAPTER TWENTY-SIX

'Just take it nice and easy,' the wolf whisperer said. 'And no one needs to get hurt.'

Ursula recalled the articles written about Stella and her friends after the Collector had been discovered, and she knew who the boy was at once.

'You're Shay Silverton Kipling!' she blurted. 'And you're Stella Starflake Pearl!'

'That's us, all right,' Shay agreed mildly. 'I guess pretty much every pirate on this island knows we're wanted thanks to those posters.'

'Oh!' Ursula was startled. 'But we're not pirates! We're explorers too!'

Stella and Shay exchanged a look.

'That's funny,' Stella said. 'Because you look exactly like pirates.'

'We're in disguise,' Jai said.

'Disguise!' his parrot squawked.

Shay raised an eyebrow. 'With talking parrots and

330

everything,' he said. 'You can't expect us to believe that? You just want to get away so you can report on us to the Collector.'

'For goodness' sake!' Max exclaimed, sweeping off his hat. 'Would a pirate have the Ocean Squid emblem shaved into the side of his head?'

He gestured at his shave fade, but it was starting to grow out and Stella and Shay squinted at it dubiously.

'Just looks like a squid to me,' Stella said. 'Which seems *exactly* like the sort of thing a pirate would have. Besides –' her eyes lingered on Ursula and Genie – 'everyone knows the Ocean Squid Explorers' Club doesn't admit female members.'

'We're the first,' Genie said. 'Just like you were for your club. You inspired us, Stella! You've got to believe we're explorers. You've spoken to us on the radio. We're the crew of the *Blowfish*.'

At the mention of the submarine's name, Stella's eyes widened slightly. 'The *Blowfish*?' She glanced at Shay. 'That *is* the name of the submarine we were in contact with.'

The wolf whisperer still looked uncertain. 'Ursula Jellyfin is half mermaid,' he said. 'So if you really are her and not a pirate then you can prove it by turning into a mermaid for us now.'

'I can't,' Ursula replied. 'It doesn't work like that. I can only transform if my legs touch saltwater.'

'That seems mighty convenient,' Shay said.

'Actually, it's not convenient at all.'

'Look, if you really are explorers then why are you dressed as pirates?' Stella asked.

'Scarlett kidnapped some children and we came here in disguise to rescue them,' Jai said.

'One of them is my sister,' Max said.

'I really am Ursula Jellyfin,' Ursula said, looking at Stella. 'Is Ethan with you? He met me at the club. He can vouch for me. He'd probably recognise Max and Jai too.'

'He's back at our hideout,' Shay said. 'Probably getting bitten by some sort of rare bat.'

One corner of his mouth twitched, as if he rather liked the idea.

'Well, take us to him then,' Jai said. 'And he can confirm who we are.'

Stella shook her head. 'We can't – we're on a rescue mission too. Our friend Beanie is in the cells.'

'Not any more he isn't,' Jai replied. 'I've just been inside the fort. All the prisoners have escaped. The guards know and have raised the alarm. These trees will be swarming with pirates any second, so if you really do have somewhere safe to hide then we all need to go there *right now.*'

Stella frowned. Ursula wasn't sure whether they'd done a good enough job of convincing her or not, but just then they heard a pirate shout from the other side of the fort. His words carried over to them clearly in the trees.

'The kids have escaped! Scarlett says to turn the island inside out until we find them!'

Stella and Shay exchanged a startled glance.

'OK, we believe you!' Stella said, her voice low. 'We've got to get back to the cave. Quick! Come with us!'

She snatched the tiara from her head and thrust it into her bag, looking relieved to be rid of it. Then the children were racing through the palm grove as fast as they could go. The pirates were blundering around in the trees too, but fortunately for the explorers they didn't make any attempt at stealth and it was easy enough to hear where they were and avoid them.

Ursula and her friends followed Stella and Shay as they wound their way back down the hill towards the water. When they reached the shore, the Polar Bear explorers hunted around in the underbrush until they found the little rowing boat they'd hidden there. There was just about enough room for them all to squeeze into it, although the boat sat worryingly close to the waterline.

'The cave is just around the corner from those rocks,' Stella said. 'You can only access it from the water.'

She and Shay both snatched up a pair of oars and started to row. The boat was heavy with so many people in it, and Ursula worried they weren't going fast enough. She could see the leaves of the trees moving nearby as if someone was pushing through them. If a pirate reached the shoreline they'd see them at once, but there were only two pairs of oars. Stella must have been thinking the same thing because she snapped her fingers. At once, six small trolls made from snow appeared on the sides of the boat, each clutching a small snow paddle. They dipped these in the water and began to row energetically. In no time at all, the boat had passed round the rocks.

'That was awesome,' Ursula said, admiring the trolls.

Stella gave her a smile. 'Thanks. I've been practising magic with permafrost. It's a bit harder than regular frost – more like ice. The trolls don't last long in this heat, but they help a bit.'

As she spoke, the trolls melted away, leaving pools of icy, sparkling water behind them. The explorers could see the cave mouth now, although only because they knew to look for it. The entrance was several feet above the water and blended in with the rocks. When they got nearer, they saw that a rope stretched down the side of the rocks towards them.

'Can you all climb a rope?' Stella asked.

'We're explorers,' Jai replied, looking offended. 'Of course we can.'

'Just checking,' she replied.

Perhaps Stella had thought that Jai might have some difficulty, having only one arm, but in fact he had taught himself to compensate for this by relying more on his feet. There was quite a knack to it, but Jai had never yet found a challenge he couldn't overcome.

Shay tied the boat up to the end of the rope and then the children all climbed to the cave mouth. Stella and Shay went first, followed by the Ocean Squid explorers. Ursula had expected the cave to be deep, but in fact it was barely more than a narrow ledge, with only just enough room for a tent.

It was an extremely shabby, moth-eaten sort of tent too. Ursula couldn't help being a little shocked, as well as disappointed. She knew that the other clubs tended to rough it on expeditions, going for weeks on end without washing, and sleeping on dirty floors and all that business, but the tent was even more sorry-looking than she had expected.

'Come on in.' Stella lifted one of the tent flaps.

Ursula wondered whether she was joking. 'But ... there won't be room for all of us in there,' she said.

Stella smiled. 'It's bigger than it appears from the outside.'

The Ocean Squid explorers gave each other dubious looks. It seemed to them that even two people would be a squeeze in a space so small, but they ducked their heads and followed Stella and Shay inside anyway. And that was when they realised that this was no ordinary tent. Inside, it was massive. There was an entire living-room area filled with overstuffed cushions and colourful silk curtains. Pith helmets hung on the walls, along with maps of faraway deserts. Not only that, but they could see other rooms through open doorways too – a kitchen and at least one bedroom. Strangely, the entire place smelled strongly of rum.

'But ... but how?' Jai asked.

'It's a magic fort blanket,' Shay explained. 'The Desert Jackal Explorers' Club uses them. We traded for it at Witch Mountain when we—'

'Where's Beanie?' an irritated voice demanded. 'And who the heck are all these people?'

They turned to see Ethan Edward Rook standing in the doorway to the kitchen part of the tent. His pale blond hair was dishevelled and his fair skin was covered in angry-looking mosquito bites.

'Honestly!' he exclaimed. 'You two had the easy job! All you needed to do was use that enchanted rum I gave you and the guards would have walked Beanie right out of the cells. I couldn't have made it any simpler, yet somehow here you are with four pirates and their horrid parrots. I've already been bitten by parrots three times since we got here, and I don't intend to go through it all again.'

'Salty!' Ursula's parrot screeched.

'Settle down, Prawn,' Shay said mildly. 'We couldn't get Beanie because the prisoners have already escaped. And these kids say they're not pirates at all, but Ocean Squid explorers and that you can vouch for them.'

'What?' Ethan snapped crossly. 'What are you talking about?'

Ursula swept the pirate hat from her head. 'Ethan, it's me, Ursula,' she said. 'The engineer from the club?'

Ethan narrowed his eyes at her for a moment, before a startled look flashed across his face. '*Ursula?*' he said. 'Why are you dressed as a pirate, for goodness' sake?'

Ursula had been hoping that he would be pleased to see her, or might even congratulate her on managing to become an explorer after all, even if she wasn't an official member of the club yet. But instead he just looked irritated, as usual.

'Why can't anything ever go as planned?' he complained, without waiting for her answer. 'What are you even doing here?'

'So this really *is* Ursula Jellyfin then?' Stella asked eagerly. 'These are the Ocean Squid explorers who've been helping us?'

Ethan nodded. He pointed at Genie. 'I'm not sure who she is, but I know the others.' He looked at Jai. 'I don't think we've ever met in person, but you're Jai Bartholomew Singh, aren't you? The club is fond of using your image on their posters. Quite the golden boy.'

'That's right,' Jai said. 'And this is my sister, Genie Delilah Singh.'

Ethan frowned slightly as his gaze fell on Max. 'And you're ... well, I don't remember your name, but you're the one who's always getting into trouble for breaking the rules. And you sniggered at me while I was trying to recount the tale of the Black Ice Bridge.'

'It wasn't the tale I was sniggering at,' Max said. 'It was the spiky starfish you accidentally made while trying to show off in the telling of it.'

Shay gave a snort, which he turned into a cough. 'Sounds about right.'

Ethan's frown deepened. 'Weren't you expelled from the club?'

'I prefer to think of it as a temporary suspension,' Max replied. 'They'll have no choice but to reinstate me once we perform our daring rescue of the club. My name is Maxwell Xavier Clark, by the way. Robot inventor.' He gestured at his robot shark T-shirt. 'At your service.'

'*Robot* inventor?' Ethan pulled a face. 'What kind of speciality is that?'

'A pretty useful one, if my sister's escape from Scarlett's cells is anything to go by,' Max said, in a waspish tone.

'Well, a fat lot of good that's done!' Ethan exclaimed. 'Now they're roaming the island by themselves and are probably being herded up like goats as we speak.'

'Ethan, don't be so melodramatic,' Stella replied. 'Beanie knows where we are. If he's escaped, then he'll come straight here with the children.' She glanced at the others. 'Look, we obviously have some catching up to do, but before anyone says another word, I just want to say thank you for warning us about the Collector's new psychic spies. We couldn't work out how she was managing to keep track of us and sending pirates and sea gremlins after us all the time until you sent that message. Cool dolphin too, by the way.'

Ursula was delighted to hear that it had been helpful, as they had hoped.

'We managed to get all the way to Pirate Island in secret,' Stella went on. 'We came in Ethan's family's submarine.'

'Ahem!' Ethan coughed loudly.

Stella rolled her eyes. 'We managed to get here without discovery because Ethan performed a cloaking spell on the sub,' she said.

The magician puffed up his chest importantly until Shay added, 'Well, he did eventually. And the less said about the time he managed to create a hoard of biting wombats instead, the better.'

Ethan glared at him and looked about to say something insulting, but Stella hurried on with the story before he could do so.

'*Anyway*,' she said, 'we've been using this cave as a hideout and were scoping out the fort when we were ambushed by pirates and poor Beanie was captured. Ethan's made some magic rum that makes the pirates follow our orders for a few minutes after they drink it. We were hoping to get Beanie out with that.'

'Seems like I'm pretty indispensable to the team, for all the mockery I have to put up with,' Ethan sniffed, shooting Shay a dirty look. 'It takes a lot of time and effort to make that rum, you know. Why do you think I was back here rather than part of the rescue mission? The way we're getting through the stuff, I can barely keep up.'

'Everyone thinks you're doing a wonderful job,' Stella soothed.

'Yeah, I was only kidding about the biting wombats, Prawn,' Shay said.

He reached over to ruffle the magician's hair affectionately, but Ethan flinched away. 'Don't touch my hair!' he snapped. 'I've told you before, you'll mess it up!'

Ursula was surprised by Ethan's abrupt tone. If she hadn't known any better, she would have thought they weren't friends at all.

'We came by submarine too,' she said. 'And Ethan, we have some really important news for you. You'll never believe who we found in the Poison Tentacle Sea. It was—'

She was absolutely bursting to share the news of Julian's rescue, but right at that moment they became aware of a chatter of voices from the water below. Fearing pirates, they all rushed to the entrance, only to see a boat full of children.

Ursula would have recognised Beanie from Scarlett's

reward poster even without his Polar Bear explorer's cloak. He had spiky dark hair tipped in blue, as well as pointed ears inherited from his elf mother. With him were six children, the kidnapped relatives of inventors. Ursula spotted Jada at once – the resemblance to Max was unmistakeable. She had black hair arranged in Bantu knots and wore a T-shirt with a robot unicorn on it.

'Jada!' Max gasped, his voice full of relief.

He called down to get her attention. She grinned back and raised her hand in a wave.

Climbing ropes was an explorer's skill and the children couldn't quite manage it, so they got some sheets from the tent for the children to tie themselves into and then organised a pulley system to fetch them up. Soon, everyone had gathered together in the magic fort blanket, and there were glad reunions on all sides.

'Scarlett didn't hurt you, did she?' Max asked anxiously, crouching down in front of Jada.

'No, actually she treated us pretty well. We were even allowed to use one of the fort's bathrooms and take exercise breaks outside.'

'That makes sense,' Stella said. 'Scarlett doesn't think of herself as a villain, after all. She believes she's saving the planet.'

'What about pirate fairies?' Zara asked eagerly, fluttering over to Jada. 'Did you see any down in the cells?'

The little girl shook her head. 'We haven't seen any fairies. Sorry.'

Zara's face fell. 'Scarlett must be keeping them somewhere else,' she said. 'Or perhaps she never let them out of that snow globe to begin with.'

'Sorry, Zara.' Max gave her a sympathetic look. 'We'll keep looking for your crew.' Then he turned back to his sister and tried to sweep her up in a hug, but she wasn't having any of it and loudly berated him in front of everyone for taking so long to get there.

'We came as fast as we could,' Max said, rolling his eyes. 'And we risked life and limb, so a thank you would be nice!'

'A *thank* you!' Jada looked incredulous. 'Why, what have you done? Did *you* manage to make a robot crab out of a spoon and a few bits of wire? I don't think so! Did *you* manage to dig a secret tunnel under the beds and hide it from the pirate guards? I don't think so! Did *you*—'

'All right, we get the idea.' Max looked faintly annoyed. 'You're the superstar inventor. But we're here with our submarine, aren't we? You got yourself out of the fort, but how were you planning to get off the island, genius? Fashion a robot shark out of a coconut?'

'I hadn't got to that bit yet,' Jada admitted. She set her jaw stubbornly. 'I'd have come up with something, though. But if you've got a submarine then I suppose you may as well take us home in it. It'll save me having to make a whole new robot.'

'You're too kind,' Max said, rolling his eyes again. 'Also, it's really annoying that you can make a robot out of a spoon and some wires.'

He sounded cross, but there was pride in his voice too. The explorers checked that the other children – two more girls and three boys around Jada's age – were all unharmed. It seemed that Scarlett had treated them kindly and everyone was clean and well fed. Despite her threats, no one had been made to join pirate crews or walk the plank.

'I don't think Scarlett likes the pirates much,' Jada said. 'She always talks to them in a snappy kind of way.'

'It probably doesn't sit well with her, having to work with criminals,' Stella said. 'But now that everyone's here, we can get on with our mission to—'

'Actually, not *everyone* is here,' Ursula interrupted.

344

She looked at Ethan. 'It's what I started to tell you earlier. We found your brother Julian in the Bone Current.'

She expected Ethan to be overcome with delight, but instead he looked as if someone had struck him across the face. For a long moment he didn't speak at all.

'You mean you found his body?' he finally said.

'Oh!' Ursula was startled. She realised she hadn't phrased the news very well and hurried to correct herself. 'No, we found *him*. He survived. He's been living in the wreck of the *Silent Eel*. There were air pockets and leftover food. He's alive, Ethan!'

The magician's face was a stone. 'I don't believe you,' he said. 'My brother drowned. I saw it happen.'

'It really was him,' Jai said. 'He told us all about how he used a bubble crab to breathe until he reached the submarine wreck. It was quite ingenious.'

'Oh, Ethan!' Stella looked delighted. 'This is wonderful!'

Ethan shook his head. 'No,' he said. 'Don't. Just . . . please don't say anything like that. I won't believe it,' he said. 'Not until I've seen him for myself. None of you know what Julian looks like. It could have been some other explorer you found, passing himself off as Julian for some reason.'

'He looked just like you,' Max said. 'He sounded like you too. Only, you know, a lot more polite. Less complaining.'

'If what you say is true then where is he?' Ethan demanded.

Ursula explained what had happened and how Julian had disguised himself as a pirate, only to be taken into the fort.

'We've got to rescue him,' she said. 'Then you'll see that what we're saying is true.'

After a quick discussion, the explorers decided that the children should be taken back to the Rook family's submarine, where they'd be out of harm's way, while the explorers would use the magic rum to infiltrate the fort, rescue Julian, find the Ocean Squid Explorers' Club snow globe, free Zara's crew and – hopefully – capture Scarlett too.

'I'm glad we haven't set ourselves too ambitious a task,' Ethan said with a curl of his lip.

Beanie looked faintly troubled. 'It seems highly ambitious to me,' he said.

Ethan sighed. 'I know. I was being sarcastic to try to make myself feel better.'

'Oh.' Beanie frowned. 'Did it work?'

'No.'

'Well, I'm not surprised,' Beanie said. 'It's a fort. It's designed to be impenetrable.'

'But we know that it's not,' Ursula said. 'If one young girl with a robot crab can get out, then a group of intrepid explorers can get *in*.'

'Well said.' Shay gave her an approving look. 'Especially if two of them are an ice princess and a mermaid.'

'Don't forget magician,' Ethan sniffed. 'I'm the one with the magic rum.'

'You haven't let us forget it for a moment,' Shay replied. His eyes fell on Genie, then he smiled and said, 'Do you have a speciality? Or are you hoping to learn one if you get admitted to the club?'

Genie glanced at the kidnapped children, who were now sitting around the table drinking hot chocolate. Then she lowered her voice and said, 'Actually, I'm a whisperer. I've asked my shadow animal to stay away for now so she doesn't frighten the children.'

'Oh!' Shay looked immediately happy to meet another whisperer and his eyes went to the clockwork pendant he knew Genie would have to match his own. 'An octopus whisperer!' he exclaimed. 'How fascinating! I'm a wolf whisperer, and this is Koa.'

He indicated the shadow wolf lying at his feet.

'She's beautiful,' Genie said. Her hand went to her pendant. 'This isn't an octopus, though,' she said. 'It's a kraken.'

'Impossible!' Ethan scoffed. 'There's not a person alive who can speak to a monster as fearsome as that.'

'No one but me,' Genie said, quietly but firmly. 'My shadow kraken is called Bess.'

Ethan shook his head and it was clear that he didn't believe Genie. Ursula felt a little offended on her behalf but her friend didn't seem to mind, and she supposed it didn't much matter what Ethan thought. As soon as he saw Bess he would realise the truth soon enough, but for now it was better that she stayed hidden.

CHAPTER TWENTY-SEVEN

The Polar Bear team's submarine was hidden in a cave similar to the one the Ocean Squid club had used. Fortunately, Beanie's uncle was an entomologist, so Beanie knew all about the treasure butterflies and they had used the submarine's metal detector to find a cave just below the waterline. Ethan's father was on board because he had the same penchant for getting attacked by things as his younger son, and was nursing a jellyfish sting that Beanie's magic had been unable to heal. He'd made such a fuss about it that Stella's father Felix had stayed behind to look after him.

The two teams of explorers spent the time until sunset discussing their next moves. Finally, it was decided that they would all head to the fort together. But first they briefly split up to return to their respective submarines. The Polar Bear explorers dropped the rescued children off at Ethan's submarine so the adults could look after them, while Ursula and her friends returned to the *Blowfish* to swap their pirate disguises for their explorers' cloaks. There seemed little point trying to continue with the disguises now that the alarm had been raised. Ursula took the opportunity to collect her trident too.

A short while later, the Ocean Squid team found themselves creeping back through the jungle alongside the Polar Bear explorers. They'd expected to see and hear pirates moving about, but the island was eerily quiet.

'I don't like this,' Ethan muttered. 'Where have they all gone? The other nights we've heard them doing their pirate karaoke down on the beach, but tonight there's nothing. It's like they've all left.'

'Well, maybe Scarlett's sent them to search the surrounding ocean?' Ursula suggested. 'Perhaps it's a good thing? It might make it easier for us to get into the fort.'

'Unlikely,' Ethan grunted. 'Our luck doesn't run like that. If past experience is anything to go by, then anything that can go wrong will.'

'But you've had some incredible successes,' Genie protested. 'So incredible that the whole world knows about them.' She nudged Ursula. 'This is a prime example of a crying shrimp.'

'What's a crying shrimp?' Stella asked, immediately looking interested.

Ursula explained and the ice princess grinned. 'Oh, I see. Yes, Ethan is definitely a crying shrimp at times.'

'I am not—' the magician began to protest.

'Shh!' Stella said. 'You know you are. And look, we've reached the fort and the guards have gone.'

They peered through the palms and saw that she was right.

Ethan frowned. 'Perhaps they've all gone,' he said. 'Not just the pirates, but Scarlett Sauvage as well.' His face darkened. 'In which case, we'll have to begin our search for her all over again. And *if* what you say about my brother is true, then he's lost too.'

'We don't know what's happened yet,' Stella said. 'So let's not jump to conclusions.'

'Well, come on then,' Ethan said, already heading towards the fort. 'Let's get inside while we can. Before something else goes wrong.'

'Definitely a crying shrimp,' Stella said to the other two girls under her breath.

Genie and Ursula both giggled.

'I heard that,' Ethan said with a sigh.

They all felt a deep thrill of danger as they passed through the gates of the fort. Everyone tried to move as silently as possible, but they soon realised there was no need. When they entered the grand front lobby, it wasn't still and dark, as they had expected. Instead, every candle and lantern was lit, providing enough light for them to see all the spider webs and each dusty coat of armour. The sound of jazz playing on a scratchy record player reached them from down the corridor. And hung up in the middle of the wall before them was a banner that said: *Welcome, explorers!*

They all stared at it for a moment.

'This isn't good,' Ethan finally said. 'You can call me a crying shrimp all you like, but if Scarlett's expecting us then we're in big trouble.'

Ursula couldn't help thinking he was right. The corridors leading off from the lobby were locked up tight with iron gates, but there was one that was brightly lit. At its entrance there was a sign with an arrow on it and words that read: *Explorers, please come this way for the inaugural Phantom Atlas Society dinner.*

'Come on,' Stella said. 'We won't achieve anything by standing around here.'

Ursula could feel her hands sweating where they gripped her trident as they made their way down the corridor. Candles flickered from every holder, casting dancing lights across the stone walls. The fort had the musty feeling of a place that had been shut up for a long time. There was even wet straw strewn across the flagstones in places, and the rustling of rats darting from one corner to the other. As they continued walking, the music got louder and clearer until, finally, they reached a doorway with light spilling from it.

'I know you're out there,' a female voice called. 'Stop dawdling and come in.'

'Stay close together,' Stella said quietly. 'And . . . don't trust anything she says.'

She pushed open the door to reveal a grand banqueting hall. Or at least what had *once* been a grand banqueting hall. Like the rest of the fort, it was now dilapidated and disused, but Scarlett had made some effort to make it habitable. A cheerful fire crackled in the huge fireplace and the record player filled the space with the sound of jazz. Beneath the music was another sound, one Ursula couldn't quite identify – a sort of crunching that seemed to come from underneath the table. Emerald-green banners hung from the walls, proudly displaying the emblem of the Phantom Atlas Society, and a long wooden dining table stretched from almost one end of the room to the other. Garlands of rare sea flowers hung from the ceiling and were scattered over the table. Candles flickered in the sconces, but they could only partially light such a massive room, and much of it remained in shadow. Ursula could only just make out the silhouettes of the suits of armour lined up along the furthest wall.

But the most striking thing was the collection of exhibits. Placed at intervals around the room, surrounded by candles, were the enchanted snow globes the explorers had heard so much about. There must have been twenty or so, and they were all filled with the most glorious, wondrous things. In one, Ursula saw a whole flock of tiger-striped flamingos, long thought extinct. Another held an endangered Jaltease panther, while still another contained the flapping sails of the lost Floating City of Kanga. Finally, her eye fell on one containing a beautiful water horse, its mane shimmering in the candlelight. She caught her breath as she remembered what Princess Coral had said about the water foal having its mother snatched away. Could this be the horse?

'Not quite what you're used to, is it?' a female voice said. 'Where you come from, your halls are decorated with stuffed animals and stolen relics, not live creatures and preserved cities.'

The explorers turned to the speaker. Scarlett Sauvage sat at the head of the table, which was set for dinner with a variety of china, cutlery, chunky goblets and elegant candlesticks. The table was so long that one end stretched into the shadows at the edge of the room. And in the very centre of the table was one final snow globe containing the Ocean Squid Explorers' Club itself.

Ursula's heart seemed to swell with longing as she took in the starfish-shaped clubhouse, and the jellyfish nursery and sea-flower garden. She thought of Old Joe and Mutt, and all the others trapped inside, and longed to snatch the globe from the table, along with the captive water horse. But Scarlett certainly wouldn't allow that.

The Collector wore a white shirt tucked into dark trousers and was leaning back so far in her chair that the front legs had come off the floor. Her booted feet were crossed at the ankle and resting on the table in a way that would have made Mrs Soames incandescent with rage if Ursula had ever dared attempt such a thing. Scarlett's black hair was scraped back in a scruffy ponytail and she regarded them calmly with a look of keen intelligence in her dark eyes.

'Where's my fleet?' Zara demanded, fluttering forwards to land her booted feet on the table.

Scarlett raised an eyebrow at her. 'I'm sure I have no idea,' she said. 'Have you lost them? How careless of you. But welcome, everyone, to the inaugural Phantom Atlas Society dinner. It's just grog and fried fish, I'm afraid. My pirate chef is somewhat limited in his repertoire.'

'How did you know we were still on the island?' Stella asked.

Scarlett's eyes widened slightly in mock hurt. 'What, no happy reunion?' she asked. 'No *How are you, Scarlett*? *Long time, no see*? It seems a little ungrateful, given that I'm the one who made you famous.'

'I don't care about being famous,' Stella said quietly. 'I never asked for that, or wanted it.'

'Then you're a fool,' Scarlett said sharply. 'But as for your question, the pirates assured me you couldn't possibly be on the island because they had searched every inch. I guess I made the bounty on you a little too generous because they simply wouldn't listen when I insisted you were still here.' She shook her head. 'Useless, stupid bunch. They've taken off in their galleons to search the surrounding ocean, but I knew you hadn't left because you were hardly going to leave behind one of your own. You didn't honestly expect me to believe that that explorer was a pirate, did you? He couldn't even swear without blushing. Could you, *Julian*?'

Ursula jumped, startled. She had thought there was no one else in the room, but now she followed the direction of Scarlett's gaze. She had to strain her eyes into the shadows, but she saw there was someone sitting at the other end of the table. She could just make out his fair hair and thin features.

'Julian?' Ethan's voice was a hoarse croak. When Ursula glanced at him she saw that he'd gone so deathly pale that he looked in danger of keeling over on the spot. Shay noticed too and put a steadying hand on the magician's arm.

'Well, speak up,' Scarlett said in a lazy drawl. 'Aren't you pleased to see your companions?'

Ursula felt a sudden sense of wrongness. She didn't like the way Julian sat so motionless and that he hadn't spoken since they walked into the room, not even to his brother. She didn't like that weird crunching noise she could still hear from underneath the table either, and she didn't like that they could only see a small part of the room. This time she didn't hesitate, but gripped her trident more tightly and sang the appropriate magic scale. Almost at once, the trident lit up with bright, golden light that dispersed the shadows and finally allowed them to see the entire room properly.

The explorers gasped as several things became

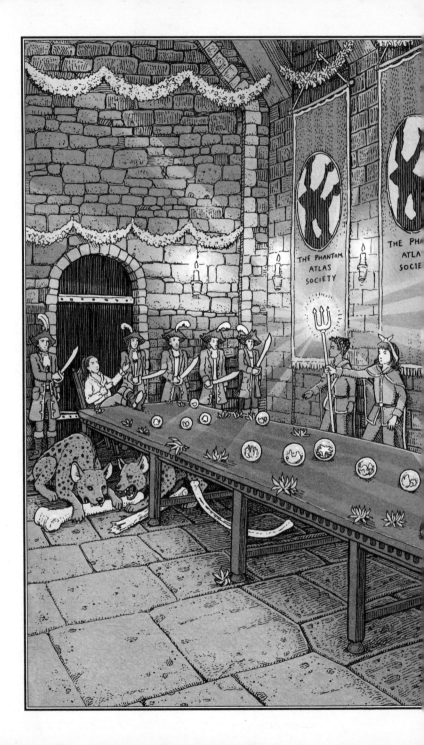

apparent at once, none of which were good. The first was that the strange crunching sound they'd heard was from a pair of massive hyenas lurking beneath the table at Scarlett's feet, their powerful jaws gnawing on a couple of huge bones that Ursula thought must have come from a whale. The hyenas were even larger than Koa, and Ursula identified them as cackling devil hyenas from the Ottoway Mountains, thought to be extinct.

The second disturbing thing she noticed was that Julian was tied to the chair he occupied and that he hadn't spoken because there was a gag in his mouth. There was a large black bruise spreading around one of his eyes too. And, finally, the silhouettes Ursula had taken for suits of armour were actually nothing of the kind – they were pirates lined up against the wall, armed to the teeth and grinning at them.

'I thought you said the pirates had gone!' Jai exclaimed.

Scarlett smiled. 'Well,' she said. 'I guess I lied.'

CHAPTER TWENTY-EIGHT

Ethan immediately began hurrying towards Julian, but Scarlett's voice stopped him.

'I wouldn't do that if I were you,' she said. 'Haven't you noticed his animal upgrade? Perhaps you can't see it from there. I thought the parrot a little pedestrian for an explorer, so I added it to my aviary and gave your friend something else instead.' She looked at the pirates standing behind Julian and said, 'Go ahead and remove his gag so he can tell his friends the happy news himself.'

With a cruel grin, one of the pirates stepped forwards to whip off Julian's gag. The explorer gave them a bleak look and spoke in a strange, strained voice, while keeping his body still as a statue. 'There's a golden scorpion,' he said through gritted teeth, 'on my sleeve.'

Ursula looked and groaned aloud in horror. The scorpion was right there, glittering on Julian's cuff. It was small but extraordinarily deadly – one of the rarest and most dangerous scorpions on the planet. There was no known antidote for its venom, and there would be no time to administer it anyway. One sting from the golden scorpion and it would stop a man's heart within seconds. No wonder there were beads of sweat forming on Julian's hairline.

Ethan looked like he was about to be sick and Beanie, inexplicably, began muttering unpleasant scorpion facts under his breath. Ursula recalled how he'd explained back in the cave that this was something he sometimes did to try to calm himself, but it was having the opposite effect on her. Stella, meanwhile, simply looked furious.

'How dare you treat an explorer this way!' she exclaimed. 'You say you're not a villain, but you're certainly acting like one!'

'But *you* are the ones who are trespassing!' Scarlett replied. She swung her boots off the table and leaned forward to stroke one of the hyena's ears. 'If you explorers had your way, you'd carry on stuffing animals until kingdom come.'

'We're trying to change that,' Stella said. 'The clubs can do things differently. They can be better.'

'They've had every chance to improve,' Scarlett replied. 'And I'm sick of waiting for changes that never come. I intend to protect all the beautiful creatures and places in this world, whether the explorers' clubs want me to or not.' Her eyes gleamed. 'And that's where you come in, Stella. You refused to work with me once, but perhaps now you will change your mind.'

'Just ... take the scorpion off Julian,' Stella pleaded. 'And then we'll talk.'

'Oh, will we?' Scarlett asked. 'Or will you simply try to double-cross me? No, I think the scorpion will stay where it is for now.' Her eyes flicked to Ethan, who'd started to raise his hands. 'And I wouldn't think of throwing any spells at it either,' she said. 'It's got an anti-magic charm on it, so if you try anything like that you'll probably just make it angry. And scorpions are liable to sting when they're angry.'

Ethan swallowed hard and slowly lowered his hands. The golden scorpion began to gradually scuttle up Julian's sleeve and there was nothing anyone could do to stop it.

'For what it's worth, Julian, I'd try not to tremble like that either.' Scarlett rolled her eyes. 'Good grief, I can see you shaking from here. You explorers are all the same. Terribly brave if you're pointing a gun at a defenceless animal, but absolute cowards as soon as you find yourselves in any real danger.'

Ursula felt a sudden surge of anger race up through

her body, making her fingertips tingle where they gripped the trident.

'He's *not* a coward!' she snapped. 'He's one of the bravest explorers I've ever met and he's done things you can only dream of!'

She wanted to add that Julian hadn't been well and that was why he was so pale and shaky, but she was worried this wouldn't stir any sympathy in Scarlett and would only give her more ammunition to use against them.

'Who is this now?' Scarlett asked, turning her gaze to Ursula before settling on the trident. 'Don't tell me. You're the mermaid girl.' She gave a great sigh. 'Of all people, I'd expect an ice princess and a mermaid to understand what I'm trying to do. You both know what it's like to be treated as villains and you both have every reason to dislike explorers.'

Ursula's eyes went back to the scorpion. It had continued to climb Julian's sleeve and was almost at his collar. She knew they were running out of time. Sooner or later, even if Julian didn't do anything, the scorpion would sting him because that's what golden scorpions did. She thought of trying to use her singing voice to persuade one of the pirates to remove the scorpion, but she hadn't practised that spell on a person before and was afraid he'd act too clumsily and end up causing the scorpion to sting.

'Using scorpions to threaten people is barbaric,' Max said.

Scarlett's gaze went to him. 'Ah, Max,' she said. 'My greatest disappointment. I had such high hopes that you'd be the first to create a weapon for me. It's such a shame. Still, at least your sister breaking everyone out saved me the job of disposing of them now that their usefulness has expired.'

'What do you mean?' Jai suddenly looked wary.

'One of the inventors finally came through for me.' Scarlett smiled. With a flick of her wrist, she removed her napkin from the table to reveal a pair of unusual handcuffs. On first glance it looked as if they were made from gold, but Ursula saw they were actually hollow glass filled with dancing flames.

'A gift from a fire magician who wanted his kidnapped granddaughter back,' Scarlett said. 'He assures me that once the fire cuffs are on an ice princess, she will do exactly what I tell her to. There's just one snag,' she said softly. 'They'll only work if an ice princess puts them on willingly.'

'Why would Stella do that?' Shay demanded, looking angry.

'Well, that's what I've been trying to work out,' Scarlett said. 'And then you played right into my hands by giving me a brand-new hostage. One of your own.' Her eyes went to Julian. The scorpion was on the bare skin of his neck now and Julian was shaking so badly that the scorpion would surely sting him at any moment.

'Because if she doesn't, then I won't give you the antidote for the golden scorpion venom,' Scarlett said.

'You're lying!' Ethan burst out savagely. 'There *is* no antidote. Not for that scorpion! Everyone knows that.'

'Just because explorers have no knowledge of a thing doesn't mean it doesn't exist,' Scarlett replied with a sneer. 'I give you my word that there is an antidote. And if Stella puts on the cuffs then I'll give it to you.'

'Don't,' Julian breathed out the word in a whisper as he looked right at Stella with sudden fierceness. 'Don't do it.'

They all knew at once that he shouldn't have talked. The vibrations from his throat irritated the scorpion and they watched in helpless horror as its tail uncurled and it delivered the deadly sting. Julian gave one dreadful gasping groan and then his eyes rolled back in his head and he slumped in his chair.

Ethan raced forwards at once, hurling a spell at the

scorpion, which immediately turned into solid gold. He snatched it from his brother and threw it into the corner of the room.

'Julian!' he exclaimed. 'Julian!' He gripped his shoulders and shook him, but Julian remained completely limp. 'Oh my gods,' Ethan whispered. He stared up at his friends and Ursula didn't think she'd ever seen a person look more wretched. 'He's not breathing.'

'Best make your decision quickly then,' Scarlett said, standing up. She picked up the Ocean Squid Explorers' Club snow globe. 'The antidote only works if it's administered within three minutes of the sting. Good Lord, did I forget to mention that? How careless of me.'

Time seemed to slow down inside the hall. The fire spat out a shower of sparks that smouldered on the flagstones. The pirates had a watchful look of excitement, their hands straying to the pistols and cutlasses at their sides. One of the hyenas cackled under the table – a terrible, devilish sound that made the hairs on Ursula's arms stand on end. She shuddered. Her eyes fell on Stella's face and she was shocked by the grim determination she saw there.

'You give your word that you'll hand over the antidote?' she asked.

Scarlett placed her free hand on her chest. 'My solemn vow,' she said.

'Stella!' Ethan said.

Ursula wasn't sure whether he was going to beg her to do it, or plead with her not to. It seemed the magician couldn't make up his mind either. An agonised look of confusion flashed over his face and he just gazed at Stella helplessly.

She gave him a warm smile. 'It's all right,' she said softly. 'It's all right.'

In one movement Stella slipped off her charm bracelet and thrust it into Ursula's hand before striding towards the table and reaching for the cuffs. Shay cried out to stop her but it was too late. The moment she touched them, the cuffs snapped around her wrists. Stella gasped and Scarlett laughed in delight.

'I did what you asked!' Stella said. 'Now give him the antidote!'

'Certainly. I'm a woman of my word.' Scarlett took a small bottle from her pocket and threw it down on the table. Her eyes gleamed as she looked at Stella. 'Now,' she said. 'Come with me.'

Stella's feet stumbled over themselves in a jerky fashion as the magic cuffs forced her to obey Scarlett's instruction at once. The Collector laughed again, and the hyenas cackled with her. Shay snatched up the antidote and threw it down the room to Ethan, who caught it in one hand and quickly opened the bottle.

'Wait!' Ursula began, stepping forwards, raising her trident.

She had some vague idea of trying to force Scarlett to stay and release Stella, but before she could say another word, Scarlett turned back to the pirates and said, 'Round them up. I don't care what you do with them. Force them into your crews, lock them in the cells, whatever. Just see to it that they don't disturb me.'

'But you promised!' Stella gasped, outraged.

'I promised to give you the antidote and I did,' Scarlett replied. 'See, it's working already.'

She was right. Ethan had dribbled the contents into Julian's mouth, causing him to immediately start coughing and retching. He looked terrible, but he was alive.

'I never said anything about letting your friends walk free, however,' Scarlett went on. 'They'd be mounting a rescue mission for you in no time, and that I just can't have. You children have caused me enough bother as it is. Now come along, Stella.'

She swept from the room with the hyenas at her side and, casting a final bleak look at her friends, Stella had no choice but to follow, tears pouring freely down her face. Shay lunged after her, but was immediately blocked by a pirate. The other pirates all fell on them at once and pandemonium broke out.

The explorers found themselves fighting against a foe that was only too happy to play dirty. There were too many of them for Ursula to attempt to charm with singing, so she turned her trident on them instead. Thanks to all the hours of practice she'd put in back on the *Blowfish*, she was much better at controlling the blast this time, and the pirates scattered right and left from her lightning forks. The pirates' parrots filled the air above their heads, squawking in panic.

Out of the corner of her eye she saw that Genie and Beanie had run over to help Ethan with Julian. The others were fighting – Jai with his harpoon gun, Max with his robots and Shay with his boomerang. They were having some success in driving back the pirates, but it was Ursula's trident the pirates were really frightened of, especially after one lightning bolt set a pirate's coat on fire. He put it out by snatching up a water jug from the table, but he seemed to lose his taste for the explorers after that, and fled the room. Seeing what had happened, several other pirates followed his lead.

'They're fleeing!' Jai gasped. 'Come on, let's go! We might still be in time to stop Scarlett.'

Ursula paused only to snatch up the water horse snow globe, and then they all raced from the fort. There was no sign of the Collector anywhere. If she was leaving the island, it seemed likely that she would do so by sea, so they hurried back through the palms towards the cave where the *Blowfish* was hidden.

But then Bess suddenly materialised beside Genie, causing the Polar Bear explorers to cry out in shock. Even though they'd been told Genie was a kraken whisperer, it was still startling to have a great sea monster sprawl around them out of nowhere, tentacles flailing. The eyes of Genie's clockwork pendant gleamed as she spoke to the kraken inside her head, then she groaned aloud before turning to the others.

'It's no use,' she said. 'Bess says the pirates have discovered the *Blowfish*. They worked out she was a shadow animal when their cannonballs passed straight through her. They've taken the submarine. It's moored out to sea. Bess will show us.'

The shadow kraken drifted ahead of them, showing the way to the nearest beach, where they saw what Genie had said was true. The *Blowfish* had been removed from the cave and was now moored out at sea, completely surrounded by pirate galleons. One of these ships had a dirigible tethered to its mast, with the Phantom Atlas Society crest emblazoned on its balloon.

Scarlett stood on the ship's deck, with Stella looking wretched by her side.

'You didn't think you'd found a secret cave, did you?' she sneered, her voice carrying easily across the water. 'Pirate Island is full of them. And we knew exactly where your submarine was the whole time.'

Chapter Twenty-nine

Ursula felt a crippling sense of dismay wash over her. Even her trident wouldn't be able to attack so many pirates at the same time, and without their submarine, they were trapped on the island.

'Blast!' Zara hissed. 'I was sure that cave was a fairy secret!'

'It's not your fault,' Jai said, but he looked as despondent as Ursula felt.

It really seemed as if they had come all this way for nothing and that Scarlett was going to get away scot-free with Stella and the Ocean Squid Explorers' Club, and all the other stolen snow globes.

'There must be something we can do,' Max said.

Genie turned to them with a sudden smile. 'There is,' she said. She held up the necklace with the miniature kraken floating in it. Her eyes met Zara's. 'I need you to return Jodie to her true size. As soon as I throw her into the water.'

The pirate fairy gave her a sudden grin. 'Right you are,' she said.

Genie straightened her shoulders, walked to the edge of the pier and raised her voice. 'If you let Stella go and return the snow globes to us, then I won't ask my kraken to attack your fleet.'

'You must think we were born yesterday, girl,' Scarlett called back. She'd pulled down the dirigible's rope ladder and was forcing Stella to climb it. 'We all know you're a kraken whisperer. Your shadow monster has no substance and is no threat to us.'

'I'm not talking about Bess,' Genie said. 'I'm talking about the kraken in this bottle.'

She held the necklace up to the sunlight, the glass sparkling where it dangled from her fingers. Her proclamation was immediately met with jeers and laughter from the pirates.

'A pygmy kraken!' one of them shrieked in mock horror. 'How terrifying! Run for your lives!'

Scarlett began climbing the rope ladder after Stella.

Genie glanced back at Zara.

'Now!' she said, as she threw the necklace out towards the water.

The pirate fairy sent a blast of magic after it and before their eyes a gigantic kraken erupted from the bottle, smashing it into a thousand pieces. Jodie was much larger even than Bess, and it was immediately obvious that she was a fighting kraken. Her huge body landed in the ocean, creating such a great wave that Genie was drenched from head to toe. The kraken's body was covered in scars from all her old battles and there was an angry look in her eyes. She looked like a monster that *wanted* something to attack, and she found the perfect target in the pirate fleet.

The pirates weren't prepared and scrambled to man their cannons, their terrified yells filling the air. Scarlett paused to give one appalled look at the kraken before racing up the last few rungs of the ladder to join Stella on the deck of her dirigible. In contrast to the Collector, Stella didn't look horrified by the kraken at all, but awed and impressed instead.

Ursula could tell that Genie was talking to the kraken inside her head as her soaked friend gestured towards the galleon attached to Scarlett's dirigible. Jodie plunged beneath the sea so fast that the surface bubbled in her wake, as if it were boiling. Moments later, the sea around the pirate ship erupted in great sprays of foam as the battle kraken burst out from beneath the waves, wrapping her tentacles around the galleon. They heard the crunch of wood splintering and beams breaking as one tentacle punched a hole straight through the hold, and dozens of snow globes came pouring out.

Ursula gave a yell of triumph, but then she saw that Scarlett had untied the ropes tethering the dirigible to the ship and it was already starting to rise higher in the sky, away from their reach. The explorers raced down the pier to join Genie. Some of the pirates had opened fire on the kraken, disregarding the panic-stricken yells of their comrades on the besieged ship. Ursula raised her trident and directed lightning blasts at the attacking fleet, which immediately set their sails alight in a blaze of fire.

Ethan helped Julian to sit down with his back against a post and then joined the other two, throwing magic spells across the water, which turned every pirate they hit into frogs. The other explorers all dived straight into the water and began rounding up the snow globes. They couldn't afford for any to sink to the bottom of the sea, or be carried away on the waves and lost forever. Zara flew out to join them too, flitting and skimming about the surface as she looked for her crew.

All the while, Scarlett's dirigible rose higher into the sky, further away from the battle. Soon it would be lost to the clouds altogether and Stella would be gone.

Ursula thought of aiming her trident at the balloon, but if she crashed the dirigible then Stella could be hurt too. And besides, they had their hands full with the pirates. Even with the kraken ripping into the ships and making the water bubble and foam, they still had a lot of cannon fire between them. Iron balls landed in the water all around, sending up great wet sprays and narrowly missing the explorers. Ursula could see that Jai was trying to swim to the *Blowfish*, but the pirates were keeping a tight perimeter around the submarine.

Genie saw this too and called to Jodie, telling her to abandon Scarlett's ship and help Jai reach the *Blowfish* instead. The kraken disappeared beneath the water for a moment before erupting from the sea a short distance away, winding her tentacles around another pirate ship. She was immensely strong and able to break apart a galleon with ease, but she could only deal with one at a time and there must have been twenty ships there. Ursula was worried that the others might get the better of her now that they were all manning their cannons.

But just then, she noticed Zara swoop down suddenly towards the surface, going after one of the snow globes bobbing in the water. The next second Ursula realised Zara had found the missing part of her fleet. The air shimmered with magic as she opened the globe, releasing the fairy ships from their glass prison. The miniature galleons bobbed on the surface and the rescued fairies cheered and whooped from the decks. Taking the situation in at speed, the fairies lost no time and immediately raced to their own cannons, firing magic at the pirates.

With the fairies' help, the tide at last began to turn in the explorers' favour. They saw a repeat of what had happened at Starfish Island, with pirates being turned into hamsters and sails into mushrooms. Finally, the water was still and there were no more foes left to fight.

But there was no sign of the dirigible either.

'We've lost her,' Ursula said, crestfallen. 'We've lost Stella.'

'We'll find her again.'

They turned around to see Julian standing behind them on the boardwalk. He still looked pale and unsteady on his feet, but at least he was standing up by himself. Ethan rushed to him, throwing his arms round his older brother and squeezing him tight.

'I just can't believe it,' he said. 'I thought you were gone – that I'd never see you again.'

'It's nice to know you missed me, kiddo,' Julian said, ruffling his hair. 'And it's good to be back. We have Ursula and her team to thank for that.'

He'd barely finished speaking before Ethan let him go and whirled round to face Ursula.

'You!' he said, staring at her as if seeing her for the first time. He looked so intense that she almost wondered whether he was about to tell her off, but instead he said, 'If you ever need anything ... if I can ever do anything for you, then tell me at once. I'll never be able to repay what you've done for my family, but I swear on the Ocean Squid Explorers' Club itself that I'll be your friend for life.'

Ursula smiled and started to say something modest, but Ethan put his arms round her in a tight hug before she could finish.

'Oof, watch out for the trident,' she said, narrowly missing jabbing him with it.

'Is Ethan *hugging* someone of his own accord?' Shay asked, as he pulled himself out of the water and on to the boardwalk. 'I never thought I'd see *that* happen.'

'And speaking of the Ocean Squid Explorers' Club,' Jai said, coming up beside him. 'It's one of the globes we rescued from the water. Look!'

He held up the snow globe and Ursula saw that it did indeed house the club. The other explorers soon joined them on the boardwalk with more snow globes of lost cities and endangered species. They all agreed to go back to the fort and pick up any remaining snow globes there before they returned to the water. They already knew some had been left behind in the banquet room, and it was important that they rescue all the snow globes they could. Between them, they found another eight globes altogether, before heading to the pier.

'So we saved all this, but we lost Stella,' Ursula said, looking at the snow globes on the pier.

'We'll get her back,' Shay said. 'We've got to.'

'Any idea how?' Ethan asked.

'Whatever your plans, you might want to discuss them away from here,' Zara said, fluttering down to join them on the pier. 'The fairy magic will wear off soon. Those pirates won't remain hamsters forever and, trust me, you don't want to be around when they go back to being human. Being transformed into hamsters tends to put them in the most devilishly bad mood for some reason.'

The explorers didn't need telling twice. They stuffed the snow globes into their bags and, thanking Jodie for her help, bid farewell to the kraken, who had decided to make her home there. They then swam the short distance to the *Blowfish*. Once inside, it was a relief to dive back beneath the surface, set the engines to full speed and leave Pirate Island behind them.

*

A short while later, the explorers all gathered on the bridge to discuss their next move. There were things that needed to be done. They had to reconvene with the other submarine in order to return the kidnapped children to their families, but they also had to take the Ocean Squid Explorers' Club back to its rightful spot, not to mention all the other lost places, as well as stop Scarlett and, most importantly of course, save Stella.

'Scarlett will be more dangerous now than ever,' Shay said grimly. 'An ice princess at her bidding is what she's always wanted. She can force Stella to create as many snow globes as she likes. There's nothing to stop her stealing up half the world if she wants to. There could be almost nothing left by the time she's finished.'

'And we have no idea where she's gone,' Ethan said. 'We're back to square one.'

'Not quite,' Ursula said. She took Stella's charm bracelet from her pocket and held it up. 'Stella passed this to me before she put on the cuffs. I thought she was doing it to make room for them, but look! The compass charm has been lit up and sparkling since Stella left.'

She held it up for them to see. The compass charm

didn't have an N for North at its top, as most compasses did, but the initials SSP instead.

'Stella Starflake Pearl,' Beanie said eagerly. 'The compass is pointing to Stella. It can tell us where she is!'

'Still sounds like it's going to be a bit of a wild goose chase,' Ethan said, frowning.

Beanie looked confused. 'Why would we be chasing wild geese? This hardly seems like the time. We ought to go after Stella first.'

Ethan waved his hand. 'It's a figure of speech. It means we'll be running about without much idea where we're going or what we're doing. Like usual.'

'Well, it's better than nothing,' Genie said. 'And it was smart of Stella to slip it to you like that.'

'Sorry to interrupt, but I just wanted to say goodbye and thanks,' Zara said, flying into the bridge. She and the rescued pirate fairies were going to rejoin the other half of the fleet waiting at Starfish Island to continue their business of roaming the Seventeen Seas.

'Land ahoy!' Ollie shrieked.

'Oh, by the way,' Zara said. 'If I were you, I'd return the Stardust City snow globe first. I saw it in the library.' When they came on board they had placed all the snow globes there for cataloguing.

Ethan rolled his eyes. 'You're just saying that because

it's got fairies in it,' he said. 'But we've got a lot of places to return and we'll get to them when we get to them.'

Zara raised an eyebrow at him. 'You'd think being reunited with your long-lost brother would have improved your mood a bit,' she said with a sniff. 'I was only trying to give you a tip that will help with your rescue mission, but if you don't want my advice then suit yourself.'

'We don't want your advice,' Ethan snapped. 'You're a pirate, so keep your swashbuckling opinions to yourself.'

'Actually,' Jai said with a frown at Ethan. 'She's been a valuable member of our team, so please don't be rude to her.'

'We've very grateful for your help, Zara,' Ursula said, trying to be conciliatory. 'If there's any more advice you can give us, we'd really appreciate it.'

'All right.' Zara deliberately turned away from Ethan and addressed herself directly to Ursula. 'Well, it's like this. Stardust City is home to the galaxy fairies.'

'Everyone knows that,' Ethan muttered.

Shay nudged him in the ribs. 'Would you shut up?' he said. 'Do you want to rescue Stella or not?'

Ethan fell moodily silent.

'What you probably *don't* know,' Zara went on, 'is

that galaxy fairies are so-called because they can travel into space. Their wings are made from moon dust and the stories go that they even developed rockets. In fact, Stardust City was home to the oldest explorers' club in the world.'

'Are you sure?' Beanie asked. He was an expert on explorers and their clubs, but had never heard of that one. 'I thought the Desert Jackal Explorers' Club was the oldest in the world. It officially opened its doors just three days before the Jungle Cat Explorers' Club.'

'I'm only telling you what I've heard on the fairy grapevine,' Zara said with a shrug. 'Humans always think they're the first ones to invent anything or go anywhere, but that's not actually true. We've long heard stories of the Space Fairy Explorers' Club. And it struck me that if you were to release them from their prison then they might help in your search for Scarlett, and just *maybe* it might be useful to have a rocket or two on your side.' She cast Ethan a withering look. 'Even if they *weren't* invented by the Ocean Squid Explorers' Club.'

Ursula felt a sudden sense of excitement. 'I think it's a good idea,' she said. 'We can use the the Phantom Atlas to find where the city originally was.'

The Phantom Atlas was a book Stella and her friends had taken from the Collector when they'd discovered her first hideout. It contained a record of all the places that had been stolen from the world, and where they had come from.

'Our team could return the fairy city and ask for their help, while yours uses Stella's bracelet,' Ursula went on. 'Between us, we're bound to find her.'

'What about the Ocean Squid Explorers' Club?' Jai asked. 'Someone needs to take it back too'

'I've been thinking about that,' Max said. 'And I don't think it should be us. After all, you'd think we would be given a hero's welcome for rescuing them from the Collector, but they're an unpredictable bunch. Even if they are grateful to us, they might not let us carry on exploring together like this. Technically speaking, I'm still expelled from the club, and Ursula and Genie aren't even members.'

'He's right,' Genie said. 'You know how slowly things change there. Even if they eventually let us join, it would probably take them weeks to approve the new policy, and we don't have time to wait around for that.'

The Ocean Squid explorers all looked at Jai, knowing that he would find this the hardest out of all of them. Breaking a few rules in order to get the club back was one thing, but deliberately failing to report back to them and return the *Blowfish* was something else altogether.

'I don't like it,' Jai said. 'But I—'

'We haven't got any choice,' Max started to protest.

'There's always a choice,' Jai said. 'But if you'd just let me finish, I was going to say I agree with you. This is such an unprecedented situation with Scarlett and the Phantom Atlas Society. We're entering uncharted waters. You're also right about the club being slow to adapt, and we don't have time to waste. Stella needs us now. And the Collector needs to be stopped as quickly as possible too. So we're going to have to follow our own rules. I think we should forge ahead with our next expedition. And I agree that setting the space fairies free sounds like an excellent place to start.'

'My father can return the club once he's recovered from his jellyfish sting,' Ethan said. 'If we travel to a nearby island they can charter a boat and take the rescued children with them.' He glanced at his friends. 'And then we can use Stella's bracelet to follow her.'

The other explorers all agreed this was a good idea. After saying goodbye to Zara and her fleet, they lost no time in plotting a course to meet up with the other submarine. As they powered swiftly and silently through the sea, Ursula smiled. They might have lost

Stella, but all was not hopeless. They had rescued the Ocean Squid Explorers' Club and retrieved a lot of stolen places from Scarlett. And it thrilled her explorer's soul to think that she would get to see Stardust City and find out if there really was a Space Fairy Explorers' Club.

'Don't worry, Stella,' she said quietly, looking out at the dark ocean. 'We're on our way.'

Polar Bear Explorers' Club Rules

1. Polar Bear explorers will keep their moustaches trimmed, waxed and generally well-groomed at all times. Any explorer found with a slovenly moustache will be asked to withdraw from the club's public rooms immediately.

2. Explorers with disorderly moustaches or unkempt beards will also be refused entry to the members-only bar, the private dining room and the billiards room without exception.

3. All igloos on club property must contain a flask of hot chocolate and an adequate supply of marshmallows at all times.

4. Only polar-bear-shaped marshmallows are to be served on club property. Additionally, the following breakfast items will be prepared in polar-bear-shape only: pancakes, waffles, crumpets, sticky pastries, fruit jellies and doughnuts. Please do not request alternative

shapes or animals from the kitchen – including penguins, walruses, woolly mammoths or yetis – as this offends the chef.

5. Members are kindly reminded that when the chef is offended, insulted or peeved, there will be nothing on offer in the dining room whatsoever except for buttered toast. This toast will be bread-shaped.

6. Explorers must not hunt or harm unicorns under any circumstances.

7. All Polar Bear Explorers' Club sleighs must be properly decorated with seven brass bells, and must contain the following items: five fleecy blankets, three hot-water bottles in knitted jumpers, two flasks of emergency hot chocolate and a warmed basket of buttered crumpets (polar-bear-shaped).

8. Please do not take penguins into the club's saltwater baths; they *will* hog the jacuzzi.

9. All penguins are the property of the club and are not to be removed by explorers. The club reserves the right to search any suspiciously shaped bags. Any bag that moves by itself will automatically be deemed suspicious.

10. All snowmen built on club property must have appropriately groomed moustaches. Please note that a carrot is not a suitable object to use as a

moustache. Nor is an aubergine. If in doubt, the club president is always available for consultation regarding snowmen's moustaches.

11. It is considered bad form to threaten other club members with icicles, snowballs or oddly dressed snowmen.

12. Whistling ducks are not permitted on club property. Any member found with a whistling duck in his possession will be asked to leave.

UPON INITIATION, ALL POLAR BEAR EXPLORERS SHALL RECEIVE AN EXPLORER'S BAG CONTAINING THE FOLLOWING ITEMS:

- One tin of Captain Filibuster's Expedition–Strength Moustache Wax.
- One bottle of Captain Filibuster's Scented Beard Oil.
- One folding pocket moustache comb.
- One ivory-handled shaving brush, two pairs of grooming scissors and four individually wrapped cakes of luxurious foaming shaving soap.
- Two compact pocket mirrors.

Ocean Squid Explorers' Club Rules

1. Sea monsters, kraken and giant squid trophies are the private property of the club, and cannot be removed to adorn private homes. Explorers will be charged for any decorative tentacles that are found to be missing from their rooms.

2. Explorers are not to fraternise – or join forces – with pirates or smugglers during the course of any official expedition.

3. Poisonous puffer fish, barbed wire jellyfish, saltwater stingrays and electric eels are not appropriate fillings for pies and/or sandwiches. Any such requests sent to the kitchen will be politely rejected.

4. Explorers are kindly asked to refrain from offering to show the club's chef how to prepare sea snakes, sharks, crustaceans or deep-sea monsters for

human consumption. This includes the creatures listed in rule number three. Please respect the expert knowledge of the chef.

5. The Ocean Squid Explorers' Club does not consider the sea cucumber to be a trophy worthy of reward or recognition. This includes the lesser-found biting cucumber, as well as the singing cucumber and the argumentative cucumber.

6. Any Ocean Squid explorer who gifts the club with a tentacle from the screeching red devil squid will be rewarded with a year's supply of Captain Ishmael's Premium Dark Rum.

7. Please do not leave docked submarines in a submerged state – it wreaks havoc with the club's valet service.

8. Explorers are kindly asked not to leave deceased sea monsters in the hallways or any of the club's communal rooms. Unattended sea monsters are liable to be removed to the kitchens without notice.

9. The South Seas Navigation Company will not accept liability for any damage caused to their submarines. This includes damage caused by giant squid attacks, whale ambushes and jellyfish plots.

10. Explorers are not to use the map room to compare

the length of squid tentacles or other trophies. Kindly use the marked areas within the trophy rooms to settle any private wagers or bets.

11. Please note: any explorer who threatens another explorer with a harpoon cannon will be suspended from the club immediately.

UPON INITIATION, ALL OCEAN SQUID EXPLORERS SHALL RECEIVE AN EXPLORER'S BAG CONTAINING THE FOLLOWING ITEMS:

- One tin of Captain Ishmael's Kraken Bait.
- One kraken net.
- One engraved hip flask filled with Captain Ishmael's Expedition-Strength Salted Rum.
- Two sharpened fishing spears and three bags of hunting barbs.
- Five tins of Captain Ishmael's Harpoon Cannon Polish.

Desert Jackal Explorers' Club Rules

1. Magical flying carpets are to be kept tightly rolled when on club premises. Any damage caused by out-of-control flying carpets will be considered the sole responsibility of the explorer in question.

2. Enchanted genie lamps must stay in their owner's possession at all times.

3. Please note: genies are strictly prohibited at the bar and at the bridge tables.

4. Tents are for serious expedition use only, and are not to be used to host parties, gatherings, chinwags, or chit-chats.

5. Camels must not be permitted – or encouraged – to spit at other club members.

6. Jumping cactuses are not allowed inside the club unless under exceptional circumstances.

7. Please do not remove flags, maps or wallabies from the club.

8. Club members are not permitted to settle disagreements via camel racing between the hours of midnight and sunrise.

9. The club kangaroos, coyotes, sand cats and rattlesnakes are to be respected at all times.

10. Members who wish to keep all their fingers are advised not to torment the giant desert hairy scorpions, irritate the bearded vultures or vex the spotted desert recluse spiders.

11. Explorers are kindly asked to refrain from washing their feet in the drinking water tureens at the club's entrance, which are provided strictly for our members' refreshment.

12. Sand forts may be constructed on club grounds, providing explorers empty all sand from their sandals, pockets, bags, binocular cases and helmets before entering the club.

13. Explorers are asked not to take camel decoration to extremes. Desert Jackal Explorers' Club camels may wear a maximum of one jewelled necklace, one tasselled headdress and/or bandana, seven plain gold anklets, up to four knee bells and one floral snout decoration.

UPON INITIATION, ALL DESERT JACKAL EXPLORERS SHALL RECEIVE AN EXPLORER'S BAG CONTAINING THE FOLLOWING ITEMS:

- One foldable leather safari hat or one pith helmet.
- One canister of tropical-strength giant desert hairy scorpion repellent.
- One shovel (please note this object's usefulness in the event of being buried alive in a sandstorm).
- One camel-grooming kit, consisting of: organic camel shampoo, camel eyelash curlers, head brush, toenail trimmers and hoof-polishers (kindly provided by the National Camel Grooming Association).
- Two spare genie lamps and one spare genie bottle.

JUNGLE CAT EXPLORERS' CLUB RULES

1. Members of the Jungle Cat Explorers' Club shall refrain from picnicking in a slovenly manner. All expedition picnics are to be conducted with grace, poise and elegance.

2. All expedition picnicware must be made from solid silver, and kept perfectly polished at all times.

3. Champagne-carrier hampers must be constructed from high-grade wickerwork, premium leather or teak wood. Please note that champagne carriers considered 'tacky' will not be accepted onto the luggage elephant under ANY circumstances.

4. Expedition picnics will not take place unless there are scones present. Ideally, there should also be magic lanterns, pixie cakes and an assortment of fairy jellies.

5. Oriental whip snakes, alligator snapping turtles, horned baboon tarantulas and flying panthers

must be kept securely under lock and key whilst on club premises.

6. Do not torment or tease the jungle fairies. They *will* bite and may also catapult their tormentors with tiny, but extremely potent, stink-berries. Please be warned that stink-berries smell worse than anything you can imagine, including unwashed feet, mouldy cheese, elephant poo and hippopotamus burps.

7. Jungle fairies must be allowed to join expedition picnics if they bring an offering of any of the following: elephant cakes, striped giraffe scones, or fizzy tiger punch from the Forbidden Jungle Tiger Temple.

8. Jungle fairy boats have right of way on the Tikki Zikki River under *all* circumstances, including when there are piranhas present.

9. Spears are to be pointed away from other club members at all times.

10. When travelling by elephant, explorers are kindly asked to supply their own bananas.

11. If and when confronted by an enraged hippopotamus, a Jungle Cat explorer must remain calm and act with haste to avoid any damage befalling the expedition boat (please note that the

Jungle Navigation Company expects all boats to be returned to them in pristine condition).

12. Members are courteously reminded that – due to the size and smell of the beasts in question – the club's elephant house is not an appropriate venue in which to host soirees, banquets, galas or shindigs. Carousing of any kind in the elephant house is strictly prohibited.

UPON INITIATION, ALL JUNGLE CAT EXPLORERS SHALL RECEIVE AN EXPLORER'S BAG CONTAINING THE FOLLOWING ITEMS:

- An elegant mother-of-pearl knife and fork, inscribed with the explorer's initials.
- One silverware polishing kit.
- One engraved Jungle Cat Explorers' Club napkin ring and five luxury linen napkins – ironed, starched and embossed with the club's insignia.
- One magic lantern with fire pixie.
- One tin of Captain Greystoke's Expedition-Flavour Smoked Caviar.
- One corkscrew, two Scotch egg knives and three wicker grape baskets.

ACKNOWLEDGEMENTS

Many thanks to the following wonderful people:

My agent, Thérèse Coen, and the Hardman and Swainson Literary Agency.

The lovely team at Faber – especially Natasha Brown, Leah Thaxton, Sarah Lough and Susila Baybars.

My two Siameses, Suki and Misu, and my husband, Neil Dayus.

All of the children's booksellers and teachers who take the time to champion books and nurture a love of reading in young people.

And, finally, to all of the children who have read and enjoyed Polar Bears and Ocean Squid. When you dress up as the characters, or write letters to me, or create things in the classroom, or share your amazing ideas at events, you remind me of what a special thing it is to be a children's writer. I hope you enjoy this book too.

COLLECT THE EXPLORERS' CLUBS SERIES!